MW01139043

FLAME of GOD

A Love Story

ROBERT W. WILSON

E‌xulon ELITE

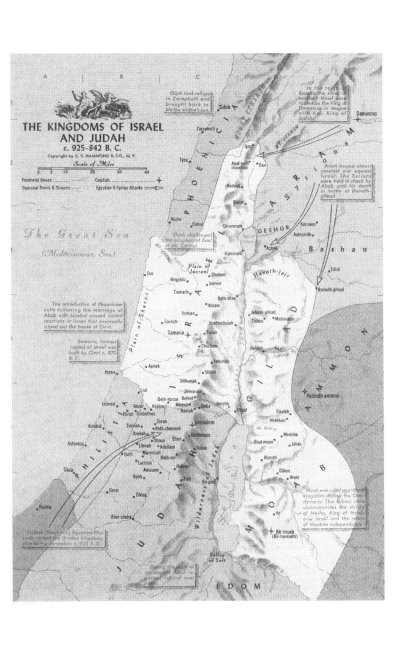

Dedication

I dedicate this book to my wife, Kathy, who taught me the real meaning of love.

Flame of God is a love story about two beautiful young people from the land of Israel. The Jewish people focus today on the renewal of life in their children.

In 1939, the Nazis ordered them to wear the Magen David as a visible yellow badge intended as a sign of shame. In 1948, the new Jewish state adopted the Star of David with two parallel lines above and below it as its official flag.

After touring the memorial to the 1.5 million children exterminated in the Holocaust, I cried to think this could happen in a civilized world.

Their message shouts out to you in their faces in the pictures and let-ters displayed in the museum. Never let it be forgotten! I also dedicate this book to them—to the children.

CONTENTS

Chapter 1—Ashur: A Beginning 9
Chapter 2—Ammi and the Pool by
          the Terebinth Tree.... 35
Chapter 3—The Black Forest 87
Chapter 4—The Death Angel 144
Chapter 5—Chariot Warriors 199
Chapter 6—Carchemish and the
          Piles of Bones....... 240
Chapter 7—The Signet Ring 270
Chapter 8—Shields of Gold 293
Chapter 9—A Sinister Plot and the
          Battle at the River .. 316
Chapter 10—The Fortress of the
          Heroes 333
Chapter 11—King Solomon's
          Harem 343
Chapter 12—Ashur Fights Pithon
          in the Ring........ 352

vii

Chapter 13—The Vineyards of
         Baal-Hamon 390
Chapter 14—Jerusalem, the Palace
and Riches Beyond Belief....... 417
Chapter 15—The Chariot Battle
         to the Death....... 484
Chapter 16—Ammi's Song 498

CHAPTER 1

Ashur: A Beginning

*N*ear the village of Solem, Israel, c.950 BC

A bloodcurdling scream pierced the night. Outside, the servant girl's husband stood, ready to go to her side.

"Relax, man," Machir said, "there is little you can do. Birthing a first baby is often difficult. You must be patient." Elkai, the expectant father, slumped in his seat on the stone bench, his head in his hands, obviously frustrated he could do nothing to help his young wife.

Machir, though childless, had attended many a new father among the servants. Elkai was the latest.

He kept a wineskin and a jug of arak available for such occasions. He handed Elkai the wineskin. "Take a big drink. The wine will calm you."

Elkai did as he had been instructed. He was used to taking orders from his master. He swallowed and gave a long sigh.

Machir took the wineskin back and drank deeply himself. Each time one of his servants brought a new child into the world, his own pain intensified. His wife, Nelmaah, would shed bitter tears because she longed to have a child of her own.

As Elkai paced around the yard, Machir tossed another log onto an already hot fire. "That ought to last the night," he commented, half to himself, half to Elkai.

Inside the house, Nelmaah wiped the brow of the young servant woman, Baara, and tried to ease her pain. The cool cloth did little or nothing to help. Nevertheless, Baara told Nelmaah, "I am grateful that you are here with me."

Off to the side, several maidservants watched anxiously.

When the midwife arrived, she uncovered the girl's swollen belly. "When was the baby conceived? Do you know?"

Nelmaah turned to Baara for the answer.

"I think it was the night of the Festival of Trumpets, the day Elkai returned from Megiddon."

"Hmm," Nelmaah mused, doubting the young woman knew exactly when she was impregnated. "I wish Machir were here in the room. He is better with figures than I am," she commented to whoever might be listening.

Machir benefited from his experience in the Gibore Hail, the regular army. He often enumerated the comparative strengths of bands of warriors, numbers of weapons, and food stores available to his men. Nelmaah, using her fingers, calculated for a moment, then said, "The baby may come too early."

Baara sat up, resting on her elbows. "What do you mean?" she asked anxiously.

Nelmaah realized she had been whispering. "Have you fallen or—?" Another scream interrupted her question. Baara quickly lay back and grabbed her abdomen with both hands as the strongest contraction yet wracked her body. She cried out so loudly that Elkai, who was waiting outside, could hear. He lifted his eyes toward heaven. "Why must she suffer so?" he asked.

Finally, after several more hours of Baara suffering the pains of the contractions and Elkai pacing outside, the midwife ordered, "Bring the birthing stool. The baby is coming."

Baara fought the efforts of Nelmaah and the midwife to get her off the soft skins and onto the stool. She sobbed uncontrollably, her body convulsed with pain. In three great surges, the baby came forth. The midwife expertly cut the cord and cleansed the baby, while Nelmaah supported a tired but happy mother.

"You have a little boy," Nelmaah announced. "He is a beautiful baby boy." She turned to the servant girls waiting in the doorway.

"Go and tell Elkai he has a son," she ordered. Then she turned to assist the midwife.

The baby had started to breathe, a rapid gasping. Then it stopped.

"The baby has quit breathing!" Nelmaah cried.

The midwife stayed calm. "All babies have an adjustment to make from the womb," she assured as she wiped moisture from the baby's mouth and pressed her own lips to the infant's. Simultaneously she pinched his nose with her thumb and finger to prevent air from escaping. She massaged his chest for a few moments. She bent over to listen to his heart. He was now breathing normally. "His heart is strong," she announced.

She completed cleaning the infant. Then she wrapped him in soft cloths and held him for Baara to see. "God makes all things, large and small," said the midwife, speaking to the maidens who had been observing.

Elkai paced outside. Machir said to him, "It is customary for the midwife to present the baby to you, the father. I don't know what is keeping her."

Losing patience, Machir went into the house to check on the condition of the mother and child. At his entry, the young servant women scattered, taking his presence as notice that the event was over.

"Come in, Elkai. Come and see your son," Machir said to the hesitant father.

***

The baby grew and prospered. Nelmaah was no longer needed, and the pain of her own barrenness intensified at this separation from the baby. Although Machir no longer mentioned a child, she knew he desperately wanted a son to preserve his name. Nelmaah dug her fist into her belly, abhorring the emptiness of the womb that betrayed her. She fell to her knees, sobbing. "Oh, Elohim, my God, I pray you will hear my prayer and remove this blight from my womb. Have pity on me. Bless me and heal me.

"The women laugh at me and hold me in derision. My husband's eyes no longer honor me. He does not seem to look on me with pleasure. My time has passed.

"The other women play joyfully with their children. My husband is called the 'father of nothing.' Have mercy on me. What sin have I committed? How have I disobeyed you?

"Yet, I praise you. You are perfect. Your words and laws are perfect. I know that you are God. Remove this curse from me.

"You alone can lift my head, which is bowed in shame. You are my only hope."

***

Machir loved to hunt and did so at every opportunity. Old war injuries made it difficult for him to bring back the meat of his kill, but he never complained. He took pride in his hunting prowess and in providing a varied menu for his household. Machir felt more comfortable alone, where he could commune with nature on a one-to-one basis. He still served King Solomon as purveyor of horses in his monarch's first district.

Returning from a fruitless hunt one afternoon, he caught a glimpse of movement on the hillside above him. His experienced eye needed only one fleeting second to identify the ibex that had disappeared. He scanned the rocky slope to determine whether other ibex were present. None were visible. They could blend in with the rocks. Only the most practiced eye could locate them.

Machir was tired and his leg ached. Nevertheless, the hunting instinct immediately rekindled. He worked his way up the slope and entered the buckthorn thicket where the animal had disappeared. The hooves of the animal made an indentation and left an obvious trail.

The ibex must water nearby at the pool of the terebinth tree, he reasoned. Living so near the village, the animal had become extremely cunning, avoiding the hunters in daylight hours. It probably drank from the pool by moonlight.

The thick brush overhead shut out most of the light. He leaned away from the thorny limbs and let them brush quietly from his shoulders.

The excitement of the hunt caused him to hold his breath and place each foot carefully, painstakingly avoiding any sudden noise. He eased forward, no more than twenty meters, and now could see a wall through the brush. As he drew closer, he noticed that the trail turned to the right, traversed the side of the mountain, and led to the entrance of a cave. The chamber opened until he could stand erect. Under closer observation, it was clear the cavernous room had been carved out or at least enlarged by human hands long ago. The walls bore the telltale scars of the tools of man. As Machir made his way through the passageway a short distance, he could see light at the other end.

When he stepped out into the daylight, he was surprised to find himself ten to twelve feet above the main trail that led to Solem. How often he had passed below, never dreaming the cave existed. The entrance was not visible from below or from the side. Sheer rock walls across the pass barred anyone from standing in front of the cave. At least, no one could stand within seeing distance of the entrance. The ibex had apparently run through the cave and leaped down the outcropping steps below.

Machir's body relaxed in disappointment at losing his quarry. He turned to examine the interior of the underground chamber. Out of the corner of his eye, he saw something that was totally out of place. His eyes came to meet little human ones staring back at him. A child—yes, a baby—was watching him from a basket lying on the floor of the chamber.

What was a baby doing here? He gazed around the cave for some clue as to how the little one had gotten there. Machir's first response was dismay, but soon it turned into anger at the mother or parents who had left the infant alone in such a secluded place. He was sure that the ibex had passed close by when it came through the cave. Wherever the mountain goats were, the leopards that stalked them would not be far away. He carefully made his way down the face of the cliff, pausing on the ledge, where he called out, "Mother, mother—father,

father. I have found the baby. Come out, please, I am a friend."

The lower part of the descent proved more hazardous because the steps carved out of the mountain were worn away, hardly recognizable. He went down the trail a short distance. Then he reversed direction, walking up the trail for a similar distance, all the time calling out to the imagined mother. "Come out, please—I will not hurt you. The baby needs you."

Machir retraced his steps and clambered back up the side of the mountain. Inside the cave, he bent over and enclosed the tiny hand in his own large one. The baby grasped his thumb. He noticed a signet ring dangling from the infant's leg. The ring was a beautiful creation, perfect in every dimension. Obviously, it had been fashioned by a superior craftsman and was nothing like any ring Machir had seen before. He examined the interior of the basket thoroughly, uncovering the infant's body in the process—a little manchild, he noted, as he replaced the coverings.

No other clue emerged as to the child's identity or origin. The basket and blankets were common. Now he began to realize that he was in a predicament, since it was not long until night would descend on the mountains. Though he was an accomplished outdoorsman, he did not relish sleeping on the hard floor in pitch-black darkness. Waiting for whoever was entrusted with this child to return was not possible. He could not leave the infant in the cave, alone and helpless. Should he take him now while he had good light, or should he wait? Why would someone leave a baby alone for any length of time? To add to his dilemma, the baby began to cry.

"What is wrong, little man? Do you miss your mother?" Increasingly loud cries hastened his decision. He put his bow over his shoulder so as not to be encumbered. With the basket under his arm, he began making his way down the side of the mountain.

"Gird them up, little man," he said, using a military phrase that meant to buckle down or to get ready for a difficult task. He immediately realized how ridiculous he would sound if someone were listening. The baby stopped crying, so he continued talking.

"My wife will want to hold you and rock you in her arms. I am going to get you to her as quickly as possible. She will know how to take care of you. We will find your mother, but my wife will probably want to keep you." His mind raced, dealing with the implications of finding this infant, considering his wife's intense desire for a child.

The possibilities frightened him. Would this mean more heartache for her when they found the parents? He wondered how his wife would react. He remembered the look on her face when she held Baara's new baby. Her eyes had misted as they met his for one painful moment.

He struggled for words, realizing that he did not know very much about babies or how to talk to them. He knew the women sang to their children, so he began belting out a ribald marching song. When he got to the chorus, his voice trailed off.

The words seemed too profane for tender ears.

Machir did not have to go far down the main trail to reach the point where he would cut across the fields to his home. Finally, he reached the familiar trail. If he did not step on a snake or encounter some wild animal in the darkness, he would reach home safely. This thought crossed his mind as he stepped into the middle of a covey of quail bedded down for the night. They burst out of the grass at his feet, with great fluttering and flapping.

The baby let out a wail, and Machir's own heart pounded violently. He wondered if anyone had ever suffered heart failure from such an experience. He kept his mind on the quail to avoid thinking of the deadly snakes, common to the area. His powerful arms and hands fumbled to find a comfortable way to hold the basket. He held it away from his side so his leg and hip would not bump or jar his precious cargo. This awkward position intensified the strain on his leg and lower back. The pain in his leg became excruciating.

Machir managed a smile as a glow of flames greeted him from the valley below. His wife had obviously ordered the servants to build a huge bonfire to guide him home. This had become a ritual, since he had once become lost years earlier. In his mind, he reproduced the scene below. From where he stood, on this high point, he could survey his lands. His house stood atop a small hill, surrounded by a wall. The house was not elaborate, but comfortable. During the day, oxen plowed the fields. Sheep and goats dotted the hillsides. Scattered buildings housed servants and workers. The houses were constructed of the same rock as the wall. On the far side, Machir had built a large barn to shelter the horses and to store grain. A common well in the center of his estate provided water for his household and the servants.

Solem had been designated a chariot village by the king. A road encircled its walls, serving as a training ground for the young men of Solem and Nahal. Machir trained the young men to handle horses and chariots.

To the west, on adjacent slopes, grew stands of vines and olive trees belonging to the residents of the village of Solem. White stripes lined the grassy heights. The white stripes were trails permanently etched into the mountain by goats' hooves, over hundreds of years. Solem's walls enclosed close-packed houses, the workshops of the local craftsmen, and a threshing floor, where each farmer took his turn according to a fixed order. The village had wine-presses and olive presses. A spring provided fresh water.

An open area and the threshing floor housed a local market. Adjoining the open area stood a fine banquet house. This collective undertaking of the entire community remained a source of pride for all of the people in and around Solem. The building served as the centerpiece for festivals and marriage celebrations.

"Machir!" a servant shouted, as his master entered the outer limits of the fire's blaze. Machir limped to meet his anxious wife and his servants.

"Look, woman," he said to his wife, as she embraced him. "See what I found in a cave over the road. It is a little baby, a boy." His wife and the servants gathered around, trying to get a look at the tiny face peeping out of the blanket. The child had been quiet for a time but now sensed nourishment nearby, for he began to cry lustily.

"This baby is starving!" Nelmaah exclaimed. "Where is his mother?"

Machir shrugged his shoulders. "I looked everywhere for her. I found no one. I could not leave such a little one there alone."

"Send someone to bring Baara here. She has enough milk for four," Nelmaah said to a servant woman. "I will bring the baby inside. You, girl, light the lamps."

The servant girl Baara was brought to Nelmaah. When she heard of the little newborn's plight, she readily volunteered one of her ample breasts. He was soon nursing hungrily.

Machir related the story of how he had found the baby. He promised his wife that he would mount a search at first light. He sent the servants

to bed and retired himself, leaving
Nelmaah to care for the baby. The
little foundling cried during the
night, and each time Nelmaah awakened immediately. Without complaint,
she gave the baby the warmth of her
own bosom. When this did not satisfy
the child, she shook Baara until she
awakened to feed him again.

In the morning, as promised, Machir
sent a messenger to the village with
word of his find. He and his servants
returned to the cave and combed the
entire area.

Machir was an excellent tracker,
but apparently the people who left
the baby had not left a trail. He
did find a rock that appeared to have
been scraped or smudged. Kneeling,
he ran his hand along it. A smudge
appeared when he brushed away loose
sand. He was almost certain it was a
bloodstain. He took his knife from
his belt and scraped some crusted
sand from around the base of the
rock. Machir rolled it around between
thumb and forefinger. More probing
with the knife suggested that the
patch was quite large. Some animal

had died here or at the least had lost a great deal of blood.

The possibility existed, however, that the blood could be of human origin. Rain had fallen about a week and a half previously, so the incident must have occurred after the rain, he reasoned. Someone had brushed sand over the area. He searched the entire vicinity again but found no other trace of human presence. At midday, men from the village, led by an elder, came out to aid in the search.

***

"Machir, what is it we hear? Now you hunt for babies—hah!" the elder said, laughing. "Have you found any more?"

"No, just one, Galal. We can find no trace of the mother. Do you know whose child it is? We have searched this whole valley and the hillsides and haven't found anything that would help explain how the baby came to be in the cave. If I had not come along, the poor little one would be near death or would have been eaten by a leopard."

"I do not know whose child it is," Galal said, his voice becoming more sympathetic. "We called a meeting of the elders when your messenger came to me, but no one knows anything. Someone has done a terrible thing, to leave a defenseless little baby alone like this."

"That is what I told my wife," Machir said, his voice reflecting anger. "For me to come along when I did was an act of divine intervention."

Late that afternoon, they gave up the search. Machir sent a servant to the cave the next morning. For days, he kept a watch. Finally, when the vigil became impractical, he returned the basket to the cave, with a message telling where the baby could be found.

In Nelmaah's eyes, the infant had been given to her. He certainly did not lack for attention. From the first day he was with them, Nelmaah accepted him as her own. She never appeared to fear he would be taken away. Machir, however, could not accept the circumstances surrounding the child's discovery.

"The baby we have in our house is not ours," he reminded her. He could not rest until he exhausted every possibility of locating the little foundling's parents. He sent servants with messages to all of the surrounding villages and to Hazor and Megiddon, telling of the child they had found. Machir's strong sense of values demanded that he return the child to his family, if possible. Nelmaah's attitude only served to deepen his resolve to find the child's parents. He could see that she loved him as her own. He was afraid he would see his wife deeply hurt if the baby was claimed. Every day that passed forged a stronger bond between Nelmaah and the baby.

"A son was given to me without the travail and pangs of labor," Nelmaah avowed.

"Foolish woman," Machir mumbled under his breath. Although Machir had desperately wanted a son, he did not have much interest in someone else's baby. In an idealistic way, he had viewed himself teaching his son of horses and shepherd dogs, and roaming the hills and forests to hunt game. At first, he showed only a passing interest in the small stranger.

The tiny face was blank and inscrutable and displayed little interest in his surroundings. Occasionally, he would bring a smile to Machir's face as he rooted for a nipple or sucked noisily on his own thumb. On one occasion, the servant woman was tardy in delivering her breast for sustenance. The infant clenched his fists, churned his feet, and angrily denounced all in charge. Machir laughed aloud. Later the child's face began to respond with a smile to Machir's familiar form and voice.

The servant girl's nursing of the baby proved to be difficult for his wife to accept. Baara had finished nursing the baby and had been gone for quite a while, but Nelmaah did not emerge from their sleeping quarters. Upon entering the room, he found her sitting, holding the baby. She had pulled her loose-fitting tunic down, exposing her breast to the infant. She was so completely engrossed in the baby, she was unaware he had entered.

His first response was a feeling that he had come upon a scene where he did not belong. This little foreign creature, not the issue from his loins, shared the intimacy of his wife's breast. He thought the experience was sensual. The light in the room was not good, so he knelt to see her face clearly. He watched as the baby tried to nurse at her barren breast. The child burrowed into the warmth and fell asleep.

Nelmaah turned her head to face Machir but said nothing. A tear brimmed over and traced down her cheek. He wiped it away with his hand and bent over to kiss the warm, damp place where the tear had stained her face. "Are you all right, my love?"

She did not reply but nodded to show that she was. She obviously did not want to discuss her feelings. He kissed her on the lips and then left her alone with the infant.

Several months elapsed, and Nelmaah's frustration slowly passed. She enjoyed mothering the boy. Machir paused from his work to watch as Nelmaah gently cradled him on her lap, unwinding the soft bands of swaddling. A woman servant held him while she lined the rock tub with soft cloths, then poured heated water from the hearth into the tub. Nelmaah washed and caressed him as he waved his arms, splashing and squealing joyfully at the sensations he experienced from the warm water and the midmorning sun. After Nelmaah dried him with loving care, she sat cross-legged on the mat as he crawled about. She appeared younger and happier than Machir had seen her in years. He approached them and knelt down on the edge of the mat. The infant grunted manfully at the effort expended to look up at him. Machir laughed as the baby tumbled over backward. He laid the new arrow shafts on the mat and watched with amusement as the baby discovered the delight of banging a headless shaft against the others.

The baby's crying during the nights proved a difficult adjustment for him. Nonetheless, one particular night proved to be an unforgettable milestone in their relationship.

"Waa-uh, waah-uh, waah-uh!" Machir tossed and turned, trying to escape the incessant noise. Finally, he went into the living area of their home. He found his wife holding the child. Baara was nearby. Both looked worried.

"He has a high fever. I hope it is not something serious," Nelmaah said.

Machir, seeing the women exhausted from their late night's vigil, offered to hold the child. He found that as long as he walked around the room with him, he seemed to quiet his crying. Few things had frightened Machir in his lifetime. However, the thought that this helpless little baby might have some life-threatening illness was a new terror that he had never confronted. The old warrior pressed his lips against the feverish brow and kissed the tiny head.

Praying fervently, he asked Elohim to spare the child for his wife's sake, never realizing that he had forever bonded to him as his own. The fever quickly passed, and the little boy child rapidly regained his color and good health. Nelmaah succeeded

in getting Machir to name the foundling Ashur, meaning "free man."

Months and years passed without
any word about the little manchild whose beginning was without
beginning.

CHAPTER 2

Ammi and the Pool by the Terebinth Tree

*I*n the village of Solem, a very active little girl pulled aside the curtain across a doorway. Her impish face peered out at her father, then disappeared from view with the musical giggle that he loved. She hid her face and burst out laughing when discovered.

"I saw you, Ammi," Dedan said. It was her own special game of peek-a-boo, and one that was fast becoming an afternoon ritual as she watched him count the shekels from his collections. She soon tired of the game and came to rest against his leg. Dedan put his arm around her shoulders and caressed her face and hair. She waited patiently for a while, content with being close to her father. Finally, he finished with the tally and lifted her into the considerable bulk of his lap. "Come give me a big hug, Katan-Ammi," he said, using his favorite term of endearment, meaning "little one of my people."

Little Ammi responded as she always did, with a hug and a tiny kiss so soft that he leaned into it so that his rough cheek would not miss it altogether. He looked down at her in wonder and joy. The child had a cherub's face, flawless skin and perfect features, except for a tiny, unique curl at the corner of her lips. This gave her face a captivating look, especially when she smiled. He never tired of hugging her and kissing her beautiful face. He loved her affectionate ways that were so different from her older brothers'. They preferred rough-and-tumble play and seldom stood still long enough to allow him to hug them.

King Solomon recognized a group of men as his Royal K'nani, or royal merchants. Dedan enjoyed this official designation. He procured foreign goods for the home market and sold goods to Tyre and Egypt.

Ammi worshiped her father and wanted to be with him everywhere he went. She followed him as he made his daily rounds to the shops. The merchant smiled to himself because now he was known more as the father of the beautiful Ammi than as the successful merchant. Amazingly, the precocious Ammi remembered names and facts about people very well. The child hurried along after him, her short legs taking several steps to every one of his strides. As they entered the tanning shop, Dedan greeted the owner. "How are you, Kabar?" The grumpy old merchant only grunted.

"Hello, Mr. Kabar," Ammi offered.

"Well, hello there, Ammi. I am glad to see you," Kabar replied.

"How is your son?" Ammi asked.

"He is getting better, Ammi," Kabar said. "How are you doing?"

"Fine, sir. I brought some mandrakes for you to give him," Ammi said, turning over her carefully wrapped bundle to Kabar.

"Thank you, Ammi," Kabar laughed. "Yes, indeed! I think the mandrakes are just what he needs."

Dedan also began to laugh. People believed that mandrakes enhanced sexual desire and fertility. Kabar's son suffered from a severe respiratory ailment. "Ammi heard the men joking," he said to Kabar by way of explanation.

When Ammi was excited, the words came so fast he could understand only a part of what she was saying. Dedan was sure that old Kabar understood even less. When Ammi finished a sentence, Kabar always made some exclamation that encouraged another animated exchange from her. The gruff shopkeeper would brush Dedan aside when he tried to get on with business. He almost always had flatbread and honey for Ammi. Kabar's wife prepared bread differently from the way Ammi's mother baked bread, and Ammi considered it a treat.

"Ammi is describing a very special tree beside a pool and the flowers. There will be plenty of time for business later," insisted Kabar crossly. Dedan was surprised that Kabar understood what she was talking about. Obviously, he did though, for Ammi's favorite place was a pool by a terebinth tree where the wild flowers grew profusely in the spring. She and her brothers loved to play under the shade of the huge tree. Perhaps the sly old merchant was not as hard of hearing as Dedan thought and only pretended to be so when it was to his benefit.

Kabar stopped what he was doing to spend a few minutes with her. Dedan suspected that Kabar and the other shopkeepers also found Ammi's visit to be the high point of their day. The crusty storekeepers had only to watch the charming girl bouncing and skipping along behind her father to bring a smile to their faces.

"Bring her to see me again," Kabar said when they had concluded their business. "Always she has a smile on her face."

"She is a happy girl," Dedan replied proudly.

***

"Softens them up, she does," her father said to his wife when they returned home. "They do not complain as loudly about the price of my goods with Ammi along. My daughter's smile brightens the darkest day and the darkest of men, even that black-hearted Kabar. The king's men have to threaten him with death every year to collect the taxes from him. He has contributed nothing toward the banquet hall, and I dare say he is the wealthiest man in the province."

***

Ammi never grew tired or complained, though her short legs and tiny feet had to take several steps for every one of her father's. She would play on the floor of the shops or among the store goods with her favorite toy, a terra-cotta doll that she dressed in rags. The doll, which Ammi had named Abi, accompanied them on their rounds. Dedan had obtained the doll from Egypt. Immediately it had found great favor with Ammi because of its lifelike features.

Ammi and another girl the same age often played together in her father's walled garden. Ammi's brothers interrupted their play. "See, it's not moving. The doll is dead, I say," one of her brothers taunted.

"Abi is not dead," Ammi declared angrily.

"Yes she is—it's a dead person—a dead thing. She was always dead," her brother insisted. He hesitated a moment, searching for words. "And it will forever be dead," he declared with triumphant finality. At this, Ammi fled in defeat into the house to her father.

"What is wrong, Katan-Ammi?" her father asked as he gathered her into the warmth of his big arms. "What has your brother done?"

"He said that Abi was dead," Ammi sniffled.

"Whose doll is this?"

"Mine," she said.

"And who gave it to you?"

"You did."

"And who named it Abi?"

"I did." More sniffling.

"Well then, if it is your doll and I gave it to you and you want to pretend that it is alive, then that is fine. You return to the garden when you are ready and tell your brothers to come here. I want to speak to them."

***

"She is my heart-friend," Ammi would say, referring to her friend Merab. Hand and hand they went, skipping about. The two playmates got along very well. However, Ammi's love for the doll developed into a problem. Merab viewed her toy as inferior because it did not have the lifelike features of the terra-cotta doll. She would play practically any game, but her distaste for dolls grew, finally leading to a quarrel that took place in the courtyard of Merab's father.

"No! I do not want to play this game ever again," Merab declared.

Merab's mother, overhearing her daughter's angry voice, intervened. "Merab, why are you speaking in that tone of voice? Ammi is your best friend. Why are you angry?"

"I do not want to play dolls!"

"We have played everything Merab wanted to play, and she will not do anything I want to," Ammi complained. She enumerated all the games of Merab's choice. Merab's mother ordered her daughter to play dolls with Ammi. While Ammi was in the house getting a drink of water, Merab took a wooden spade and dug a hole in the sand. Ammi returned to play and immediately missed Abi.

"Where is my Abi?" Ammi demanded. Merab folded her hands across her chest and refused to speak. Ammi could tell from her attitude that she knew the whereabouts of the missing doll.

"You better tell me, or I will go to your mother."

"I will not!" Merab responded defiantly, finally breaking her silence.

Ammi's eyes grew large. Her fists clinched, and she began to breathe rapidly. Merab was about six months older than Ammi. In the past, she had succeeded in bullying Ammi into submission. Merab stepped forward and gave Ammi a hard pinch on her arm. This time, however, Ammi responded by pinching her back. Merab retaliated with a harder and longer pinch. Ammi screamed and did a little dance in place, then went after Merab. Merab tried to evade her, but Ammi successfully cornered her against the house. She gathered a soft flap of skin on Merab's upper arm between her thumb and forefinger. Her fingers squeezed with all her might, bringing her thumbnail into play. Merab's eyes grew large at this sharper pain. She, too, began crying. The loud and angry voices brought Merab's mother into the courtyard. Under her stern interrogation, Merab confessed.

"I buried her," she admitted, openly exultant at Ammi's discomfort.

"You buried Ammi's doll! Where did you put her? You are going to be punished for this."

"I do not remember."

"Well, you had better remember in a hurry, or you will be punished more severely," Merab's mother demanded.

When her father was called to the scene, Merab finally broke down and confessed. "I heard Ammi's brother say her doll was dead. My doll was dead, too, so I buried them in the sand by the wall, where we play."

Ammi's doll was recovered, none the worse for its short interment. Neither of the girls harbored a lasting grudge, and a few days later they were playing together again as if nothing had happened. The incident proved to be one of Ammi's earliest lessons in human nature. Merab viewed Ammi with new respect.

***

Ammi climbed into her father's lap. Her father had given her an ornately carved ivory comb for her own. She found great fun in combing everything. She combed his beard, his head, and even the hair on the back of his arms.

Over the years this scene was repeated often.

Dedan sat on a stone bench by a water cistern, with his back against the courtyard wall, watching the children play. Ammi jumped down from his lap. A tuft of hair was out of place on her brother's head. She determinedly tried to get her brother to stand still long enough to conquer the rebellious strand of hair. Finally, her brother turned and ran, with Ammi in pursuit.

***

Another incident occurred involving Ammi and her friend Merab. The girls received new dresses for the religious festival of Sukkot. Their mothers allowed them to walk alone the short distance to the village Hekal. Proud as double-crested hoopoe birds in all their finery, they marched hand in hand down the street, basking in compliments. Several adults took time to stop and praise their fashionable attire.

"Look at the little girls strut, Pithon," said Sabta.

"Oh, no, not them," Ammi said to Merab, catching sight of the two boys in an alley between two rows of houses. She knew both of them. They were older than Ammi and Merab, and the only two people in the village that she did not like. They were troublemakers. Pithon qualified as the bully of the village. Sabta lied about anything and everything.

"Leave us alone," Ammi ordered. "I know you are up to no good."

Sabta belched loudly in reply and cackled in self- appreciation. Pithon joined in, locked arm in arm with Sabta, mocking and taunting them as he and Sabta followed the girls down the street.

They endured the abuse until the usually imperturbable Ammi could take no more. She turned to confront their tormenters. The plucky girl threatened to tell her father, the elders of the village, the *mazkir*, the king, and everybody else in authority she could think of. The girls marched on, and Sabta and Pithon fell back, discouraged by the furious outburst from Ammi.

The two boys noticed several fallen figs under a tree. Sabta leaped forward and began gathering a handful of the rotten figs. Pithon joined him, giggling at the mischief they planned. The two boys ran ahead through the alleys to intercept Ammi and Merab at the next street crossing. The ambush was a complete success. Sabta and Pithon both scored direct hits on the girl's new dresses with the rotten fruit.

Ammi was heartbroken. She and Merab returned to their homes in tears. It took her father quite a while to console her. "Do not cry, Katan-Ammi. I will bring you another new tunic. It will be even more beautiful than this one," he said as he wiped the tears away with the fingertips of his big hand. "Your mother will wash this one, and it will be as good as new. Is it not so, Mother?" said Dedan, silently berating himself for allowing the girls to go to the temple alone.

"Here, Ammi," her mother said, "I have another pretty tunic for you to wear. Come in and I will help you put it on."

After she had changed and her mother had combed her hair again, her mother led the dejected Ammi to her father. He held up a new blue sash to tie around her waist. "I put this back to give to you when you were older, but I've decided to go ahead and give it to you now. It might cheer your spirits to wear it today." He tied it around her waist. Ammi gave her father a big hug. The sudden appearance of the new sash dried her tears.

"Come now. Your mother and I will walk you to the festival. I have a crimson sash for you to give Merab. We will see if she will go with us now."

Shortly after, Pithon and Sabta were caught stealing from the village silversmith. Ammi and Merab gained some measure of revenge when they saw the two boys publicly flogged at the city gates. Ammi watched as Pithon and Sabta were brought before the village elders. "You two have embarked on a path of evil doings," the elder said. "If you boys do not change your ways, you will certainly come to no good. You would do better to follow Malta's example or the example of young Ashur, the son of Machir. The boy comes all the way from his father's land to sit at the feet of the reader of the code of law."

The code of law protected the rights of the poor, the orphan, the widow, and the foreigner. It guarded slaves from abuse. Outside of Israel, the rich could pay bribes to avoid punishment, but under the code, wealthy and poor alike were punished for their crimes. Unlike the laws of other lands, the code valued the life of a woman.

"Now, be off with you," the elder said. Do not find yourselves here again, guilty of wrongdoing. I warn you, next time the punishment will be severe."

Pithon had endured his whipping in silence, but Sabta had shrieked and yelled as though he were being murdered. Ammi thought surely that from the punishment they received,

Sabta and Pithon would change their attitudes. The public flogging cured Pithon of stealing. He knew he would have to find another way to advance his position and carefully avoid, by threat or bribery, appearing before the village elders again.

After the public flogging, the wily Sabta planned his own thievery, blaming his accomplice for their being caught. Sabta carried on alone, but he continued to follow Pithon around. He bribed the larger youth into protecting him when his obnoxious and cowardly nature got him into trouble.

Ammi knew Malta, but the elder's praise of the boy Ashur made her curious about him. If this Ashur was different from Pithon and Sabta, she was sure she would like him. She would make a point of watching for him when he came to listen to the reader of the code and the elders at the village gates.

***

As she grew older, Ammi's curiosity and thirst to learn led her to cross the distinct lines drawn for the behavior of women. This began innocently enough. Ammi and Merab were playing behind a wall on the east side of her house. The wall provided shade and a windbreak and was near enough to the house so that she could hear her mother call for her. The ancient intersecting wall had partially collapsed. She heard the sound of voices on the other side and climbed up the rubble to see who was speaking. From her vantage point, she could see the reader of the code sitting on a raised platform. At his side was a low rack containing the scrolls. His pupils sat on the ground about him.

"You, girl! Get down from that wall!" the elder ordered. "You know that you are forbidden to take part in the lessons."

Later, when she was playing alone, she began to eavesdrop on the elders. She hid behind the low wall of her father's estate and pretended to play with her seashell collection. At the sound of the ram's horn or a call by the elders, boys of all ages gathered to study their lessons.

The letters were a great mystery to her. After the elders and their students left the courtyard, she went in to pick up discarded pieces of potsherds. Then she retreated to her place of safety behind the wall, where she would practice her own letters. Her pen was a sharpened stick. She made ink from crushed gallnuts and fireplace soot. The ink stains on her hands became her downfall. Her mother discovered her secret cache of potsherds by the wall, and this led to a confrontation.

"Ammi, how long have you studied the boys' lessons?"

"Ever since my brothers began their lessons. I did not think it would hurt anything."

"You know there are some people in the village who would strongly object—your father, for one."

"Are you going to tell Father?"

"I do not know. I think you should tell him. He may be very hurt. How much of the letters do you know?"

"I know all of the letters and I can read the words, except the big words and the ones I have not seen before."

"Ammi, none of the other girls want to learn to read. Why are you doing this?" her mother questioned.

"I do not know," Ammi lamented, obviously repentant. "Is something wrong with me? Once, Mother, there was a great woman named Deborah, who led our people when the men were afraid to go to war. The elders teach the young men about her."

"Yes, I know." Ammi's mother shrugged her shoulders, at a loss to explain. "Nevertheless, Solem and the elders are very traditional."

Ammi was not easily consoled. It was as though she had permission to be enormously courageous, but only while being totally submissive. In her culture, choices were limited. The father or the oldest male in the family made the decisions, and the women had very little to say about any situation. A girl was to obey her father without question. When she married, she was expected to obey her husband in the same way. Only when a man and his wife had no sons was the daughter allowed to receive an inheritance. A father could cancel a contract or vow made by a woman.

After being discovered by her mother, Ammi found herself in more trouble when her brothers found her reading their father's papers. She was trying to read the scrolls of the code but had become frustrated with her inability to master certain words and therefore the meaning of the passage. She had no one she could go to for a translation of difficult words.

"What are you doing with our father's papers?" her brother demanded. "You cannot read."

"I know," Ammi stammered defensively. If only they knew the half of it, she thought. "I can pretend. I like to look at the letters."

"You had better leave Father's scrolls alone. After all, you are only a girl."

"If it were not for a woman, you would not be here," Ammi shot back, repeating what she had once heard her grandmother say. "I bet you cannot read this," Ammi challenged.

"Yes, we can," the older brother responded confidently. The younger brother was not so certain.

"Show me." Ammi coaxed the boys to her side and was successful in getting them to translate the scroll for her. She discovered that she compared very favorably with the speed with which her younger brother read.

She became more careful of discovery by her brothers. Covertly, she began to read the Book of the Heroes and other works, while carefully feigning indifference in the presence of her brothers. Their jealousy and attempts to put her in her place only intensified her desire to learn.

One day when her father was away from Solem and her mother was with the brothers visiting the tanning shop, Ammi was reading from the Book of Jashur, seeking to prove to herself that she could read faster than her brothers. She read aloud, trying to give the words the proper inflection. Dedan returned earlier than expected and paused in the doorway to listen in amazement.

"What are you doing, Katan-Ammi?" Although her father used the term of endearment in addressing her, his tone held obvious anger. There was a long silence as fear gripped her. "You have never kept anything from me before. Did you fear me so much that you could not tell me?"

"Yes, Father." Ammi clutched the side of her head, a fearful look in her eyes as though she expected him to strike her. She watched as he sat heavily on a bench beside the scrolls.

"We must talk about this. Does your mother know that you can read?"

"Yes, sir," she answered tremulously, not wanting to implicate her mother, but too frightened to consider lying to him. Dedan did not appear to know what to do. She guessed that he was surprised to learn that he had been a victim of conspiracy between his wife and daughter.

"How did you learn to read, Ammi?" he probed, thinking that perhaps she had memorized the scroll.

"I listened while you were teaching my brothers and to the elders giving lessons to the boys behind our wall."

"Why did you do it? None of the other young women of the village are interested in learning to read."

"I wanted to learn the wisdom of Elohim, Father," she answered wisely.

No other statement could have so fully disarmed him.

"It is all right. I think I will allow it."

Ammi brightened as though a tremendous burden had been lifted from her shoulders.

"To tell you the truth," he said, "I have long disagreed with the elders of the village. I said to myself, 'I have sons, and there is no need for my daughter to learn.' I was wrong. Nothing in the code prohibits a woman from learning to read and write. Let us keep this a secret, even from the boys. You know how the village feels about this. Perhaps, though, one day you will help your husband in teaching your own children. Promise me that you will never hide anything from me again."

"I promise, Father." She went into his arms, sobbing tears of relief.

***

Later in the year, the boys of the village were having footraces in the courtyard near the city's gates. The participants lined up, one foot touching the wall. On the starter's signal, they sprinted across the courtyard and around a hitching post. The first one to return to touch the wall would be declared the winner. Despite his large frame, Pithon ran very well. Only Malta could outdistance him in a fair race. On this day, Ammi and two of her friends were playing on the steps leading to the wall above them.

"You cheated, Pithon," Malta cried. "You tripped me and you did it on purpose! You started early. You did not have your foot against the wall."

Upon hearing Pithon's name shouted in anger, Ammi stopped her play to watch what was happening. Malta lay writhing on the ground, holding his ankle. Pain and anger contorted his face. Bravely he fought back tears. He regained his composure and climbed to his feet. Pithon decided to silence his main accuser. He grabbed Malta by his tunic and throat and slammed him against the hard stones.

"Let go of me, Pithon," Malta ordered, finally pushed to the limit. Pithon shoved Malta again, and the fight began. The boys struggled, pushing and flailing at one another. Most of the blows were ineffectual. Pithon used his superior strength to his advantage. He, after all, had much more experience fighting than did the good-hearted Malta. Pithon's fist landed on the side of Malta's jaw, and the boy collapsed in a heap.

Ammi, concerned that Pithon would continue beating the helpless boy, leaped down from the steps and ran to his side.

"Pithon, you . . . you brute. You are going to get it now. Call the guard. Go get Malta's father."

"Shut up, you little tramp. You are nothing but a girl, "Pithon snarled.

Ammi let out a piercing scream and then another louder one. Pithon blinked at the shrill blasts.

Confusion and apprehension replaced the threatening look on his face.

The guard on the wall had ignored the usual sounds of boys playing and quarreling. The sound of a young female in distress, however, brought him to the inner edge of the wall.

"Stop that, you down there. Stop it right now!"

Ammi watched as Pithon beat a hasty retreat. She knew, as he did, that he had no defenders in this group.

***

King Solomon compiled a book of laws and edicts from those handed down through the years by his own people. He also incorporated the best of the laws of Egypt. Where none existed, he formulated new ones. To every city he sent an appointed holy man called the *mazkir*, or "reader of the code."

The holy man of Solem was a stern but kindly man who spoke of holiness and responsibility. As the men sat at his feet, he read the code for hours at the city's gate. From the highest-ranking elder to the lowest free servant, all were expected to know the first book of the code. The other books, which were read later, were learned more or less on a voluntary basis. Rules defined the punishment and fine meted out to a man striking a pregnant woman, causing a miscarriage. The code dealt with situations such as an ox that gored a neighbor.

***

Ashur gathered with the men in an open-air meeting by the city gate.

One of the elders stood to speak. "On the third day of the month, a great pack of wolves swept down on the house of Ashbel of Nahal. The wolves slaughtered more than a dozen sheep in his sheepfold. The wolves killed for the sheer joy of killing."

"We must not alarm the people," another elder interjected. "There were only five or six wolves, by witnesses' accounts."

"That may be true," the first elder rejoined, "but we must alert the people to this danger. The walls of Solem were built years ago for this very reason. A great pack of wolves swept down on the village. I was there. I was a boy, but I remember the sound of the wolves tearing at the door of my father's house, trying to get inside. Our people were so terrified that they would not go out into the streets. The wolves slaughtered the sheep and goats, even the dogs. We lived in terror. The packs left only when nothing else remained for them to kill."

Another man of the village, who had several daughters—one of them particularly homely— and no sons stood to speak. "Sometimes having daughters is a nuisance," he began. "The father gets up in the middle of the night at the cry of his girl baby, losing his sleep." A ripple of sympathetic laughter ran through the assembled group of men. "When she is a young woman, he worries she will pass the flower of her age and no one will call her to marry. If she marries, the father worries that her husband may hate her or divorce her. In her virginity, he worries that she may become defiled and pregnant in her father's house. If she becomes married, he worries that she will be barren in her husband's house. Alas, it is better to have no daughters at all," he said remorsefully. The man with the daughters sat down amid applause and laughter.

Another man stood to speak. Ashur knew him to be the father of two particularly troublesome boys. "The ears of boys are on their backsides," he said wearily, "and they listen when the backside is beaten." After a period of laughter and reflection, one and then another offered comments, such as, "Every man knows that he must die, but no one believes it," followed by, "Better a noble death than a wretched life."

The thoughts were not always connected. "Men should be careful not to give their wives any cause for tears, for Elohim counts their tears," said another man whose wife brought this thought to mind.

***

Ashur had received rigorous instruction in the code of law leading to the ritual of blood sacrifice. A young bullock was selected from a herd penned outside the city's walls. The priests led the bullock through the sheep gate, inside the tabernacle, and into the presence of the high priest. They tied the animal to the altar. The high priest motioned Ashur to come forward. As instructed, Ashur approached the altar and laid his hands on the head of the sacrificial bull. By this act, the sins of the offerer transferred to the bullock. The innocent beast died for the sins of the offerer. By substitution, the death of the animal satisfied God's perfect righteousness.

A priest put his arm around the bullock's neck and tilted the animal's muzzle toward the ceiling. The high priest lifted the knife above his head and buried the blade into the animal's neck. In spite of the careful placement, the point of the blade struck bone and temporarily lodged. Ashur gasped as the blood spurted forth, spattering at his feet. He watched the terrified animal plunge against the restraining rope, threatening to break free.

The high priest held onto the knife as the powerful beast severed his own jugular. With each heart-beat, the dying animal literally pumped his own life's blood upon the altar and the floor of the tabernacle. The animal's tongue lolled out, and he finally expired. The priest collected blood in a basin, then pulled aside the veil and went into the Holy of Holies, approaching another altar. He dipped his fingers into the blood and sprinkled it on all sides. Then he poured out the remainder of the blood at the foot of the altar.

The priest skinned the bullock and carved it into pieces. The wood of the altar was set on fire. The oppressive heat in the building and the sweet odor of burning flesh made Ashur uncomfortable. His eyes swept the room, finally meeting those of his father. He detected a slight smile on Machir's face. The rituals taught the people the purity and holiness of God.

***

A man named Jubal Ben-Adah became one of Ashur's favorite visitors. The purveyor loved to tell long, fascinating stories of his travels. He had crossed the length and breadth of the continent and was accomplished in several languages.

According to Ashur's father, Jubal Ben-Adah was a shrewd trader of horses. "He is prone to exaggeration, but fearless, and many of his escapades are true."

The man found an attentive audience in Ashur and the other young people around Solem. He embellished his stories with descriptions of exotic cities such as Senjirli and Hordofan. Not particularly receptive to lessons taught by the reader of the code, he would appear within the group at the precise moment the elders were finishing their instruction. The old rogue would weather the withering stares from the elders and enter into the storytelling.

"The forest bok is the shyest creature on the face of the earth," he would intone in a conspiring way. "You might see it slipping through the forest as silently as a spirit.

Its hooves make not a whisper in the driest of leaves before it vanishes before your very eyes. Years past, I was stalking one in the Black Forest the year after the great wolves came to Solem. I had drawn my bow to let fly my arrow. Suddenly I saw movement out of the corner of my eye. I looked to my left and there appeared the huntress of the Black Forest moving through the trees. The forest bok and the huntress vanished before my very eyes as if she had stolen him away. That night she appeared to me in a dream and revealed answers to my innermost thoughts."

"Please, Jubal Ben-Adah," an elder said. "Consider the young men. The testimony of a drunkard is uncalled for. You probably stumbled upon a youth with long hair."

"Is it wrong for the man who has no wife to seek the warmth of strong drink?" Jubal seemed genuinely hurt by the elder's response.

"It is wrong in the quantity that you have been observed ingesting. The drunkard shall have no place in the kingdom of God."

"I drink against the miseries of life. Once I had a great love in my life, but, alas . . ." Jubal gestured sadly.

On the way home, Ashur's father assured his dubious son that some tales might actually have occurred as Jubal Ben-Adah had related them.

"The meat of the forest bok is delicious, as he said. I wish I could walk like I used to. We would go into the Black Forest and not return until you had tasted the best of the best. As for the existence of a huntress in the forest, I doubt that."

"I like Jubal Ben-Adah, Father. Do you believe he is a drunkard?"

His father was silent for a moment and seemed to measure his words before replying. "I enjoy Jubal Ben-Adah, too. I have no doubt that he has, at times, had too much to drink. Nevertheless, it is not our place to judge him for his shortcomings. We do not know what manner of hurt he has suffered. It is our place to be his friend. I see no harm in that. You know better than to make the same mistakes, do you not?"

"Yes, Father."

* * *

The air was fresh with the dew of early morning as Ammi and her brothers went out through Solem's main gate. Ammi lagged behind for most of the way, for her legs were not as long as those of her brothers. When the solitary old terebinth tree came into view, she ran forward. However, the brothers, sensing some sort of competition, raced ahead and threw their arms around the trunk. The three spent the morning playing under the great tree. They tossed rocks into the pool, climbed onto low branches, and rested in the shade of the tamarisk grove nearby.

Ammi thought of her new hero, Ashur, the son of Machir, the young man the elders praised. She imagined Ashur striking out alone, across the wilderness, with the admirable goal of sitting at the feet of the reader of the code. She pictured him now, braving wild animals and snakes. She became so involved in her thoughts that she spoke aloud as though she addressed him.

"Do you go home in the dark, at night?"

"Who are you talking to?" her older brother asked.

"You don't need to know," Ammi snapped.

She fantasized that one day a prince of her people would carry her away in his chariot. At the same time, this prince would put Pithon in his place. Her hero would teach him a lesson that would render her tormentor permanently reformed. She hoped to catch a glimpse of this young Ashur. Then she could put a face on her dream prince.

Malta did not fit the image of her prince. Though Malta was a fine young man, he had already been vanquished and bloodied by the bully. Malta would not serve as her champion.

Before the children realized it, the sun had reached a certain point in the sky, and they sensed they should return home. Ammi straggled behind.

"Come on," one of her brothers shouted irritably. "Mother will be angry at you if you do not come."

Ammi cast one last look back toward the tree and the pool. Surely this was her favorite place in the world, she thought. Reluctantly she turned and ran after her brothers.

***

The singsong calls of the reader of the code brought Ammi's head peeking out the door of her father's house that afternoon. She ran down the street to the steps of the temple where she could watch the men gather in the shade of the village gates. She soon became bored with the proceedings. No young stranger appeared. She wandered back down the street until she found her friend Merab. They played together for a while.

Sensing that her mother might be concerned over her absence, she ran home to let her know what she had been doing. Her mother sent her out to get some flowers for the table. She gathered several desert gardenias from their garden. Then she placed one of the delicate flowers in her hair. She was standing in the doorway when she caught sight of Malta and another young boy. The stranger must be Ashur, the boy the elders had praised, she thought. Malta's father and another man followed them down the street.

The boy was slim and dark-skinned, with large eyes. Locks of thick, wavy hair curled in ringlets over his forehead and framed a ruddy, finely tanned face. A signet ring hung from his neck. He was slighter in build than Ammi had imagined, smaller in frame than one accustomed to subduing wild animals, but no less heroic in her child's mind.

Both of the boys carried bows and quivers of arrows secured by leather straps. Ammi's eyes widened as they met his. She knew she was staring and that Malta saw her, for she heard him laugh. "You have an admirer, Ashur," she heard Malta say to the boy.

"Oh, no," Ammi muttered. She turned and fled into the house.

***

Ashur and Malta left the village together. They separated, however, when they reached the area they planned to hunt, having found it more effective to hunt alone. Ashur felt more secure in knowing his friend was nearby. He carefully worked his way through scattered euphorbia and buck brush on the edge of a field and flushed a single hen quail. The bird flew only a short distance before it dropped to the earth, running from him on wobbly legs, dragging a wing along the ground.

He drew his bowstring to the corner of his mouth, found his aim point for the distance, and released the arrow toward his target. The flight of the arrow was straight and true until it struck the ground under the startled bird.

The bird recovered enough to make another short flight. It plummeted to earth and again trailed the crippled wing, clucking weakly. Ashur followed and was almost close enough to get off another shot. However, the bird flew a short span and again dropped to the ground, trailing the supposedly injured wing. He continued the stalk until he had closed the distance sufficiently to loose another arrow at the bird. As he was drawing the bow, the hen launched herself into flight. She gained altitude rapidly, the injured wing now miraculously healed. The quail made a wide arc to the right, sailed over his head, and flew all the way back to the place where he had first seen her.

That evening he told his father the story. Machir was unable to contain himself and laughed aloud as his son completed the story. "I am glad you did not kill the mother quail. She had a nest nearby or chicks hidden there. She was taking you away from her nest or her chicks. Normally, if you flush a covey of quail, the best thing to do is to kneel behind a bush. Wait a few minutes for them to calm down, then begin to call softly to the scattered birds."

Demonstrating, he whistled, "Whoo-whitt, whoo-whitt," imitating the male bird, then "Twooey-thi, twoo-ey-thi," the hen. "First, one of the birds will answer you, then another, and soon the entire covey will begin to run toward you. You can probably get a shot at one of the birds—sometimes a couple of shots. Now you try it."

They laughed together at his first feeble attempts. "You sound more like a lovesick owl," Machir said. "Listen to the quail call to one another in the fields. Call to them and practice your calls. When they begin to answer, then you will know that you have it right."

***

Occasionally Machir was unable to go into the village because of pain in his leg. Ashur, eager for more latitude as a young man, persuaded his father to allow him to go into Solem alone.

"But the boy is too young to go to Solem by himself," Nelmaah argued.

"No, I'm not, Mother," Ashur insisted, fearing she would persuade his father to withdraw his permission for him to go into the village alone. "I will be staying with Malta. His father will look after me. I do not need anyone to care for me, anyway. Father and I have been in the forest together, at night, and

I was not afraid. It will be in the daytime. I will have my knife and my bow."

"The boy must continue to grow," Machir replied. "I want him to sit at the feet of the elders. He will soon be a young man and must be pre- pared for greater responsibilities. I do not have time to go with him to the village, nor can we spare anyone from work. He will be all right."

He turned to address Ashur. "The desert people have a saying 'Elohim takes care of all things, but remember to tie your camel.'" This was his father's way of telling him to be careful.

***

Early the following morning, Ashur left for Solem. The journey was not long, but it was the first time he had made it alone; therefore, it was more on the order of an adventure for him. He did not stop along the way, even at his favorite place, the pool by the terebinth tree, but went straightway to the village.

As Ashur entered the gates and walked down the street toward the temple, he noticed a young girl watching him from the doorway of one of the houses. He was struck by the beauty of the little girl with the white flower in her raven-black hair. He noticed the unique curl at the corner of her lips. Not yet having more than a passing interest in young girls, Ashur ignored her. He laid his knapsack on the threshold of the temple, where he thought it would be safe. Malta joined him, and they went to sit at the feet of the elders gathered at the city gates.

When he returned to the steps of the temple, a white flower lay on his knapsack. Ashur picked it up and inhaled the delicate fragrance of the desert gardenia. The little black-haired girl must have placed it there. He looked around, but she was nowhere in sight. This must be the flower she was wearing in her hair, he thought, smiling. He walked toward Malta's home with a bit more swagger in his step. The girl's attention had made him feel very special.

***

Orders from the king had directed Dedan to depart from Solem immediately for his new post.

"Be careful with that!" Ammi cautioned, as she watched servants load their possessions onto wagons. A few items of furniture were elaborate. She knew her mother wanted them to be undamaged for her role as wife of the new royal merchant of Megiddon. Her mother and brothers already awaited them there, having left Solem two weeks earlier. Two of the four wagons had returned to transport the rest of her father's goods. Ammi had stayed with Merab as long as possible. She waited patiently until a place for her was made on the wagon.

While she waited, Ammi occupied herself with observing the two men who would serve as guards for their two-wagon caravan. The rough, bearded men were imposing. The taller of the two, the Nubian, carried a long spear and shield. A long sword hung from his belt. He wore a plumed headdress and carried the skin of a black-maned lion draped over his shoulder.

The other man was not as large, but was solidly built. The man saw her eyeing the wicked dagger at his belt, and he began to finger the ornate gold handle. Ammi averted her eyes.

When the wagons were loaded, Ammi took her place beside Dedan. She waved good-bye to Merab.

"Good-bye, Ammi," her friend said, "I wish you didn't have to go."

"I know. I feel the same way." She glanced around the familiar surroundings. Ammi did not share her brothers' sense of adventure. She would never see Merab again, nor the pool by the terebinth tree. Worst of all, she would never get to know the boy called Ashur. The wagon lurched forward, and she tightly clutched the edge of her seat.

"May Elohim smooth the road before you," she heard an elder say as they left the village of Solem.

For most of the day, Ammi enjoyed her greatest adventure to date, but the continuous jolting of the wagon took a toll on her enthusiasm. The trail seemed endless. The wagons halted when they reached a tree fallen across the road.

"How much longer before we can stop, Papa?" Ammi asked.

"We will camp near the river, where we will have plenty of water and firewood," Dedan replied. "When the sun sets on the—"

The hiss and thunk of the arrow into the side of the wagon cut off his sentence.

"Papa!" Ammi screamed, clutching his arm. Men ran toward them from out of the forest. She saw the huge Nubian guard leap to the ground. He threw his spear at the men, then drew his sword and swung it with all his might. The long, curved blade felled the first of the robbers to reach the wagons. Another of the attackers shot an arrow into the black man at point-blank range. Others rushed him, slashing and hacking, and she saw him go down.

Her father and the other driver fought valiantly, but they proved no match for the fierce brigands. The driver perished, writhing on the end of a spear. Her father stumbled and fell from the wagon, losing hold of his sword. One of the thieves raised his axe high to finish him, but their leader stopped the man.

Rough, bloodstained hands reached and dragged Ammi from the wagon seat. She struggled weakly as the powerful leader tied her to a limb of the fallen tree. The men tied her father's hands behind him. Loud voices laughed and cursed in turn as the men rummaged through the wagons.

As darkness gathered, the robber band built a large fire and cast lots, gambling for the most prized of her father's goods. When the outcome was decided, the majority of the band left. However, three members remained with the leader to divide her father's purse of gold and to decide Ammi's fate. She listened in horror as the leader of the band described what they intended doing with her father. They proposed to sell her in the slave market in Edom.

The men gambled again to decide who got to kill her father. The winner must decapitate him with one blow of the sword to complete the wager. If the first try was not successful, then the purse and Ammi went to the man who completed the beheading. Ammi hugged the tree trunk tightly. She feared the worst things her mother had ever warned of were about to happen.

***

Machir and Ashur were hunting on the opposite slope when they heard the sounds of the ambush. Machir had ordered Ashur to stay put and climbed to the hill's crest. The odds were too great to attempt a rescue. They had remained nearby, watching for an opportunity. When the gang of bandits divided, Machir decided that they must risk their lives to try to save Dedan and his daughter. He and Ashur approached the camp with practiced stealth. Machir hated to put his son at risk, but there was no other way.

"Listen to me carefully," Machir whispered. "Wait until I strike one of the men on the left. See the big man on the right? When he stands to his feet, shoot him in the chest. Place the arrow in his chest just as you would hit a target. Don't look into the fire. It will ruin your night vision," he reminded. "After you put an arrow in him, run into the forest as if you were running your fastest race. Don't stop until you get back to the oasis house. Wait there for me. If I don't get back before morning, go to Solem and tell the elders what happened here."

Machir gripped his son's shoulder. "Steady now."

"I'm not afraid, Father," Ashur whispered.

Machir advanced quickly to the fire's side and killed the first man before the man could react. He whirled and brought the heavy sword across the second man's face. The man's shield partially blocked the blow. He was stunned, and he dropped his shield into the fire, reducing the brightness. Machir struggled with the injured thief, his back exposed to the huge man that was Ashur's target.

As Machir had said, the man stood to his feet and drew his sword. Ashur's arrow arrived simultaneously, piercing the man's shoulder.

The man's scream aided Machir in locating him. His sword blow was expert and unerring, slicing deeply into the man's face and neck. The leader of the band fell heavily, blood spurting from the fatal wound.

Ashur forgot to run. He stumbled into the light of the camp, dazed with the terrible violence he had witnessed. "You killed them all, Father," Ashur said, numbly.

Machir jabbed the big man with the point of his sword to make sure he was dead. Then he wiped the blood from the blade upon the man's tunic.

"You did well, my son." He noticed that Ashur's hand on the bow was shaking, and he softened his voice. "We did what we had to do. Come now. We must get Dedan and his daughter back to Solem." He cut the bindings that held them, selected the cleanest of the swords, and handed it to Dedan.

"The king's men will want to know about this. The chariot warriors may be able to catch the rest of them. Quickly now, help me drag this one to that ravine over there. We will cave in the side of the bank and cover them with dirt and rocks."

Ashur came forward and grabbed one of the men by the leg. As he did, he met Ammi's eyes. She said nothing, nor did Dedan. They both appeared to be in shock. Her face was pale and her arms wrapped tightly around her father's arm. Ashur steadied his trembling hand and tried to act as though this was routine for a young warrior.

CHAPTER 3

The Black Forest

Ashur's boyhood had been a happy one. Under Machir's watchful eye, he explored expanding boundaries each day. He wrestled and ran footraces with the other boys his age. He learned to use a spear and bow and to trap wild animals.

Machir instructed Ashur, while he was still at an early age, in driving the chariot, Machir's own first love. Ashur exhibited a natural instinct for handling the horses. When the boy grew older, Machir decided to give him a horse of his own.

When King Solomon's father conquered Zobah and secured the northern borders of Israel, he took more than one thousand fine chariot horses. The horses were hamstrung so that they could not be used in war. Solomon ignored the admonition of his religious advisors and the written code, and he bred these horses with ones purchased from Egypt and Kue. Some of the finest of these horses were entrusted to Machir. The offspring of this breeding proved equal or superior to any other horses in the world.

The colt he gave Ashur was a foal of one of the finest chariot horses from those that had been hamstrung by the king. How the stallion managed to service the mares with his weakened legs was a mystery. Nevertheless, Machir had only to put the selected mares into a separate corral with the stallion. The mares somehow squatted for the beautiful stallion or perhaps went to their knees to help him.

"The mare is most important in producing fine offspring," Machir instructed. "Your colt has his mother's kind eyes and friendly disposition. No matter how fine a foal is physically, he will be useless if he inherits his mother's bad temper."

Ashur loved the colt. For the first
time in his son's life, Machir had
trouble getting him to do his chores
and other duties. The boy wanted to
be with the horse every moment of
the day. He groomed the horse until
his silky coat, mane and tail flashed
in the sun.

As his confidence grew, Ashur wandered further and further from home
on his hunting trips. Ashur decided
to visit the area his father called
the Black Forest. This forest was
so far from home that it was necessary for him to make camp two
nights on the way. He ran across
forest and fields with his faithful
dog, Chazad, loping easily at his
side. The first night, he bedded down
in an old oasis house on the edge of
his father's land. The second night
he set up camp near the Black Forest
and gathered wood to build a small
fire to ward off the cool of the evening. Any wandering beast would be
afraid to approach the fire.

Fallen limbs provided kindling
for an old hardwood stump he wrestled from the ground. He stuffed dry
leaves underneath. Using hardwood

shavings and flint from his pouch, he produced a tiny flame. Ashur shielded the smoldering leaves from the wind with his body. The flames leaped up, chasing back the shadows, reflecting eerily in the dog's eyes. After a time, the fire died down to a glowing bed of coals. Beyond the shadows it was pitch-black.

The warmth of the fire comforted them. He wrapped himself in a blanket, arms under his head. Chazad put his head on Ashur's knee and snuffled contentedly by the campfire. Ashur reached down and patted him on the head. He ran his hand over the dog's black face and smoothed the soft white hair on his haunches and his one white leg. The young explorer did not feel so alone with the devoted dog by his side. He had camped out before with Machir, but he had not spent nights out without a human companion.

Gazing up at the vast expanse of sky and the stars, he felt very small. Words of the old prophet Iddon came to him: "The fool hath said in his heart, there is no God." Looking out into the darkness, he experienced a moment of panic, but the excitement and test of his courage were stronger than the fear. "There is nothing out there in the night that isn't there in the daytime," Machir had said when Ashur had expressed his anxiety as a young boy.

At dawn, Ashur trotted out across the plain with Chazad loping easily at his side. He had resolved that he would explore this forest area that he had never entered before, not even with Machir. He went through some euphorbia bushes and stood quietly looking down into the heart of the glade that opened before them. The breathtaking beauty of the place awed him.

A drop of moisture on a leaf caught the sun's rays and flashed more brilliantly than the purest diamond in the king's coffers. A misty haze rising from the springs gave the Eden-like glen a mystical quality. The smell of the forest was different from anything he had ever experienced. Magnificent Aleppo pines, oaks, and tamarisk trees formed a giant canopy overhead. Rotting leaves and logs all contributed to the pungent odor that filled his senses with excitement. Sounds of wildlife were everywhere.

He glanced down at Chazad. The dog was motionless, his nose and ears working, trying to take in all that was happening around them. The dog's attention was riveted to the sound of rustling leaves off to Ashur's left. Ashur had already identified an agur, a type of hermit thrush as the source of this rustling. He could observe the bird scratching in the leaves from his more elevated viewpoint. One of the euphorbia bushes beside him housed a deserted bird's nest, but he could see that it did not belong to the agur. Only the bush robin had the distinct habit of lining its nest with a snakeskin.

Machir had often mentioned the succulent meat of the forest bok. Ashur was intrigued and determined to bring back the rare trophy. "Nothing can match the taste of the forest bok. I wish they were not so hard to come by," Machir had said wistfully, capturing Ashur's imagination with tales of the illusive quarry of the forest. "If not for my old war wound, I would go with you."

Ashur took a vial of liquid from his belt. The concoction was a secret formula that Jubal Ben-Adah had made from a doe in estrous. He called Chazad to him and released a couple of malodorous drops of deer urine onto his back. The dog had come to him expecting to be petted. When he turned to smell the drops on his back, he reacted as though it were burning. Chazad rolled onto his back and twisted from side to side, trying to rid himself of the smell. The dog finally settled down, giving his master an injured look. Ashur put a couple of drops of the liquid onto a piece of deerskin his mother had sewn to his tunic for that purpose. He hated the stuff himself, but it was effective in masking his scent.

Ashur took some special powdered leaves from a leather pouch at his belt. He held out his arm and watched carefully as they fell toward the forest floor. Assured that the wind was still blowing toward him, he and Chazad advanced through the forest.

Ashur saw a deer move on the far side of the spring, but he could not make out the species because a bit of foliage partially obscured it. Chazad followed quietly at his heels. Each time the deer raised its head, Ashur froze and Chazad did the same. They progressed to a point where the stalk became more difficult. Ashur pushed down on Chazad's hindquarters, which meant he should assume a sitting position. He signaled for the dog to wait.

Carefully Ashur stalked the deer. Finally, he judged that he could get off a clear bowshot. He drew the bow as the buck stepped into the clearing. To his disappointment, the hoped-for forest bok was a common deer that he had taken often. Ashur turned and called to the dog as the deer bounded away. "Come, Chazad." The dog immediately appeared at his side. "Well, Chazad, I guess it was foolish of me to expect the first animal we saw to be a forest bok. We'll have to find another one."

Ashur and Chazad went down to the spring to drink. They continued hunting along the bed of the dry wadi deeper into the forest. Machir referred to this heavily wooded area as the Black Forest. This ominous name had piqued Ashur's interest for some time. When Machir gave his permission for Ashur to explore it, his mother was greatly chagrined.

Machir had taught Ashur the lore of hunting in woods and fields. He knew never to camp in a wadi. The deceitfully dry riverbed could immediately transform into a torrent of water from rains upstream. He knew to shuffle his feet and to make as much noise as possible when traveling a bushy trail where he could not see the ground. This warned the fanged serpent and allowed it time to get out of the way.

Spellbound as he was with the Black Forest, Ashur was unprepared for the hard lessons that he would learn this day. These were lessons hunters had confronted since the beginning of time. Deeper and deeper the boy and his dog went into the forest in search of the elusive bok. Ashur followed the dry wadi. His ears strained to distinguish the sound of a fallen leaf or

the wind from what might be a care-
lessly placed hoof. The forest was
alive with game. Nevertheless, they
hunted the whole day without seeing
their quarry.

They were on their way back to
camp when he finally sighted the
bok. Chazad, of course, first heard
the soft steps of some animal
approaching. Ashur tested the wind
again and left Chazad resting behind
a fallen tree. He saw movement and
believed the creature to be a deer.
However, he was amazed an animal of
such size could negotiate the dry
leaves, twigs, and branches without
making more noise.

Now he could make out distinctive
horns through the underbrush. He
drew the bow but was unable to get
a clear shot through the branches.
He weighed his chances that the buck
would step out into the opening. The
animal's actions indicated that he
had either picked up Ashur's scent
or sensed danger. The scent of a doe
in estrous must have confused the
bok because he continued forward a
few more steps. Before Ashur stood a
magnificent forest bok. Another body

length and he would be in the open. His coveted trophy stood frozen for what seemed to Ashur an eternity, but actually was only a few moments. The bok finally looked back in the direction from which he had come. Ashur knew it was now or never.

When he loosed the arrow, he knew it was on a perfect course. However, it struck a small limb and rattled harmlessly through the forest, sending the bok fleeing to safer haunts. What a disappointing conclusion to an exciting day, the boy thought. He called the dog to him and disgustedly began to search for his lost arrow.

Ashur noticed with a start that the forest was becoming darker. The sun was beginning to set. He abandoned the search for the lost arrow and cut back toward the bed of the dry wadi, which he thought was off to his right. The further he went into the forest, the more his confidence waned.

Ashur began to get more panicky the longer he walked without intersecting the dry wadi. Darkness closed in rapidly, and soon he could no

longer see where he was going. His
father had taught him to find directions by the stars, but here the
trees completely obscured the sky.
His father had once told him that a
hunter lost in the woods would probably circle to his left. He tried
to compensate for this tendency, but
soon saw that it was futile.

The most imposing landmark near
Solem was Mount Tabor, which marked
the border between the northern
tribes. Here, there were no hills
to climb where he could see the
familiar outline on the horizon. He
began to run blindly through the
woods. Finally, he halted under a
large tree, realizing that he was
not being rational. He held his hand
in front of his face but could not
see it. He sat against the trunk of
a tree. Chazad slipped in beside
him. He now had to face the prospect
of spending the night in the damp
forest with no fire to ward off the
cold or a prowling leopard or wolf.

Ashur sat for perhaps five minutes to gather his nerves. Again he
tried to find the wadi. From there,
he was sure he could get out of the

forest. Keeping a tight rein on panicky emotions, he began to feel his way through the darkness. He and Chazad had gone a few hundred yards farther through the blackness when suddenly the firm floor of the ground dropped out from under him. He fell into nothingness. To his horror, he found himself jammed tightly in a hole with his hands forced up over his head. Much worse, his feet were not touching the bottom of the hole. Nor could he reach the ground level above him with his hands. He struggled to contract his body and gain some kind of foothold, but to his sheer terror, he felt his body slip a few inches deeper into the pit.

Ashur stopped struggling and began to consider a need for outside help. He screamed loudly, but he knew that no one could hear him. The only sound he could hear was Chazad whining softly above him. He wondered if he could get Chazad to drag a limb to the hole. That would be useless. His hand could not reach the top of the hole anyway. He tried to get a hand down to reach his knife, but it was jammed tightly against his hip. Ashur began to fully comprehend the hopelessness of his situation. He thought of his quiver of arrows. They were not attached to his back. The leather string must have torn loose from the quiver when he fell into the hole. Either the quiver of arrows had fallen down into the pit, or they were somewhere above him. All sorts of ominous thoughts went through his mind when he tried to visualize what might be below him. A den of vipers might await him. He might slide right into the bottomless pit leading to the nether world.

Groping above him, he located the arrows. They had lodged crossways in the shaft above him. Cautiously he removed the arrows from the quiver. He placed the notched end of the arrows against the side of the hole and carefully began to pull downward on the point end. He put more of his weight on the arrows and struggled mightily to free his thighs and hips. This allowed him a few inches of progress, but the arrows gave way and he slipped back. Carefully clustering the arrows together again, he positioned them against

the side of the hole. The arrows
cracked and creaked under the pressure. Nevertheless, he began to inch
toward the ground's surface.

From the sound of the whines above
him, he could tell that Chazad was
leaning into the hole. Chazad was
also loosening some earth on the
side of the shaft. Dirt fell on his
head and into his face, giving him
more to worry about. While trying to
reach him, the dog might fall on top
of him. "Get back!" he shouted to
the dog. The harshness of his master's voice sent Chazad retreating
from the area of the hole.

Ashur contorted his body, alter-
nately digging heel, toes, and knees
into the sides of the shaft until
he could free his wedged hips. He
slowly inched upward until he could
reach the surface and felt around
carefully outside for a handhold.
His groping hand brushed and finally
grasped a root. He tested it with
his weight and pulled himself upward.
Sweating freely from the exertion,
Ashur emerged from the confines of
the hole. Chazad could restrain himself no longer. He was all over his

master, licking his hands, his arms,
and his face, threatening to topple
him back into the hole.

Ashur emerged completely exhausted.
He crawled a short distance away
from the pit, feeling carefully with
his hands. He found the trunk of a
large tree. Clutching Chazad and the
tree in the darkness, he finally fell
asleep. Chazad would have to warn
him of any danger. He was in no condition to defend himself.

Ashur was already awake as the
morning's first rays of sunlight penetrated the thick canopy overhead.
"Come, Chazad. We are going home,"
Ashur called to the dog. His desire
to hunt the forest bok had vanished.
They backtracked to the place where
Ashur suspected he had taken a wrong
turn. His sense of direction returned
with the daylight. He found the dry
wadi and the trail leading out of
the Black Forest.

When Ashur returned to his home,
he did not mention his misadventure
in the forest to either Machir or
Nelmaah. If he told his mother, he
knew there would be no such future
expeditions. He wondered if the first

hunter to become lost in the Black Forest had given it the name. He had learned several lessons. He never again wanted to be in this forest at night—nor to go to the forest alone. He now knew what it meant to be in total darkness.

***

Ashur wore the signet ring around his neck on a leather thong. Everywhere he went, he asked every stranger he met if he recognized the ring. However, the years passed and no one could give him any information that would lead him to the identity of his true father. He treasured the memento from his past, the only link with his unknown parents. That mystery became an obsession with him. He spent days and days in the area of the cave, throwing his knife against a fallen log or practicing with bow and arrow. Sometimes he sat on the ledge, brooding about how his father and mother had abandoned him there. He knew Machir and Machir's wife loved him and treated him as their own son. Nevertheless, Machir was in some ways a stern and distant father figure, and Ashur longed to have his adopted father hug him and confide in him.

Whoever had left the ring must have expected the baby to be found. Why would they not leave the baby in a more populated area? In the village or by someone's door would have made more sense.

Perhaps his mother had been a leper and was afraid to approach the village, he thought morosely. When she had seen Machir enter the cave, she may have fled out the other side and watched from some hidden vantage point as Machir took the baby. This line of thought was too depressing, so Ashur's mind shifted to his father. He surmised that his father must have been someone of prominence, for the ring was excellent and therefore expensive. However, it was not completely beyond the reach of the average person, so this line of thinking was not conclusive, either. Maybe the ring had not belonged to his father, he thought.

In frustration Ashur threw the knife with such force that it overturned its point in flight. The point glanced off the tree, and the knife skimmed out through the rocks. He searched and searched but was unable to find it. He poked around between the rocks and brush until the coming dusk forced him to abandon the search. Feeling quite sorry for himself, he trudged home. The knife had been a gift from Machir and was among his most prized possessions. He was determined to find the knife and vowed to return at first light to search the area again.

As he made his way through some buck brush, the leather string of his signet ring caught on a limb, yanking him to a stop. Carefully he freed the cord and grasped the ring tightly. He must never lose the signet ring as he had lost his knife, he thought. Then he would have no hope of finding his origins.

The signet ring was an emblem of authority in neighboring Egypt. The most popular form of seal was the scarab, a likeness of the sacred beetle. On the lower flat side were the inscriptions.

The people of Israel had adopted the practice of using a signet ring and wore the seal suspended from a string about the neck or arm. They carried it with them wherever they went. They cared for it as a very valuable possession. Used to stamp documents, this seal had the same legal validity as a signature. Without a seal, no document was considered authentic.

***

Nelmaah had never considered herself a beautiful woman. Even when young, she had been short and plump. Her shoulders were slightly too broad and her legs too thick. Short, blunt hands and fingers showed signs of constant use. Nevertheless, she had healthy hair and skin and an able look. The love in her eyes for her husband was all Machir needed to perpetuate the love he had for his wife. Nelmaah was a woman who was most happy doing things for those she loved.

Ashur's adopted mother had grown up working in the vineyards in a village near En-gedi. Although she readily adopted her husband's lifestyle, she often reminisced about her childhood. She often recalled memories of the vineyards, tramping the grapes, and the odor of the crushed grapes.

As Ashur grew older, he became vaguely aware of Nelmaah's tireless ability to perform the monotonous tasks of the home. She was up before dawn to light a fire in the hearth. He watched her working with her hands with wool and flax and laboring in the fields with the servants. When Machir was away, she handled the supervision of the servants and the hired men. In spite of these tasks, she still found time to nurture and instruct him.

Ashur grew to love Nelmaah as the only mother he had ever known. He loved both of his adoptive parents, but the presence of the signet ring was a lingering distraction in his remarkable and exemplary growth. Nelmaah and Machir had made no secret of his beginnings. From his earliest memories, Ashur knew the story of his discovery in the cave.

Ashur had casually called Machir's attention to Nelmaah's untiring devotion to him. Pleased with the boy's early maturity, Machir had told him a story of a woman he thought best symbolized the undying strength of a mother's love.

"Once a woman named Rizpah was concubine to the king of Israel. He was king before Solomon's father. Rizpah was a very beautiful woman. When the king died, there was nearly civil war over her. She had two sons by the king and loved them greatly. Solomon's father allowed Rizpah's sons to be killed by the people of Gibeah as redress for the bloody crimes of their father. You see, when the boys' father was king, he had most of the people of Gibeah killed without cause. He took their lands and belongings for himself. In recompense for this crime, the remnant of the people of Gibeah took Rizpah's sons and hanged them on the gallows tree. The king decreed that their bodies were to hang in shame until the rains came and Elohim washed this transgression away.

"Rizpah, the mother of the two boys, took her shawl or cloak, covered herself with it, and stayed beside the bodies of her sons. She kept away the carrion birds and the jackals, every day and every night for six months. Finally, the king had their bodies taken down and buried where she wished."

This touching story his father had told him of Rizpah's love for her sons was forever imprinted in his mind. He could imagine the horror of this scene. A brokenhearted mother desperately fought off the vultures and jackals to keep the decaying bodies of her sons from being torn and their bones scattered.

Ashur wondered about the mother who had abandoned him. He looked over at Nelmaah. She would never forsake him.

She and Ashur were walking together one afternoon after taking water to Machir and the men who were working in the fields. Nelmaah stopped to rest on a large boulder on the side of the hill. As usual, their conversation was about her home and the vineyards of En-gedi.

"Where would you plant the vines if we were to have a vineyard, Mother?" asked Ashur.

"On the east slope," she replied. "The soil is best there, but the rocks are many, and your father says we cannot spare the men to clear the ground."

Ashur went down the slope to the place she indicated. "Where would you put the rocks, Mother?" he asked.

"Over there. I would start a wall there," she said, pointing to a huge rock, one that was too large to move.

Ashur picked up a large rock and placed it beside the large boulder she had indicated. "This rock begins the wall," he said. "That boulder will be the cornerstone of the wall." Ashur shed his tunic and began carrying rocks to build the wall.

Nelmaah sought to humor him by joining in. She carried a few of the smaller stones to pile with the ones he had gathered. The oppressive heat soon caused her to abandon the task and return to the house, leaving Ashur on the hillside.

Late that afternoon, as the sun set, Ashur was still struggling with the heavy rocks. Early the next morning, he was back on the slope again, toiling under the hot sun through midday. The third day it was difficult for the boy to rise from his bed. Very little was accomplished on that day or the next. Ashur's right foot was bruised by a large rock that had fallen from the pile. His fingers were raw from scraping dirt away from the rocks imbedded in the ground.

"Will you help him, Machir?" Nelmaah said.

"The boy will soon tire of the rocks," Machir said. "You have said so yourself. A vineyard takes years to bear fruit. It will take him months to clear the rocks away, even years. He will soon realize the task is hopeless and abandon the clearing of the hill. I do not think he realizes what he has begun. Wait until he tries to move some big rocks that are in the ground."

"You talk to him," Nelmaah said, feeling responsible for letting the boy begin the impossible task and now being unable to persuade him to abandon the clearing of the slope.

"No, let him alone," Machir said. "He must learn for himself and learn his own limitations."

Nevertheless, as the days passed, Ashur did not waver from his task. His hands and body hardened. His ravenous appetite was a good measure of how hard he was working. He was almost always hungry now, and the food he devoured converted into muscle. He learned to use a tool to dig the rocks from the ground. In the evenings, his mother and the other women joined him on the hillside. Day by day, the rock walls grew.

When Machir saw the progress made, he gradually lessened the boy's required duties, allowing him more time to work on the hillside. After all, the boy should have some privilege as son of the master, he reasoned. He would not mind having a fine vineyard. He enjoyed the sweet wine as much as any man. Not to excess, of course. He was a man of discipline.

"The love he has for his mother drives him," Machir said one evening. He and Nelmaah stood side by side on the hill, watching their young son struggle to dislodge a large rock from the ground. "Now he is like a hoop rolling downhill, like the little wheel he played with as a child. A touch of the hand and he stays on track."

"Yes," Nelmaah said, hugging close to the side of her husband. "The vineyard must be completely enclosed by a fence or terraced with walls to keep the rains from washing the rich soil away," Nelmaah explained to Machir.

The large stones were moved, but the small stones that would retain moisture were left. Dew would settle on the rocks in the cool of the night. The vines would be trailed on the wall, keeping them off the ground.

"We will bring the choicest vines from En-gedi and will build a wine-press for the grapes. There must be two troughs. Bunches of grapes are put into the upper vat. They are trodden by the women, and the juice flows into the lower vat." She never tired of explaining the growing of grapes to her husband.

Ashur came to stand beside them to rest for a moment. "Another day in the future," she said in a louder

voice to include Ashur, "perhaps
Ashur will take a wife, and the two
of them will build their own room on
the house. I could watch my grand-
children play there and work in
the vineyard. She may be of my own
people, from En-gedi."

Ashur understood the underlying
meaning Nelmaah intimated when she
suggested that Ashur might take a
wife from the vineyard country of
En-gedi. The father of a lovely young
woman in Solem was from the area where
Nelmaah had been born. The girl's
name was Shoshanna. The charming
daughter of this distant kinsman had
delighted Nelmaah by bringing them
the sweet grapes of their vineyard
several times. Nelmaah had hinted
that she would not be in the least
unhappy if some day Ashur chose this
young woman for his bride. "Did you
not see the way she was looking at
you, Ashur?" she would ask, after
Shoshanna returned home.

"Shoshanna is a fine girl, lovely
and thoughtful," she now said.

"Yes, she is." Ashur only laughed
at his mother's plans for him and
returned to the rocks.

"The work of removing the rocks has made a man of our son. Look how strong he has become," Machir said proudly. Muscle now shaped Ashur's lean frame.

On one of Shoshanna's visits, she had asked to see the horses, to be alone with Ashur. He walked to the stables with her, intending upon letting her ride Tirsah as he led him about. Tirsah was nowhere in sight. Ashur was occupied with getting hay from a stable room and intended on calling Tirsah into the corral. Then Shoshanna could pet him and rub his velvet-smooth nose. He had been working Tirsah so hard it might take a bribe to entice him. He was unaware that there were already horses in the corral, obscured from his sight by the buildings.

Shoshanna was wearing a long, loose-fitting robe. As she wandered toward the gate of the corral, a strong breeze blew the garment, causing it to flap. Precisely then a brindle-faced stallion rounded the corner of the building. Fearing that he was trapped in the corral by this strange creature, he neighed in fear, and all the horses bolted for the gate, straight for Shoshanna. She screamed and turned to run. Ashur immediately realized the danger and leaped through the doorway to sweep her into his arms. He forced Shoshanna to stand still as the horses charged by on either side of them. It had not been necessary to hold her. She had a death grip around his neck. She was breathless for a moment, eyes wide with fear.

"Oh, Ashur, you saved my life!" she gasped, relaxing her hold on him, but not drawing away.

He shrugged his shoulders and took a step backwards, well aware of her softness and nearness. "They will not run over you if you stand still. If you run in the path of the stallions, that is dangerous. They might not have time to avoid you."

He was going to kiss her forehead in a brotherly way, but Shoshanna completely misjudged his actions, thinking he intended on kissing her on the lips. She threw herself into his arms again, locking her arms around his neck. Ashur was completely surprised and stepped back.

"Please, Ashur, do not tell anyone about this."

"There is nothing to tell," he exclaimed with a nervous laugh.

The moment passed, but neither forgot the incident.

* * *

One day Ashur was in the village of Nahal, talking to an old man, a transient, about the signet ring. "I know of a man that could probably help you," conceded the old man reluctantly. "He is a wise man, a fakir. Little goes on in this area that he does not know. He lives in the village of Endor." Ashur knew of Endor, a small village a day's march north of Solem, but he had never been there before.

"I will leave at once. I know that someone somewhere must know about my father," Ashur said. The old man said no more. He had told the boy of the fakir only to rid himself of Ashur's persistent questioning.

Ashur hurried home to tell Machir and Nelmaah that he planned to visit Endor. The village of Endor had enjoyed a dubious reputation in the past because of the fortune-tellers and mystics who plied their craft there. Machir looked on these fakirs and mystics with contempt and distrust. Ashur did not tell him that he was going to Endor to consult a mystic. He only told him a man in Endor might know something about his natural parents. Machir did not forbid him to go. He secretly hoped Ashur would learn something that would cause him to permanently put the past to rest. Despite Nelmaah's pleading, the usual fear of a mother for a venturesome son, Ashur left for Endor the next morning.

As Ashur walked down the street and rounded the corner of the last building, two unveiled women beckoned to him from a darkened doorway. "Come inside. I have many pleasures for you," one invited.

When Ashur lengthened his stride and passed by without acknowledging them, the young women angrily denounced him. He realized that these were probably the brothels that Sabta and Pithon were said to visit. On a more serious note, it was here that Pithon was rumored to have killed a man in a fight over a woman.

"You think you are too good for us, don't you?" one of the women shouted as she flung a rock in his direction. Fortunately, the prostitute's aim was as poor as her character. The rock bounced harmlessly along the ground. Ashur was looking back over his shoulder to see if any more rocks were coming his way when he stumbled over a man lying in the street.

The man cursed him. "Watch where you are going, you clumsy oaf!" The man tried to rise to his knees but tilted over, falling against the side of a building. His words slurred, and it was obvious to Ashur that he was drunk. The man did not attempt to rise again. Ashur continued down the street until he came to a sullen storekeeper of whom he asked direction to the home of the old fakir.

When he had found the mystic and paid his price in gold, the old man began to consult his supposed mediums. He poured a thick liquid into a bowl and began to stir it in spirals with a carved stick, mumbling incantations. After a while, he paused to peer intently into the center of the foul-smelling mixture.

"A young man loved a young woman," the old fakir said haltingly. "I see him now. He looks a great deal like you. He has thick black hair. The ringlets of his hair are tied out of his eyes with a leather thong. He has a dark, ruddy complexion like yours. He wears a signet ring on his hand. The young woman is beautiful and desirable. They are betrothed and very happy. The man's father is wealthy. His only son will inherit a vast estate.

"Wait! Someone else finds the young woman desirable, and she commits an indiscretion with the second man during a moment of weakness. She is now with child and not sure which man is the father of the baby. She runs away. The first young man does not understand why she has run away. He seeks her everywhere. The woman cannot be found. He never sees her again, nor does he ever learn that he is the father of a child.

"A hunter finds the baby in a cave. The mother, when she sees that the baby is found, goes away alone. She hurls herself off that mountain to her death. It is a sad and tragic story," the old man said sardonically. "I am sorry to have to tell it to you."

He clinked the gold pieces together in his hand and would have walked away. Ashur listened disconsolately to the old man's story but pressed him for more. "What of my father? What happened to my father?" Ashur insisted, his voice hoarse with emotion.

"I am unable to see any more. The spell is broken." The old fakir was unable to put together another story on the spot. "You must come back another time and bring more gold." He would have turned away, but Ashur grabbed him by the arm.

"You must not touch me. I am a holy man," warned the old fakir. He winced at Ashur's strong grip.

"You said that you would tell me where I could find my father. Now you have told me that my mother is dead and have told me nothing of my father," Ashur persisted.

"Come to me again next week and bring more gold. I will try to contact the spirit again."

Ashur's eyes met the fakir's for a moment, and he tightened his grip on the old man's arm. He realized disgustedly that the old man was a fraud. He had fabricated the story from what Ashur had told him.

"You have no idea what happened to my father, do you?" Ashur snapped explosively. "Nor do you know anything about my mother. You cannot concoct another story on such short notice.

"Tell me about my signet ring before I break your worthless old neck. On which leg did I wear the ring? If what you saw is true, you will know which leg I was wearing the signet ring when I was found." Demanding an answer, he tightened his grip on the back of the man's neck.

The old fakir took only a few seconds to contemplate an answer. When he considered the several possibilities for the location of the ring, he immediately decided that the safest course of action was to admit his falsehood. Fearing a trick question, he quickly noted that the ring could have been attached to either an arm or a leg, to the basket, or wherever. He decided that it was best to return the gold to Ashur.

"Here, take your gold and go. I am an old man and my heart is weak," said the fakir. He vowed never to attempt to deceive a vigorous young man again. "I must confine my divination to the elderly and widows," he thought.

Ashur learned a lesson from the experience. "Now I know why the code forbids divining," he thought. In his defense, though, he had not known the man was a diviner when he had gone to him. He muttered to himself as he headed homeward. "My emotions overruled my head. I must never be this foolish again."

He had stopped on the outskirts of Endor to drink from a raised cistern when one of a gang of cutthroats shouted, "There he is!" They began running toward him. Ashur realized immediately that the old fakir must have told them of the gold he carried. He ran along a street where rows of houses and shops lined the sides.

"Now we have him," the thug shouted, catching sight of two of his comrades blocking Ashur's path ahead. Ashur did not slow his gait. He dipped low and threw his weight into the first of the men. The point of his shoulder caught the ruffian in the middle of his chest, flipping him onto his back. The second man stumbled over his fallen companion. Ashur shoved the man aside and dashed on. The band of cutthroats let out a collective shout of outrage at his escape. It was quickly evident to his pursuers that none of them was a match for the superbly conditioned Ashur. Beyond the outskirts of Endor he paused to be sure that he was no longer being followed. He did not slow his pace again and vowed never to return to this evil place.

***

When not at work, Ashur spent time training the young stallion, Tirsah, with the chariot. He had neglected the horse while building the vine- yard. Now, with its completion, his main interest focused on Tirsah. The stallion seemed to enjoy the attention but wanted it on his terms. His training proved most difficult.

Laboring in the vineyard had hardened and strengthened Ashur and given him more confidence in handling Tirsah and the chariot. The horse possessed speed and stamina. However, he showed no sense of location for the chariot behind him. Day after day, Ashur worked with him, and finally in frustration he asked Machir to try his hand at taking the stallion around the course. Tirsah destroyed a wheel on Machir's chariot, trying to negotiate the curves.

Equally baffled, Machir observed, "He seems to ignore the obstacles at the edge of the track. He is so strong he is not afraid of the rocks. Tirsah may run right over a wall and kill himself. I am sorry, my son. I have seen one other horse like him. We could never do anything with him. I do not believe he will ever be fit for the races, the way he veers to the side."

Ashur led the horse into his stall. Tirsah rumbled approvingly as Ashur freed him from the halter, patted him, and brushed his hand across his smooth muzzle. A bond of affection continued to grow between the two.

Machir retreated to the house, and Ashur stood studying Tirsah as he fed on the barley that Ashur had handpicked to remove any stinkweed. "You are a spoiled, useless donkey," Ashur said, half seriously. "When will you learn to obey my commands?"

***

Ashur was determined, however, and continued his attempts at training Tirsah. Another incident occurred on the road to Solem. They passed two tamarisk trees growing beside the road. He turned Tirsah around and decided to try to drive the chariot between the trees. There was just enough room for the wheels to pass between them without striking one or the other. Tirsah, as usual, failed to respond quickly enough to the reins. The left wheel of the chariot crashed into the tree, bringing the chariot to an abrupt halt. Tirsah snorted his annoyance, backed up a few feet, and again pulled the chariot forward, causing the wheel to strike the tree. This happened several times. Finally, the horse turned around and looked back at his master with a look that seemed to express the thought, "What in the world is going on back there?"

Ashur considered another possible solution. He backed up the chariot, took a length of rope, and tied one end to Tirsah's head. Then he pulled Tirsah's head to the side and tied it to the chariot. If Tirsah could see what was going on behind him, it might help. He flicked Tirsah again with the reins, and after much coaxing from Ashur and balking on Tirsah's part, they started forward, but again the stallion pulled the chariot into a tree. The horse became so agitated at this treatment that Ashur feared he would hurt himself.

"Steady, boy, steady now," he coaxed, releasing the rope. He was fortunate that Machir was not present to witness him doing such a foolish thing. Again Ashur tried unsuccessfully, but Tirsah could not or would not acknowledge the presence of the chariot. Finally, Ashur shrugged his shoulders in defeat. "We will try again another day," he vowed stubbornly.

He returned the horse to the pasture, pulled the halter over his head, and turned him loose. The stallion trotted away from him a few steps and then returned to shove his nose playfully against his shoulder. Tirsah turned and bolted away at a gallop, sprinting around the field, his mane and tail flying behind him. Ashur watched with a shared understanding of the pleasure of exercising young muscles as the horse swept by him with powerful strides.

Ashur remembered the frail little colt that had frisked around the field on unsteady and spindly legs that looked out of proportion to the rest of his body. It was hard to imagine this was the same horse. Now Tirsah displayed a deep, broad chest and powerful legs. Muscles rippled as he arched his massive neck, tossing his glistening mane. He had the power to pull the chariot and the endurance seemingly to run forever. His physical perfection was a result of blending the finest of bloodlines.

***

Several days of rain interrupted the training sessions. When the chariot course dried out, Ashur asked Elkai, his father's best chariot driver, to accompany him. They went to the spot where he had tried to teach Tirsah to go between the two trees. Elkai was driving Challa, Machir's finest chariot horse. Ashur told Elkai to take his chariot with Challa through first, but to turn too sharply, making the chariot purposely strike the tree. As expected, Elkai's chariot struck the tree, causing Challa to rear and neigh in alarm. Tirsah watched as Elkai backed the horse and continued until the chariot wheels cleared both trees. When it was Tirsah's turn, the result was the same.

This time when he struck the tree, Tirsah looked around at the offending wheel. When Ashur backed him away from the tree, he responded to the reins. He guided the young stallion forward again. Although the wheel struck one of the trees a glancing blow at the trunk, the chariot passed through. They practiced this repeatedly, with Tirsah following Challa. Soon Tirsah was negotiating the trees without touching a wheel to them. Miraculously, he instantly responded to every signal of the reins. A near-fatal flaw had become a great strength. Tirsah developed an uncanny awareness of the wheels of the chariot. Whether from watching Challa go through the trees or from the long hours of practice, he finally caught on.

"I knew he was smart enough to learn if I kept trying," Ashur said to his father, who remained unconvinced at this point. Ashur continued to train his young charger on the roads around his home. Now that he acknowledged the presence of the chariot behind him, the horse improved by great leaps and bounds. Ashur began to boast to his father. "I bet he could even beat Challa," he said, gloating over Tirsah's achievements.

Machir could no longer refuse the challenge. Ignoring the objections of Nelmaah, he agreed to a race. "I will allow you to race, but not against Challa. Tirsah has no chance against Challa."

Ashur struggled to control his emotions. Racing the chariots around the outside of the walls was not a child's game. Machir acknowledged the fact that his son was becoming a man.

Machir chose Parsah, the only horse that could challenge Challa. Parsah would be driven by one of the best of the chariot men.

Tirsah reared at the start of the race and fell behind. Much to Machir's amazement, when they had completed the first half of the race, Tirsah ran only slightly behind Parsah. Around the final turn, Tirsah took the lead and pulled away. The result stunned Machir.

Ashur knew better than to boast over his victory. He bided his time before bringing up the subject of racing against Challa.

***

Ashur's thinly veiled challenges hastened the inevitable. Ashur prepared Tirsah early in the morning and had him waiting at the starting line. He stood at his horse's head, holding his halter as Challa, driven by Elkai, came into view. Machir and some of the other men approached on foot.

Ashur greeted them respectfully. "Health be with you, Elkai, and with you, Father."

His young stallion sensed the impending race and fidgeted nervously, struggling to free himself from his master's grip. When the older and equally large Challa drew near, Tirsah half reared and rumbled a challenge.

"Steady boy, steady!" Ashur pleaded, pulling Tirsah's head down, then stroking his sleek neck and shoulders. Muscles quivered under his hand.

The experienced and well-trained Challa ignored the threat and allowed Elkai to guide the chariot alongside. A servant took hold of Tirsah's halter, and Ashur mounted the chariot. He had no sooner picked up the reins than Tirsah reared, lifting the servant from his feet.

The horse's shoulder caught the man in his chest, sending him sprawling. Seizing the opportunity, Tirsah bolted down the track.

"Hold, Tirsah, hold!" Ashur shouted, struggling to rein him in. His words whipped away in the wind. The horse ignored his efforts, lengthened his stride, and propelled the chariot forward at ever-increasing speed.

Ashur cast a glance behind at his father. His heart sank. Machir appeared visibly angry at the young stallion's behavior and would likely cancel the race.

The horse and chariot completed more than half the distance around the estate before Ashur could slow him. He allowed Tirsah to run all the way around to the point where they had started. There he reined hard, and two of the servants came forward to grab the stallion's halter.

"We may as well cancel the race," Machir said. "Tirsah will not have enough left to give Challa a good race."

"No, please, Father. He will be all right. He is not tired."

Ashur watched anxiously as Machir cast a glance toward the morning sun. He knew his father was eager to get the men working.

Machir relented. "Walk him down to the quarter pole," he said. "Then bring him back. We can't wait all day for him."

Again they took their places at the starting line. Still Tirsah wanted to run and again tried to rear. The rope fell, and Machir gave a loud shout. Tirsah got off to a good start. The horses swept down the track side by side, hooves pounding the ground.

At first, Ashur was exhilarated in the awesome experience of hurtling along in the chariot. Fear replaced this feeling as the chariot wheel grazed the rock wall. Out of the corner of his eye, he saw Elkai apply the whip. Challa responded, quickening his strides and opening a lead over his opponent. He heard his father's supporters scream their approval. Sand thrown up by the older horse's hoofs burned his face.

"Run, Tirsah, run!" Ashur urged. His young steed answered the call and came up alongside his rival. The two horses pounded down the track, with the chariots abreast, bobbing head to head.

Again Elkai applied the whip, and the magnificent horse responded, extending his lead to a full length. Desperately Ashur went to his own whip. Already they were running as fast as he had ever experienced.

The two horses began the final circuit of the track, neck and neck. Tirsah drifted wide on the high-banked turn, taking the chariot into deeper sand. He felt the horse stumble and momentarily falter. Again they fell behind. Struggling courageously, Tirsah regained his balance and lengthened his stride. They moved up even with Challa's hindquarters and then edged into the lead. As they rounded the far turn, they began the home stretch with a two-length lead.

The young stallion's endurance faded toward the finish, allowing Challa to gain on him, but he held on for the win. As they crossed the finish line, Ashur screamed at the top of his lungs, raising his arms in victory.

Down the track he slowed his victorious charger and turned around. He climbed down from the chariot and took hold of the bridle, walking Tirsah back toward the starting point to accept his father's congratulations.

"What heart and endurance he has!" Machir exclaimed with grudging admiration. "Well done, my son."

When Machir spoke again, his tone held a new respect for Tirsah. "If Tirsah continues to gain strength, there is no other horse in our part of the land that can beat him. You see the way he places his hooves directly in front as he moves toward you. He does not toe out or place one hoof in front of the other to toe in."

"Yes, Father." The instruction was repetitive, but Ashur never tired of the lessons. Machir had continued to repeat them until they became second nature. "He has his father's head and carriage. That is the Arabian in him. See how he carries his head and tail high and arches his neck?"

Ashur knew the other characteristics by heart. Tirsah's head was wedge-shaped. His neck was attached high on his chest. He possessed the large flared nostrils essential in allowing him to breathe easily while he ran.

***

The return of Jubal Ben-Adah temporarily diverted Ashur's attention from Tirsah. He captured Ashur's imagination with yarns of the great chariot wars of the Hyksos shepherd kings, stories his people had passed down through the years. A short sideline story, however, stayed with Ashur. The purveyor related a fascinating story of a woman that he had encountered in his travels.

"There is a woman who lives near Anothoth, alone and outcast. People say she came from around here—or Nahal. I cannot remember. They say she is infirm of mind. A scandal occurred. They call her the Ez woman, the goat woman, for she lives in a cave with the goats. She grazes in the field and eats grass, imitating the animals. Her nails grow long like a bird's claws."

Ashur could not get the woman out of his mind. The man said the woman came from somewhere around Solem. He had to know more about her. He decided to go to Anothoth, where he would try to talk to her himself.

***

She was sitting on a log when he found her, moaning to herself and rocking her body back and forth in misery. Ashur stood looking down at her. The woman peered up at him through scraggly locks of gray-streaked hair.

Surely this dirty, disheveled creature could not be his mother, he thought, repelled by her appearance. She exuded an odor even worse than the goats with which she shared the cave. She had, however, a remarkable countenance. Her eyes expressed intense pain.

Finally, he gathered his courage, tearing his eyes away from the grievous face. He took two objects from a bag at his belt, holding them out to the woman. One item was a small piece of cake, and the other, the signet ring. The woman's eyes went first to the objects and then to his face. Ignoring the signet ring, she reached hesitantly for the cake. She took it and devoured it with greedy gulps. She showed no interest in the signet ring.

Looking around, Ashur wondered how the woman survived her wretched existence. Her only comforts were a ramshackle lean-to and the cave. The goats were her companions. Surely the people of the village must feed her, he thought. He began to question her about her past.

To his amazement, the woman gave very lucid answers to his questions. However, as he continued questioning her, she would ignore the current one and repeat her answer to a previous query. He could see that her mind was truly damaged. From what cause, he could only guess. She was evidently fond of talking, for she went on and on. It was a simple thing for Ashur to cue her to speak on the subjects of his choice.

The story that he had heard was true. From her own lips, the tale spilled out. She came from a village somewhere in the north country, one unknown to Ashur. She had been engaged to the son of an elder of the village. When providing the dowry, her father had attempted to defraud her betrothed one's family. When the marriage was canceled and her young man took another bride, she had left her family and the village in self-imposed exile. Her fragile spirit was unable to cope with the loss. Somehow she managed to work out her miserable existence alone. Now she was a broken old woman whose mind came and went, unbidden by her. When she related the story of her lost lover, it seemed as if the events had taken place yesterday. Her anguished eyes filled with tears at recounting the experience.

However, Ashur pieced together most of her story and established that there had been no child. He returned to Solem both depressed and relieved. He was downcast at being no closer to solving the mystery of the signet ring. The hopeless condition of the Ez woman disturbed him. One good thing remained, however—the woman had not turned out to be his lost mother.

***

Ashur sat at his father's feet, urging a continuation of stories of Solomon's exploits. He had heard most of the stories before. Each time he could persuade his father to repeat his descriptions of Jerusalem, Megiddon, the palace, and the battles of the Book of the Heroes. Each time his father would recall a little embellishment that rewarded Ashur for his effort.

"Solomon is king of a vast and powerful kingdom. More than two million mighty warriors stand ready at his command," his father said. Universal and required military service meant that another five million males in the kingdom were familiar with the weapons of war. His army consisted of all men in the kingdom between the ages of twenty and fifty.

"Tell me more, Father. Tell me about the palace at Jerusalem."

"Well, son," said Machir, "Solomon's great palace at Jerusalem is a magnificent thing. It is very difficult to describe the magnitude and beauty of it and the city. Solomon is erecting buildings made entirely of white stone, cedar wood, gold, and silver. Massive pillars support the buildings. The roofs and walls are adorned with precious stones set in gold. Solomon sits on a throne constructed of ivory and gold. He hears the causes of both the rich and poor. Six steps lead to his throne. On every step, at each end stand two lions of fierce countenance. The guilty tremble before the grandeur of Solomon and babble out the truth.

"Inside the palace," Machir continued, "are beautiful gardens and a variety of royal apartments, some below ground and others at higher levels. Many rooms have unique plastered ceilings embroidered with colors and paintings. The walls are sweet, scented with sandalwood. He has beautiful gardens and a glorious dining room for feasting. The rooms are full of gold—even the vessels are gold. Not one is of silver, for silver has become so common to Solomon as to be of little account."

"Describe Megiddon to me, Father. Tell me about the horses and the chariots." When his father ended his description, Ashur would bring up a new topic.

"In Megiddon, the young warriors learn to drive war chariots and care for their horses. They become skilled in use of the spear, sword, and bow. You would have gone to Megiddon, but the king is building a fortress at the station near Jerusalem, where you will be sent to train."

"Are there any men that can drive the chariot as well as your son, Father?" Ashur asked haughtily.

"Ha!" his father exclaimed. "Remember this one thing, my young bull. Always someone, somewhere is a little faster or a little stronger. You are one of the best I have seen, but remember, too, that the Lord Elohim hates man's pride above all things. Humility comes before honor. I have taught you all that I know. You are better than I ever was, and I never had a horse that was the equal of Tirsah."

CHAPTER 4

The Death Angel

Ammi's family was finally reunited in Megiddon. Soon she was her old self, attacking life with enthusiasm. It helped that her brothers envied her adventure with the brigands. Dedan was the one who had the most trouble putting the harrowing experience behind him. Often he thought over what would have happened to them if Machir and his son had not rescued them. Now, when he gathered his family together, his prayers for their safety were more earnestly spoken.

"I love going to the new shops here, Father, and to the market, but

I miss old Mr. Kabar. Don't you, Father?"

"Yes, Ammi. Old Kabar sure thought a lot about you. I thought the old scoundrel was going to cry when you told him good-bye."

"What does scoundrel mean?"

"It means he is a prince of a good man," Dedan said, laughing.

"Will we go out to get water today?"

"I don't know. Ask your mother?"

As the gregarious Ammi grew older, she loved to visit around the springs where the women and other young girls lingered. As she matured, she noticed the young men of Megiddon, but no one caught her eye as had young Ashur of Solem.

"Do you think we will ever move back to Solem, Father?"

"I don't know, Ammi. We will if the king says for me to."

Ammi quickly adapted to life in Megiddon. The little girl plumpness disappeared. She became thin, and her legs and arms grew long—too long, she thought. She felt spindly and awkward.

When she was between ten and eleven, she played the little mother toward her brothers. She corrected them when she found them doing something contrary to the instructions of her mother or father. Ammi acted as an extended arm for her mother, browbeating her brothers when they misbehaved. They were well behaved at times and unruly at others. Ammi, though younger than her brothers, was the steady one. She always obeyed both her father and mother.

***

A few years later, Ammi's widowed grandmother came to live with them. Ammi's father often commented that his daughter was much like his mother—fastidious, spirited, and wise beyond her years. Dedan derived great pleasure from watching her working alongside his mother in the garden among the flowers, the grandmother singing, teaching her the songs of their people. Ammi loved the wrinkled old woman. Her grandmother had an easy naturalness with life.

By contrast, Ammi's mother, in many ways, was not a strong woman. She was devoted to Dedan and to the children, but she leaned heavily upon the grandmother's strength. Ammi's mother was a fearful person, always worrying about some unknown catastrophe and life's inequities. Dedan, like the grandmother, joked away the worries, saying that the mother took herself and life too seriously. Nor was Ammi's mother as warm and affectionate as Dedan and the grandmother, so Ammi gravitated toward them.

"It is always something that I forgot to worry about that happens anyway," the old grandmother said to Ammi. "When your grandfather died, I felt so alone that I cried every day and every night. The holy man came to speak to me, but even he could not say anything to comfort me. When he asked me if I would pray with him, I said for him to pray that Elohim would let me die. Then you came that day and found me crying, and you cried with me. You told me how much you loved me and how much you needed me. Then I realized that I did have worth and could be here for you when you were hurting. You gave me a reason for living."

***

As the boys grew older, they became more interested in their father's merchant business. They developed a sense of pride in knowing that one day they would become the king's merchants—the Royal K'nani. This was fortunate, for they did not excel at anything else and seemed to harbor old jealousies toward Ammi. As Ammi grew older, her body softly rounded, and she began to draw attention because of her beauty. Ammi was unaffected by the praise, as though she did not know how beautiful she was.

Two months short of her sixteenth birthday, the king ordered Dedan back to Solem. Ammi's elation quickly turned to despair. Merab's father ruined her long-awaited reunion with her childhood friend. When they arrived in Solem, she learned that he had promised Merab in marriage to a crusty old merchant of Shechem. Merab's husband-to-be was undoubtedly wealthy, but more than three times Merab's age. To make matters worse, he had an old shrew of a wife already.

Merab resigned herself to the marriage, ever the dutiful daughter, tearfully submissive to the wishes of her parents. Ammi was deeply moved by Merab's plight. Ammi questioned the right of the merchant of Shechem to purchase Merab as his wife. Through his superior position and strength, he could now either protect her or degrade her, as he saw fit.

This was all wrong concerning Merab, Ammi thought. Traditionally, when a man and woman from different villages were betrothed, the man returned to his own village to prepare a place for his bride. Then the bride waited in breathless anticipation. The joyful news of his return set off frenzied last-minute preparations by the bride's family and friends. At least that was the way it should be. Poor Merab burst into tears when told her husband had come to claim her.

Ammi could not believe the man's attitude toward her friend. "Merab is young of age and fresh of skin. She will warm me in my old age."

During the entire ceremony, Merab's head remained bowed. The wedding guests began to ask why the bride seemed so unhappy. Her father made excuses, explaining that her tears were because she was leaving her friends and family. However, Ammi knew the real reason for Merab's sadness. Merab loved a young man from Nahal, and she wanted to marry him.

The large virgin-bride price paid to Merab's father called for witnesses. In their wisdom, the elders required two witnesses for each family, one young and one old. Merab chose one of her mother's friends and Ammi.

Ammi learned that the elders and holy men viewed marriage as a covenant between the husband and wife, before God. This bond was stronger than a contract and could be broken only by death.

"Tell me about having babies. I have heard the women of the village scream as though they would die. Is the reward of the baby so much greater than the pain?" Ammi's eyes were large and innocent.

"Yes, my precious one," her grandmother replied. "You will not be
afraid if you are so fortunate as to
marry one like your grandfather. I
am sure that God places great importance on the covenant between the
man and the woman. Do not worry,
Ammi. Your young man will know that
your character is beyond reproach."

Despite her grandmother's reas-
surance, Ammi continued to have
fears. Almost every young woman of
her time shared fears of shame, ban-
ishment, or death.

Ammi quickly befriended another
young woman. Her name was Shoshanna.
In her, Ammi found a compassionate
listener. Open and frank discussions
greatly deepened their friendship.
Shoshanna was not as intelligent as
Ammi, but she had the same gentle
spirit. She was taller than Ammi and
larger boned. Her upper torso was
very well proportioned, and by some
quirk of nature, her hips and legs
were slightly forward of her upper
body. This resulted in a noticeable
undulating movement when she walked.
The sensuous walk was not something
Shoshanna did by design. She had

been born with this physical anatomy and was unaware of anything unusual about the way she walked.

For this, or another depraved reason, Pithon had been drawn to her. Although Shoshanna resolutely rejected all his advances, he openly boasted to the men of the village that Shoshanna was his. He physically threatened anyone who showed the slightest interest or courtesy to her. Much to Ammi's distaste, Pithon hung around, leering at Shoshanna. The women were elated when Pithon joined the Gibore Hail and left Solem. Ammi worried for Shoshanna and cautioned her to avoid him when he returned to the village.

***

Dedan sat on a rock bench in his courtyard, watching his daughter comb her long hair. He thought back to another time when he had watched Ammi as a young girl, playing in a courtyard, trying to comb her brother's hair.

Six years had now passed since the king had ordered him to Megiddon. He had served the king faithfully as royal merchant and envoy to cities and villages in the north. He had returned with his family to Solem. The house was different, the courtyard was larger, and other signs of his new affluence could be seen. They now employed a gatekeeper and servants.

His daughter had raven-black hair that caught the sunlight, flashing through the ivory comb like lightning on a dark night. She had inherited beautiful skin from her mother and a gracious spirit from her father. Dedan was proud of his young sons, but he was sure his daughter was by far the most thoughtful and beautiful maiden in the land. She was the crown of his life.

Dedan did not seem to have much energy today. He had felt tired lately. Maybe he should sit and doze here in the warmth of the sun. "Bring me a cool drink of water before you leave, daughter. My brow feels feverish."

***

The festival of Pessah commemo-
rated the liberation of the people
of Israel from slavery. Ammi eagerly
anticipated the occasion, looking
forward to seeing old friends. The
entire community celebrated the hol-
iday in the banquet house of Solem.
She prepared for hours and entered
the hall wearing her best dress
of fine blue linen. She watched as
serving men hurried about making
last-minute preparations. Musicians
gathered at one end of the hall.

Ammi and her parents were about
to take seats when she caught sight
of a young man staring at her. She
turned her eyes away, but when she
glanced his way again, his attention
remained fixed on her. She was used
to men staring at her, but no one
had ever done so in quite the same
way. He made her feel self-conscious
and a little embarrassed.

He had apparently entered the
hall with his parents because he
spoke with an older man and woman,
staying with them as they made their
way around the hall. Ammi covertly
watched him as they renewed old
friendships.

"This is our daughter, Ammi," she heard her mother say to someone somewhere beyond Ammi's foggy consciousness.

The young man coming toward them was tall, slim, and extremely handsome. Then she gasped audibly as she recognized him. The distinctive signet ring hung from his neck, visible over his smart white tunic. The young man so obviously taken with her was Ashur, the fantasy love of her childhood.

"You seem to have an admirer," her mother observed.

Ammi saw him say something to the man whom she took to be his father. He pointed toward her. Her heart leaped in her throat and beat so fast she thought her chest would burst. The young man moved toward her through the crowd, his parents following.

Her father obviously knew them because he greeted them warmly. "Machir . . . Nelmaah . . . and this must be young Ashur. What a handsome warrior he has grown to be."

Ammi tasted the new wine from the cup she held and mumbled a greeting.

She hoped the hand she extended to him did not shake. The young man flashed an enchanting smile. She hoped the one she returned could compete.

The tables of food in the banquet hall were arranged in a huge square so that all faced toward the center of the room. Most of the tables were only circular skins or pieces of leather placed on the floor. The district prefect shouted for everyone to take a seat. Ashur maneuvered quickly to be close to Ammi by placing skins for his family to sit upon. She blushed at his boldness, but a sideward glance assured her that her father did not disapprove. Her mother occupied herself with telling Nelmaah about their years away from Solem.

Ammi became more composed as time passed, and she exchanged a few sentences with the young man. She learned more about him from listening to the two fathers as they laughed and joked.

They dined on roast corn and baskets of grapes from the vineyards, followed by bread and honey, succulent meats, and fruits and fishes.

They danced and sang songs. Her father joined the barefooted young people on the threshing floor and entertained the crowd with his playful antics. They watched in alarm as he shakily executed the knee bends required by the dance. An audible gasp escaped from the revelers when it was doubtful he would regain his erect position. The villagers clapped with appreciation when he proved successful despite his increased size and years.

Other young men tried to attract Ammi's attention, but she had eyes only for Ashur. They were separated for a while as Ashur participated in a planned dance with other young men. She suffered a momentary loss of confidence.

"I am too young," Ammi said to her mother. "Only out of kindness, he shows me this attention. Perhaps he was briefly infatuated with me and it has passed."

"I don't think so," she heard her mother say as Ashur returned to her.

"I have to dance now," Ammi said as she ran forward to join the female dance group.

Their bare feet flashed in unison on the smooth stones. Already she was breathless from the exertion and his nearness. The crowd clapped appreciatively when they completed the spirited dance. Ammi thought her legs would collapse as she leaped down from the raised floor. She stayed close to Ashur, happily watching the other young people dance.

The only dissonant chord was the sight of Pithon leering at the young women as they danced.

"Do you know him?" she asked Ashur.

"Only by reputation," he replied.

She wondered what he had heard but kept the thought to herself.

* * *

A week after the festival, Ashur came to call on Ammi. Each week he returned to see her. Her father allowed her to spend time with him in the courtyard. At the very mention of Ashur's name, she became animated, speaking enthusiastically with a special glint in her eye. "You have seen him, Father," she said, as if that explained everything.

The way he looked at her and the first words he whispered to her in private both surprised and captivated her. "You are very beautiful to me," he said simply, so disarmingly direct she scarcely blushed. She delighted in the unique way he phrased the "to me." He said the words as though he did not care how others saw her.

When they first met, Ammi mentioned that one of her favorite places was the terebinth tree by the pool. Ashur immediately volunteered that the pool was one of his own favorite places. Soon the two young people were meeting at the terebinth tree. The first time they met by the pool, her brothers accompanied her, but the antagonistic attitude of her brothers led them to defy convention and meet alone.

***

Alone in his home, Ashur smiled to himself thinking of the beautiful Ammi, the girl with the raven-black hair. Only once before had he seen another woman with hair so black and beautiful, someone with hair like hers. There had been a little girl in Solem when he was a boy. She was the one who had left the desert gardenia on his knapsack. Now, he wondered, could Ammi be the little raven-haired girl? Yes, he had no doubt. The distinct little curl at the corner of her mouth was gone. Only a hint remained on full and sensuous lips, but it was enough.

When Ashur returned to the pool by the terebinth tree, he took the desert gardenia to give to her. When he gave her the flower, her eyes met his, and she knew that he remembered. The fragile scent of the flower touched tender emotions in her memory. She buried her face in the fragrant flower in her hands, embarrassed to have him know that she had loved him since the first time they met. She had always thought the moment was hers alone, never dreaming Ashur would somehow remember the little raven-haired girl who had admired him from afar so long ago. Ammi was sure that he had not noticed her. He had never spoken to her or acknowledged

her presence in any way when they
were young.

"It is true. I have loved you
since we were children." Ammi wondered if he remembered that he had
saved her and her father from the
brigands when they were on their way
to Megiddon.

Ashur interrupted her thoughts.
"You are very brave to come to meet
me alone," he said. "What would your
mother say if she knew?" He admired
her daring streak, although it did
cause him some concern.

"She would be unhappy with me."

"And your father?"

"My father would laugh and recall
the days of his youth. He would laugh
again and tease my mother. It is my
brothers, I fear, who will find me
here with you and tell my mother,"
she said, growing more serious. "Let
us leave the main trail and go there,
to the tamarisk grove."

Alone together under the leafy
arbor of trees Ashur became aware
that Ammi was standing quite close,
for her face was very near. He had
never noticed that her lower lip
was so full and smooth—and appeared

so soft. Ashur was at once about to step back and simultaneously tempted to kiss her. The latter seemed the natural course of action. Her eyes became very large as he took her in his arms and kissed her. Ammi did not pull away but cast down her eyes. He found her mouth sweet and soft. Ashur tilted her head back and sought her lips again, tentatively pulling her tighter against him. She sighed with the longer kiss. Her eyes met his, and she stepped back, her heart pounding and her face so flushed that she put her hands to her cheeks to feel the warmth. She turned and ran back to the terebinth tree. She stopped, smiled and waved, then ran down the road toward Solem.

***

A time comes when a young woman must put behind the happy, carefree days of her childhood and confront the realities of this life. Ammi had received no warning or premonition that today would be such a day for her.

She ran all the way home, bounded up the steps leading to the house, and entered the living area. Her first clue that something was wrong was the sight of old Masar, her father's personal servant, slumped in a corner, sobbing.

"Masar, what is wrong? What has happened?"

"Your father, Katan-Ammi," the old servant responded, addressing her with her father's favorite endearment for her. "His heart stopped. He has gone away from us," he went on, his voice choked with emotion. It was as though he were begging his young mistress to comfort him and offering no sympathy to her. The old man's face contorted with grief, and he again folded his arms over his face and huddled in misery. He had served her father with great devotion for many years and had been well treated in turn. The death of her father would greatly change the old man's life. He had little hope of having so kind a master again.

Ammi needed no consolation at this point, for she met the words of old Masar with disbelief. Everything around her now seemed unfamiliar, unreal. She ran through the house and into the bedchamber, where she found her mother. Seeing her mother's tear-stained face confirmed the worst.

The next day passed in a blur. People in the streets made way for the funeral procession. As the men prepared to place her father's body in the cold, rock-lined grave, her brothers tried bravely to fight back tears. Ammi stood numbly by. Dedan's friends tossed flowers onto the floor of the empty grave. She watched as old Masar ripped his tunic and others cried and tore their clothing, but she could only stand silently in disbelieving grief. Her father had always been there, and she had assumed that he always would be. Now he was gone, and she could no longer see him or be with him.

Back at her home, Ammi looked around the room at the simple things that used to give her such pleasure and warmth. A chill permeated the room. Her happiness and security were gone with the passing of her father. Only deep feelings of emptiness and despair remained. She walked to the fireplace, where they had spent so many happy evenings when the nights were cold.

***

A few days later, the old prophet Iddon came to see her. The old oracle walked over to Ammi, and she went to meet him. He hugged the distraught Ammi in his arms.

"I have lost my father," sobbed Ammi.

"He is not lost, my daughter."

"Why, Father? Why must my father go away? He was so kind. I miss him so much. Why does Elohim allow us to suffer so? Why must a good man like my father die and evil men like Pithon and Sabta live? Everyone in the village knows that Pithon and Sabta are thieves. They walk about freely, and no one does anything about it."

"Now, now, my daughter," consoled the old prophet. "I promise you that the sufferings of this present time are not worthy to be compared with the glory that will be revealed to us in Elohim. If your father had been old or suffered a long illness, he would have prepared you for his going away," old Iddon said gently.

"How can a loving God allow his people to suffer?" Ammi asked. "Is Elohim a cruel and merciless God? If I were God, I would not let my creatures suffer. I would not cast my own creation into everlasting fire." In her despair and pain, Ammi angrily accused God of injustice in taking her father and injustice in creating imperfect man. "My father was such a good man. Evil men like Sabta and Pithon go on living. Oh, holy one, I cannot tell you how terrible is my grief. I do not understand why we must suffer so much. Yet I know that Elohim can do all things," Ammi added, obviously confused.

"You speak words without knowledge, Ammi," said the old prophet. "Where were you when Elohim formed the foundation of the earth or enclosed the sea? Have you commanded the morning sun to rise or caused the dawn to know its place? Elohim is great, but we do not know him. The wicked do not always suffer in this life. They may even prosper. Elohim will judge the wicked. Death is no respecter of persons. The beginning of wisdom is to acknowledge the sovereignty of Elohim."

"If only I could see life as Elohim sees it," Ammi said. "I have said things too difficult for me to understand. Where is he that I could find him? I would fall down before him. My tears would stain his feet, and he would have compassion on me."

Iddon was surprised at this impassioned outburst from Ammi, for it was completely uncharacteristic of her. The people of Israel were unique in their monotheistic belief. Ammi's belief in Elohim was a deep, personal relationship, but the women of his day were not encouraged to speak out or to think on such lofty matters.

Iddon's old teacher, however, had related to him a story of a great and good man from a city called Uz. The man had experienced the most terrible tragedies and illness, losing everything that a man could lose. He remembered his own concerned questioning, for he had believed at that point that Elohim directly rewarded man based on his goodness. As an idealistic young man bent on good works, he himself was dismayed to learn that the godly suffer. He still remembered the old teacher's answers to his questions. His words to Ammi were a result of his own struggle with the question of suffering, learned over the years.

"Rest in the Lord Elohim, daughter. Wait patiently for him. Worry not yourself because of those who prosper in their evil way. The man who carries out wicked schemes will receive judgment. Worry only leads to evil doing. I have been young, but now I am old, yet I have not seen the righteous forsaken. Elohim loves justice and does not forsake his holy ones. Just as we do not know the way of the wind, we do not know how the bones form in the womb. We do not understand the marvelous works of Elohim, who makes all things. Remember this: people like your father live forever in our hearts. You have your whole life ahead of you. Your father would not want you to waste the good parts, forever mourning the bad."

Later, when Iddon started to leave, his parting words were a puzzle to her. "You will be richer all of your life for this sorrow," he said, and he turned and walked away without explaining his words.

***

News of the death of Ammi's father reached Ashur through a hired man of the village. "I must go to the village," Ashur said, thinking of the anguish Ammi would experience at the loss of her beloved father.

"You have responsibilities here," his father said. "You have stock to tend and other duties—to help your mother."

"Let the boy go to her," Ashur's mother said. She had observed Ashur's anxiety at being restrained from going to the girl's side. "Dedan was a good man and friend of all of the people of Solem."

Machir was always surprised when she opposed him, for she seldom did. He was a bit taken aback. It was usually Nelmaah who expressed reluctance to allow Ashur to leave the safe confines of their home.

Ashur went to Ammi but found that he had little to say that would comfort her. The loss was too great.

"One day he was here, full of life and mirth, then he was gone," Ammi grieved to Ashur. "To make matters worse, my mother has gone into a deep depression over Father's death, and she is no comfort to us. Fortunately, Father prepared my brothers to manage his business affairs. When my brothers notified the king of my father's death, authorization immediately came from Solomon designating them as the king's merchants. With the help of father's assistants, they have plunged into the work, giving them little time to dwell on their loss. There is no diversion to occupy Mother's grief. Mother and I were extremely close to father. Neither of us finds any consolation in the endless household duties we accomplished before with happy and willing hearts."

As time went on, her two brothers began to get disgusted with Ammi's continued disinterest in life around her. Their new positions as heads of the family brought them new confidence. They began ordering Ammi about in a tone of voice that they did not use even with the servants. Perhaps in this way the brothers expressed old resentments toward Ammi because she had been the favorite to whom their father expressed his love and affection. Her father would not have allowed this intolerable situation. Her mother was unable to discern through her grief what was happening.

Located near the strategic pass of Megiddon, Solem and Nahal were designated as chariot villages by the king. Almost all of the young men aspired to learn the skills of the chariot. The young women of the villages naturally admired those young men who showed promise of becoming the chariot warriors of the future.

Ammi's brothers were jealous of the attention given to Ashur and the other chariot warriors. They justified their own feelings of inadequacy by referring to Ashur as uncouth and

uncultivated. Her brothers dressed
in fine linen and no longer appeared
in public without their outer garments. Solving riddle-like anecdotes
and speaking in metaphors became
fashionable in King Solomon's court.
The brothers vainly sought to emu-
late the colorful speech.

Ammi's brothers sarcastically
called Ashur the young man who
always smelled like either a horse
or a sheep. They seized on ridiculing Ashur in this way when they
learned it never failed to infuriate
and provoke Ammi. She knew Ashur
to be usually freshly scrubbed and
wearing a clean tunic. The whole
of this spiteful teasing had come
from one incident. Ashur had been
working in the village sheepcote,
shearing the sheep, when she and the
brothers happened to pass by. He had
come from his work to speak to them.
He was covered with sweat and dirt.
There was, of course, no defense for
the odor emanating from him that day,
but Ashur had asked her pardon for
his appearance.

Ashur found it difficult to see
Ammi now. He had ample time to reflect

on Ammi's brothers' dislike for him, for his father sent him to the farthest reaches of his lands to watch the sheep.

***

Ashur left for Beten Telem sheepfold with a sense of urgency. One of the servants was ill. The man's dog refused to work the sheep without him and had returned home with him. On the way there, he and Chazad were forced to take shelter from heavy rain and winds under a rock ledge.

The sheepfold Ashur's father called Beten Telem lay in a protected valley. The one lone servant working without a herd dog tried to hold the sheep together. When Ashur arrived with Chazad, he learned that the early morning storm had scattered the sheep. A few were still missing. He followed the trail back to the fields where the flock had weathered the hard rains.

"Chazad, search! Search!" he called to the dog, waving him toward the sparsely wooded ravine. The dog stopped to acknowledge his command, then raced off in the direction of the gully. Ashur trotted across the field to the rise where he had last seen Chazad. He was alarmed to hear the dog growling at something below him, beyond his line of sight. He stopped to listen.

Hearing no sound other than Chazad's low growling, he readied his spear and advanced cautiously. He rounded the edge of the clump of euphorbia bushes that blocked his view. A big black bird startled him as it flapped its wings to rise above stunted trees. Another of the great shrivel-necked birds watched him from its perch on a dead limb. Ashur's eyes looked down to the floor of the ravine. There they met a shocking scene.

Vultures had come upon a mother ewe that had just given birth. Weakened by a difficult labor, the mother ewe was unable to defend herself. The grisly creatures were devouring the lamb and eating the hind parts of the ewe while she still struggled. Two well-placed arrows ended the lives of a vulture and the doomed ewe. Chazad scattered the others.

Ashur was so angry and sickened by the gory slaughter that he covered the carcasses with rocks to deny the cruel scavengers. He returned to the sheepcote, where he described the incident of the vultures to the servant. The man was not feeling well now. He left for Machir's estate, promising to return in a few days with replenished supplies. Ashur and Chazad remained with the sheep.

"If you hurry, you will get there before nightfall. Do not forget to see if my mother has any pudding cake." The man managed a smile. He was not likely to forget, for Ashur had reminded him three times not to forget the cake.

Ashur had little to do even without the servant. Chazad did all of the work. He raced about, keeping his charges together, administering a barking threat here and a nip there as the situation demanded. Occasionally he would return to Ashur's side for approval or to lap from the cool waters of the creek basin.

The dog's ears tilted to the side as he watched one of the ewes graze a short distance from the rest of the flock. The sheep was permanently marked on the face, probably by an infected tick bite. She preferred to graze on the shrubs on the edge of the field and frequently strayed. This did not make her one of Chazad's favorites. If she wandered a few more steps, she was sure to incur his wrath. The thought had no more than crossed Ashur's mind when Chazad leaped forward and descended on her like a black-and-white whirlwind. He grabbed her thick tail and allowed himself to be dragged a few feet before releasing the terrified ewe. One old ram charged Chazad, but he avoided him easily, almost nonchalantly.

Ashur reclined under a shade tree to savor a good laugh at the ewe's expense. She failed to stray again, now grudgingly submissive to Chazad's authority. No other incident occurred to capture his attention. He passed the time dozing under the leafy canopy of the trees while Chazad stood guard.

***

Ashur responded instantly to the dog's warning. Chazad growled into the dusk. His nose wrinkled in a snarl. The hair on the back of Ashur's neck began an involuntary crawling that finally steadied into his lean, powerful neck. The last of the evening light glinted on the tip of the spear as he moved easily from a sitting position to his feet. Shadowy shapes moving through the trees confirmed what he feared. Giant wolves moved to attack his father's flock. He could make out five of the beasts. His hand reached to position his bow across his shoulders.

"Steady, Chazad," he said, touching the dog, more to gain some measure of support for himself than to comfort the dog. He knew that the shivering of the dog was well founded. The wolves of 900 BC were formidable opponents. A youthful Ashur, with only a small dog at his side, was no match for them. Brought from their

usual haunts by the swelling of the
river, they had moved into more populated areas in search of food.

By now the lambs on the far side
of the grassy plain sensed that
something was badly amiss. They
began nervously to move away from
the small ravine where most of the
wolves gathered. Ashur moved forward
now to position himself directly in
the path of two large males that
were advancing. Carefully he put the
spear on the ground and very delib-
erately drew the bow from his shoulders. Careful not to make a sudden
movement that would provoke a charge,
he nocked an arrow without taking
his eyes from the lead wolf. A smile
almost came to his lips as he saw
Chazad out of the corner of his eye
circling to confront the second wolf.
The dog displayed great courage, far
beyond his size. Resolve and anger
welled up inside Ashur. He realized that the faithful dog and many
of his father's sheep were sure to
perish this night.

Now he could see clearly the wolf
that he must kill or that would kill
him. The eyes of the wolf fascinated

him as the translucent sideways look changed to one that fixed on him and penetrated through him. The wolf embodied everything that was evil.

"Satan," he whispered as his bow came up and he loosed the arrow in one fluid motion. As quickly as he moved, the wolf ran forward to spring at him. The arrow entered the neck lower than Ashur had aimed. He leaped aside, abandoning any hope of grabbing the spear. The wolf recovered from his missed leap and turned on him. Out of the corner of his eye, Ashur saw the second wolf knock the dog aside and grab a young ewe by the neck. The wolf snapped the struggling ewe's neck, suddenly ending her frenzied bleating.

Again the first wolf leaped upon him and fastened his jaws on the arm that Ashur had thrust out as his only defense. With horror he realized that the great wolf would tear his arm off as easily as one plucks a branch from an olive tree.

The viselike pressure began, then ended as devilish jaws relaxed and fell away. Apparently, the arrow found the jugular in the wolf's upper neck, below where he had hoped to place it. With all his strength, Ashur rolled from under the wolf, whose weight all but equaled his own. He saw the other big male dragging the dead ewe back toward the ravine and toward him. Tossing away the broken bow, he grabbed the spear and with all of his strength drove it into the second wolf.

The surge of the wolf's muscular shoulders translated up the shaft of the spear and sent another wave of terror through Ashur. He struggled to hold on to the spear and hold off the snapping jaws. Finally, the jagged spearhead sapped the wolf's strength, and the second wolf gasped out its last breath. Chazad ripped at its throat to hasten its death.

Ashur tried to withdraw the spear but was unable to do so. Weaponless, he turned to face the rest of the pack. One of the females had brought down one of the ewes. She and the two smaller wolves were dragging it away. He pulled on the spear but failed again to free it from the wolf's carcass. He could do little without risking his own life again.

He knew that wolves would frequently change territory when one of their pack was killed. They would surely do so, since he had killed both of the dominant males.

The broken bow was scarred and shattered from the wolf's powerful jaws. His body gave an involuntary shudder as he realized how close he had come to being torn apart himself. Fortunately, the bow had taken the brunt of the damage. He gathered up the dead ewe's orphaned lamb. He and Chazad passed a nervous night around the campfire, waiting to welcome the dawn of a new day.

The orphaned lamb wandered around bleating for its mother, and the old ewe that had lost her lamb would occasionally answer the cries. Ashur tried to force the issue by pushing the lamb toward the old pockmarked ewe that had lost its lamb. This maneuver also failed. He watched helplessly as ewe after ewe rejected the lamb.

The arrival of Jubal Ben-Adah with one of his father's sheepdogs was a welcome sight. "What are you doing here?" Ashur asked, delighted to see the man.

"Your father sent me here to take care of you," Jubal answered.

"Well, he must have threatened something just short of your life," Ashur grinned, knowing how the old horse trader hated working with sheep.

After he listened quietly to Ashur recounting all the things that had happened, he commented, "Somehow I knew you needed me to come to look after you." The noisy bleating of the lamb and the ewe caused Jubal to complain. "Why can't that ewe and lamb get together?"

"They do not belong together. The old ewe with the tick bite on her face lost her lamb during the storm. This lamb lost her mother to the wolves. It's a shame we cannot match the two of them."

"Why not? Do you know where the lamb died?"

"Yes, its carcass is down that rock slide, over there," he said, pointing to the edge of the cliff. "The lamb is still there if some animal did not find it during the night."

Jubal Ben-Adah did not say anything but went to the edge of the precipice and carefully began his descent. Ashur followed him to the edge.

"Careful, you could start the slide," Ashur warned as the big man reached the lamb's broken body and labored to carry it back up the slope.

"Here, hold the lamb's legs," Jubal panted from the exertion. He took his knife from its sheath and disemboweled the carcass. The sharp blade sliced through the skin with practiced ease. He rolled out the carcass and innards and separated the bloody fleece, washing it in the stream. "Now if you will have that dog of yours catch that ugly old ewe, I will get the little one."

Together the two herd dogs caught the ewe with ease. Chazad held her while Jubal Ben-Adah draped the fleece over the lamb, threading its legs through the skin. The ewe bucked nervously at first at the smell of blood but settled down when she was unable to loosen Chazad's firm hold on her ear. Jubal pulled at one of the ewe's tits to begin the flow. The odor of warm milk enticed the lamb to nurse. Ashur eased away from the ewe and called softly to Chazad to release his prisoner. She turned to smell this weird small thing nursing at her side and accepted the lamb, based on the scent of the fleece.

"They are not very intelligent. They are about the dumbest creatures on earth. We will use the fleece for a few more days until she gets her own milk into the lamb. Her senses will merge the scents, and she will accept the little beast as her own. There would be no great loss if the little varmint died. Several more of them will fall on their heads before they are weaned."

Despite his gruff comment, Ashur knew his friend shared his sense of accomplishment. He looked differently now at the old ewe with the scarred muzzle. She had adopted the little orphan, as Nelmaah had adopted him.

The ewe reminded him of another lesson he had learned from the shepherds. An extended summer drought had dried up all the available grass in the valleys. Ashur and the old shepherd were attempting to move the flock into the mountains to greener pastures. To reach better grazing, they had to negotiate dangerous trails along the cliffs. The sheep refused to follow the shepherd up the steep trails and stubbornly resisted the frantic urging of the dogs.

Finally, the old shepherd gathered a lamb under each arm and proceeded on the trail. The motherhood instinct was so strong that the ewes ignored the danger and followed the frightened bleating of their lambs up the mountain. With encouragement from Ashur and the herd dogs, the entire flock followed.

The servant finally returned. Ashur said goodbye to Jubal Ben-Adah and hurried home. He anticipated the following day and a prearranged meeting with Ammi at the pool of the terebinth tree. Saying good-bye to Chazad was particularly difficult after the frightening experience they had shared. Ashur looked back from the top of the hill. Chazad was still watching him. A word from the servant and the dog returned to his duties with the flock, quickly chastising one of the sheep for venturing too far afield.

***

Ammi was happy again waiting for Ashur to come to her. The healing process had begun. From her perch in the terebinth tree, she could look over the green valley yet be unseen by any chance passerby.

Spring had visited Israel. Tender green grasses carpeted the fields. Buds of the trees and flowers burst forth with their beauty. Birds were singing and calling to each other merrily as they flew back and forth on their busy assignments. The wonderful smell of the fields rivaled that of the fresh baked bread she helped her mother prepare. She loved the feel of the dough, molding and shaping it, wetting her hands in water to keep it from sticking, the marvelous smell as it was baking. She felt a sense of reward in seeing her mother and brothers hungrily devouring the hot bread.

When Ashur came into sight, she playfully hid from him behind the thick trunk of the old terebinth tree. Ashur had already sighted her at a distance before Ammi saw him.

"Ammi, come down. I want to tell you something, please," he called, and the tone of his voice told her that he did have something interesting to relate. Her curiosity piqued, she climbed down from the tree. Ashur related the story of the wolves to her. For emphasis he showed her the broken bow he had brought with him.

"Ashur, you could have been killed!" Ammi cried, alarmed, thinking of the loss of her father. Dedan was gone, but Ashur had brought a new and different love into her life. To think of losing him now was something Ammi found unbearable. Would she ever be completely without fear again? she wondered, her mood changing.

Ashur led her to a nearby grove of trees farther away from the road and the pool. Ammi shared the bread and honey that she had brought. He lay back, stretching comfortably under the leafy green canopy of a tamarisk tree. This particular tree formed a honey-like substance on the ends of its branches. Ashur sucked the nutritious little globules. From his position on his back, he watched a trail of ants gathering the sugary substance.

Ashur's own mood changed too. At first, their words were the usual ones of two young people in love. The conversation came around to the subject of the signet ring and the cave, as it always did. Ashur was obsessed with finding the origins of his birth.

"I want to see this place where they found you, Ashur, this secret place of the stairs. I want you to take me there tomorrow. Together we must find an answer to this compulsion of yours to find your natural father. You have talked of this place ever since I have known you," Ammi persisted. "I want to see the cave for myself." Despite his protests, Ammi insisted that he take her to see the place.

In the early morning, she met him on the main road, and they made their way to the cave. The morning was cool. They took the long way around and entered the cave from the thicket side as his father had done when he found the baby Ashur.

"The cave was made by men," Ammi conceded as they made their way through the entrance. "I see what you meant. A man or men fashioned the entrance or at least enlarged the natural passageway."

Ammi and Ashur passed through the cave and emerged again on the other side, where they could gaze down on the main road to the village. They sat quietly looking out over the road until finally Ashur began to feel foolish for making so much fuss over the cave. When he looked at his surroundings through her eyes, they did not seem so special.

Soon her beautiful face held his full attention. For the first time, he realized how much he loved this young woman and wanted her.

Ammi became aware of a new look in Ashur's eyes as he gazed on her. Not understanding fully what it meant, she said to Ashur, "I must go now. My mother will be worried about me. I told them I would not be gone long."

"Wait until I am down, and then you come," cautioned Ashur as he descended the worn stairs. To show off his agility, he actually ran down the side of the mountain. He leaped from foothold to foothold with the nimbleness of a gazelle.

"Now you come. If you slip, I will catch you," Ashur promised, reassuring her. Ammi was impressed. Carefully she made her own way on the steep slope. She made it almost to the bottom without incident. Where the stair steps were worn almost completely away, her foot slipped. She landed in Ashur's strong arms with her arms around his neck and their faces only inches apart.

Ashur and Ammi both felt an invisible shock travel through them. They separated. Nevertheless, from that point on, both knew that the physical infatuation and friendship had grown into something much deeper. Ashur had shared the secret place of the stairs.

Ammi and Ashur went several times to the cave. Gradually Ashur grew less anxious about his beginnings and more fulfilled by his growing love for Ammi and her love for him.

Each time they left the cave, Ammi would jump from the ledge the last few feet into Ashur's waiting arms. Ashur would catch her. Each time he anticipated the closeness and the excuse to touch Ammi in this innocent way and to display his strength.

* * *

Ammi and Ashur no longer went to their secret place of the stairs where the baby Ashur had been found. They returned to the pool by the terebinth tree as their meeting place. Their love was now so impassioned that they no longer trusted themselves in so secret a place. They were blind to foreboding realities of life and singular in their vision of perpetual happiness.

The pair of doves they often heard cooing in the tamarisk grove flew down and began bathing in the shallows. The springs that fed the pool bubbled up from unseen depths, swelling the waters practically at their feet. They watched a colorful little songbird fly to the ground to drink from the sweet water of the pool. They smiled at each other as the little bird fluffed up his feathers, comically fluttering his wings to create a shower of raindrops. The bird flew to a branch, where he preened in the warming sun. Occasionally a tree leaf dropped onto the surface of the pool. The wind pushed the leaves across the water like tiny sailboats.

Ashur leaned over the pool and let his lips touch the cool, clear water. He kissed the surface of the water with a loud smack. Then he raised his head to observe Ammi's response. There was no reaction from her, only puzzlement. He bent over the pool and loudly kissed the surface again.

"What are you doing?" Ammi asked, curious at this action.

"I am kissing your image in the pool," Ashur said, smiling at her.

"You are very impertinent to kiss a maiden with such deception. The maiden might not be willing," Ammi ventured.

"So the maiden is not willing?" Ashur said teasingly.

"I will not tell you," Ammi replied coyly. Ashur leaned over the pool to kiss the surface again. However, this time Ammi pushed his head under the water. She got up and ran from him.

"I will throw the unwilling maiden in the pool," Ashur called threateningly as he ran after her, trying to clear the water from his eyes. Although Ammi ran gracefully, she was not accustomed to the exertion of running over the broken terrain or of running any great distance. Ashur easily caught her. Her legs buckled, and they fell to the ground, laughing.

"So! Off to the pool with you now," Ashur said.

"Ashur, please, I am sick. I cannot breathe," Ammi gasped. She was not actually ill, of course, and quickly recovered her breath. She lay on the ground. Ashur crouched over her, gazing down into beautiful eyes, limpid and clear. A smile appeared briefly on Ammi's face then vanished as she embraced the special moment. She first felt the warmth of his hand on the side of her face, as Ashur gently guided his lips to meet hers. Despite his dip in the pool, his lips warmed over hers. For once she was speechless, frightened by the rush of new feelings.

"I feel a bit queasy, if you know what I mean," she said, leaning over as she clutched her abdomen. Ashur gave her a blank look. He had no sisters. Therefore, he was completely in the dark regarding women's unique problems. The cramps continued. Embarrassed now, Ammi ran from him.

"Ammi," he called, but she did not turn back.

Why was she always running from him, she thought, when it was the last thing she wanted to do?

***

Ammi's mother met her at the door, with some shocking news. "Merab is pregnant, and her husband accuses her of infidelity."

"No! You cannot mean it." Ammi was dumbstruck.

"I do. He brought the matter to the elders of Solem. Merab and her husband are here in Solem now. Because his wives before Merab were barren, he refuses to believe the child is his. He thinks the young man from Nahal is the father. You remember, the boy she wanted to marry."

"What will the elders do?"

"Merab and the young man vehemently deny this accusation, and there are no witnesses. She must undergo a trial. The elders will bring her before the priest. He will stand her before Elohim at the entrance to the sanctuary, with her hair unbound and a sacrificial offering in her hands. I know this trial well. A young woman was accused in Solem, when you were a little girl."

"What will happen to her then?" Ammi asked.

"The priest will take holy water and mix in dust from the floor of the tabernacle. He writes her husband's complaint on a scroll. Then he washes the scroll in the holy water. He will order Merab to make a promise proclaiming her innocence. They call this the oath of the curse. Merab must drink the bitter water. If she is guilty, she will turn ill and abort her baby. Should this be the outcome, they will stone her to death as an adulteress. If she is innocent, she will give birth to a healthy child. She can go back to her husband."

"Oh no!" Ammi sobbed, terrified of the possibilities. "I know she is innocent, but she will be so afraid. She told me she was resigned to her fate. She said that though her husband was old, he had been kind to her. He helps her parents and her sisters. Merab has twice remarked that she knew that every person has some burden to bear."

"Yes. I remember you saying that to me. Nevertheless, she wanted to marry the young man from Nahal. You do not think that he might have slipped in to lie with her, do you?"

"I cannot believe Merab would do this thing. I do not think she has seen him since she married. He is promised to a young woman from his own village. They will marry when he has worked out the bride price."

"Merab must attend the two hearings presided over by the priest," her mother said.

* * *

On the appointed day of Merab's second hearing, Ammi waited outside. Women were not allowed to attend the trial except as witnesses. The elders finally emerged from the temple. The mazkir approached them. Ammi thought that from his somber face, the news must be bad. Then a broad smile spread across his face. "Merab has passed the trial of bitter water," he said. "The elders have ruled that sufficient time has passed to satisfy the oath. There was no witness to any infidelity. Merab's husband has to pay her family a huge fine, one hundred shekels of silver. The elders scourged him with the whip. He also loses the right to divorce Merab, and he must support her for the rest of her life. Come, Mother," he said to his wife. "I want to go home. These trials make me very tired."

When Merab came out of the temple, Ammi hugged her and kissed her on the cheek. Merab nodded to acknowledge her friend, but her face remained fixed. She was large with child now and struggled to climb into the wagon. She refused her fawning husband's assistance.

"He has created a cold home for himself," Ammi remarked to her mother.

CHAPTER 5

Chariot Warriors

King Solomon's military was unsurpassed in training, morale, and tradition. He kept intact the individual units of his father's mighty warriors. Sons and brothers of men who had served his father now commanded many units. Preserving these traditions helped maintain a military so dedicated and skilled that few would challenge his rule over that region of the land.

Solomon assigned a special scribe to record the exploits of the mighty warriors, men of valor, trained for war, as swift as gazelles on the mountains. Their faces resembled the faces of lions. The warriors whose deeds were recorded in the Book of the Heroes were so esteemed that women kissed the hems of their garments when they walked down the street. The people of Israel yet remembered the stories of slavery told them by their grandfathers. To a people not long removed from enslavement, freedom was a great treasure.

The king armed his archers with the finest bows that could be fashioned with materials available to his craftsmen. They were further equipped with quivers filled with arrows of polished shafts and intricate fletching. Sharp, pointed iron heads tipped their arrows.

The Gibore Hail, the professionals of the army, trained the militia. Solomon's father, King David, had originally organized the militia into twelve divisions of twenty-four thousand men each. One division served on active duty for one month each year.

In the past, pay largely had come from plunder divided among the troops. Solomon made sure his growing army was adequately supplied by making families responsible for the provision of their kindred.

The regular army was stationed in a number of chariot cities, the principal of which were Megiddon, Hazor, and the capital, Jerusalem. Other smaller chariot stations were in the villages near Jerusalem and scattered around the countryside. Solomon commanded two million males over twenty years of age, proficient in the skills of war.

Solomon inherited his father's bodyguard, thirty men commanded by Benaiah, a mighty warrior whose father and grandfather had been soldiers. They passed on to him, not only the physical stature of the warrior, but also the knowledge of weapons and tactics, resulting in a commander without equal.

The king doubled the size of the royal guard to sixty men. These imported mercenaries were of the Karethi and Palethi and owed allegiance to no political group. They obeyed the king with absolute loyalty. From this group of mercenaries came a special escort group called the Ruts, or runners. Solomon's father used these foreigners to settle rebellion in his own family.

***

"I am very proud of you, my son," Machir said, reaching to grip Ashur's shoulder. "The training with the Gibore Hail will be difficult, but I know you will make me proud. I have prepared you well."

Ashur was ordered to report to Jerusalem in the month of Elul. The day to leave for Jerusalem and the Fortress of the Heroes arrived quickly. His tearful mother hugged him tight. She remembered oh so well the many good-byes when Machir had gone away.

The young men came from Solem and Nahal. Ashur renewed his friendship with an old acquaintance. Dekar, the son of the silversmith of Nahal, would go with him to the fortress for training. He had met Dekar when he had gone to search for the origin of the signet ring. The younger Dekar had instantly sensed a kindred spirit in Ashur and attached himself in a hero worship, or younger brother, attitude. He shared Ashur's interest in the code and often quoted from it.

The growth of this friendship and his friendship with Malta sustained Ashur through the rigorous training. Also, the friends helped him adjust to the separation from Ammi. The fun-loving Dekar always had a smile on his face. Ashur had grown to love the young man, although Dekar constantly made him the subject of good-natured teasing. He had only to catch sight of Dekar's mischievous face to bring a smile to his own.

"Remember, it is a saying," Dekar would offer. "One who looks for a friend without faults will have none."

Ashur, Dekar, Malta, and the other young men gathered around a captain of the royal guard. They began their trek in the evening. Darkness soon descended. After a prolonged march, the captain announced that they would return to Jerusalem.

"This is not the right road back," Ashur said to Malta. "I have traveled this road with my father."

"Things look very different at night. Perhaps you are mistaken," Malta said.

"I am not mistaken," Ashur said. He immediately went to the captain to bring the error to his attention.

"What is your name, young warrior?" the captain of the royal guard asked.

"My name is Ashur, son of Machir," Ashur replied.

The captain of the royal guard committed the name to memory. He was expected to report special leadership qualities to his superiors. The captain had plainly stated their destination as the Fortress of the Heroes at Jerusalem. He had purposely led the young militiamen off the right path, but this young man, Ashur, was not blindly following him down the wrong road.

Part of the training of the young warriors was learning to negotiate the terrain at night. The captain continued on the same trail. Ashur realized that their leader was purposely leading them away from the road to Jerusalem.

"Why are we going down the wrong road?" Sabta asked Malta when word circulated through the militiamen that they might be on the wrong

road. "Why don't we camp and wait
for daylight?"

Finally, they did make camp. The
young men soon learned that Ashur
was correct. They spent several more
days and nights following the captain of the royal guard through wilderness areas.

The men finally reached the Fortress
of the Heroes. Their training became
more difficult. The young men found
themselves pitted against the highly
trained warriors of the Gibore Hail.
They were sent with regular army
leaders to perform missions, with
the goal of having the young men
become familiar with the terrain
around Jerusalem.

Days and nights they marched,
climbing mountains, negotiating
canyons, familiarizing themselves
with the entire countryside. On one
occasion, their regular army officer
ordered them to split into two groups,
one under the leadership of Hattil
and one under Ashur. Ashur led his
men unerringly to their objective
and back to the river crossing.

"I swear, I don't know where we are," a young militiaman said. "How do you know, Ashur?"

"We passed the wadi that runs into the river Kidron about a half hour ago. Those broken rocks and that unusual overhang are near the Kidron crossing. Our crossing is over the rise, beyond this valley," Ashur said. The wooded valley looked to Dekar to be identical to several others they had crossed.

The other group became hopelessly lost. They waited half the day until Hattil's group finally found their way back to the river station.

"Where have you been?" Dekar asked of the tired, dust-covered wayfarers, as he lounged on the riverbank, his bare feet in the water. "Warm today, isn't it? Come and cool your feet. We've been waiting all day for you."

One of the other men collapsed on the edge of the river, bathing his face in the cool water. He washed the dust from his lips, waited a few seconds for the current to clear the water, and then drank deeply. All the young men were similarly tired. Not one responded to Dekar's jibes.

"Hattil and Malta got into a great argument over which way would lead us back here after we reached our objective," he explained. "Hattil won, so we followed him. Turns out, sure enough, we went the wrong way. We had to backtrack. Then we followed Malta, and he got us lost. I didn't think we would ever find our way here. You people can go where you want to go. I am not leaving Ashur's side again," he said defiantly, his eyes meeting with those of the smiling regular officer.

He pulled his sweat-soaked tunic over his head and threw it aside. "If I could have drunk all of the water that flowed from me, I would not be thirsty."

"You cannot drink sweat. It is salty," one of the younger men observed.

He gave the man a dirty look, not appreciating correction of what should have been obvious to all.

On another assignment with Ashur in command, they were making a particularly difficult march over mountain trails. After a rest break, one of the men refused to continue. When

Ashur took him by the arm and physically pulled him to his feet, the disgruntled man attempted to swing at him with his fist. Ashur easily dodged the punch. He did not retaliate. He simply pushed the man along ahead of him, keeping him off balance until he gave up.

Finally, realizing he was being manhandled, the man resumed the march. Ashur's easy management of this large and strong malcontent did not go unnoticed by the other men. It became evident to all concerned that Ashur intended to follow orders to the letter. All under his command would be expected to do likewise.

The young men soon learned that Ashur was as familiar with the night as he was with the day. They came to depend on him. Ashur became their unspoken leader. While the column rested, the tireless Ashur ranged out ahead, picking the best route, memorizing the terrain. He exhibited an uncanny ability to get from one place to another. This earned him the confidence of the militiamen and the grudging respect of the men of the Gibore Hail. Now when he left a small, bent-over tree to mark a trail, there were a dozen eyes searching for it. The experience of being lost in the Black Forest had provided a lesson that Ashur never forgot.

Malta was the first of the militia to be chosen captain. Malta was no dreamer like Ashur. He was all work and providing an example. He was brash, capable, and steady and spoke with an authoritative tone. Although he had gone down in defeat in his struggles with Pithon, the experience had hardened him.

Dekar liked to poke fun at his friend by deepening his voice, throwing out his chest, and ordering people about. "Come, O honored leader. We have prepared a brief ceremony to celebrate your promotion to captain."

He led Malta and Ashur down a path to the tree he had selected. The early morning rain had left the trees laden with water. The tree was slim and heavy with rain-soaked leaves. He allowed Malta to walk under the tree, then shook the trunk vigorously to bring down a cascade of water. Malta let out a roar, shaking water from his head and arms. The men enjoyed a good laugh at his expense. Ashur was concerned about how his friend would react. Finally, a smile broke out on Malta's face, and they all laughed together.

"You laugh, but you got yourself almost as wet as you did me," Malta told Dekar.

"Yes, but it was worth it," Dekar said, gasping for breath.

"Remember, Dekar, you must take orders from Malta," Ashur reminded his friend. "He will make you pay dearly for this."

"Yes, I am sure he will. I did not want him to get too swollen with his own importance. Don't worry. I am just one of the men from now on."

In a formal ceremony in the Fortress of the Heroes, the commanders of the Gibore Hail confirmed Malta and Ashur as officers of the militia.

The young men of Solem and Nahal made camp outside the fortress. "Let us pitch our tent near Malta and Ashur," Sabta said to his tent mate. The man did not object. He rightly assumed that Sabta wanted to curry favor with their new leaders.

Sabta soon learned to use Ashur's obsession with his unknown origins to stay close to him. He fabricated stories and passed on false rumors to feed Ashur's hope of finding his lost parents. Ashur tolerated him, despite his dubious character.

"Watch out for him," Malta cautioned Ashur. "He cannot be trusted." Malta knew Sabta. He had grown up with him.

Sabta had heard the stories of Ashur's beginnings, since he was a small boy. One of the young men of Solem boasted of Ashur's strength and ability around the campfire. A young militiaman from Nahal jokingly suggested that Ashur somehow drew his great strength and intelligence from the mysterious signet ring. This thought brought a devious glow of greed to Sabta's eyes. The superstitious Sabta became fascinated with the ring, believing it held some mystical power. Ashur was not much larger than the average man, yet he was endowed with all kinds of abilities and tremendous strength. Men and women alike admired him. From that day on, Sabta watched Ashur furtively, skulking about Ashur's tent, waiting for the right chance to steal the coveted ring. He waited for the right opportunity.

He wandered to the stables, where an irate officer awaited him. "Where have you been? I have been looking everywhere for you. You are supposed to be feeding the horses."

"One of the other officers had something for me to do," Sabta lied. He shoveled some barley for the horses, but when the officer was out of sight, Sabta stopped his work and draped himself over the corral gate.

Tirsah finished his mouthful of grain and whinnied softly to let the man know he wanted more to eat. Sabta ignored the horse and slumped lazily over the fence. His hand absentmindedly went to Tirsah's head, shoving him away. Tirsah laid his ears back, but Sabta was too absorbed with plots to steal the signet ring to heed the warning.

When he pushed the horse again, more roughly, Tirsah administered a sharp bite to the offending hand.

Sabta let out a scream of rage. From a safe distance, he observed that the horse that had bitten him was Ashur's own Tirsah. He wondered if somehow, through Ashur's magic, the horse was chastising him for what he was thinking. He considered getting a limb or rock to retaliate but thought better of it. Sabta had been severely punished once before for mistreating an animal. He tried to shake off the painful effects of the bite as he labored to finish his assignment. He kept a watchful eye on the great stallion.

***

After a long, forced march, Ashur, Malta, and the other men returned to camp and fell into their tents for a well-deserved rest. Sabta, who had managed to avoid the march by feigning an injury, waited for nightfall and then slipped into Ashur's tent. He judged from the heavy breathing that the exhausted Ashur and Malta were sleeping soundly. Sabta strained to distinguish Ashur's face in the faint moonlight coming through the opening of the tent. The leather thong was plainly visible around Ashur's neck. Ashur's shoulder was covering the cord and the signet ring.

Sabta began to draw his knife from his belt, but then decided against trying to cut the cord. If one or the other powerful young men found him in the tent with the knife in his hand, he might be slain himself. His greed to possess the mysterious ring was strong, but his cowardice was stronger. Sabta fled from the tent as quickly as the need for quietness would allow.

Ashur slept soundly through the night. As usual, though, he awakened long before daylight, vaguely aware that a fly had interrupted his sleep. Remembering that Malta and the other officers had the watch, he returned to the comfortable and hazy world between deep sleep and awareness of a new day.

A cool and pleasant breeze blew through the tent. He was on the edge of reentering peaceful sleep when he felt a tickling sensation around his nose and upper lip. "Cursed fly," Ashur muttered, rolling over to his other side. His one day off, his one day of quiet rest, interrupted by a fly. "We have camped too close to the stables," he thought.

The persistent pest returned. This time it seemed to be crawling on his ear. He brushed at the fly and rubbed his ear, burrowing his nose in the bend of his arm, trying to cover both his nose and his ear. The fly always found an opening, however, and continued to bedevil him. The little beast was particularly bold and determined.

Ashur's irritation grew, and he began to mumble to himself. "If only the fly would buzz or make a sound where I could retaliate," he thought. He turned over on his back to allow himself freer use of his hands. He had just about convinced himself that the fly had retreated so he could get back to sleep when the tickling sensation returned around his nose and upper lip. Ashur swatted blindly at the fly with the back of his hand, bringing sensitive knuckles into painful contact with a tent pole. Mumbling to himself, he sat up, his vengeful eyes seeking the little pest. He saw only the smiling face of Dekar, trying to hide behind the tent flap. The offending and incriminating fly was in Dekar's hand, in the form of a long, slender weed.

"You empty-headed rascal. You worthless, good-for-nothing idiot!" Ashur accused crossly. "I have enough trouble with the other men. I should not have to deal with your twisted sense of humor."

Dekar could not speak. He was bent over, on his knees, convulsed with laughter, shaking his head from side to side, gasping for breath. Ashur's anger melted as he imagined himself as he must have appeared when Dekar tickled his nose and ears with the soft end of the weed. He must have been quite comical.

***

Sabta continued watching Ashur and waiting for the right time to try again. Midmorning presented him with the rare opportunity, when Ashur was not wearing the ring. At

Dekar's urging, Ashur went swimming with some of the other men.

The men unbuckled their swords and shed sandals and tunics on a slight rise above the river. Sabta watched Ashur take the signet ring from around his neck and lay it beside his sword. Sabta's heart began pounding as he weighed his chances of crawling behind the hummock without being seen. Ashur's signet ring lay on his tunic, in plain view of Sabta's covetous eyes.

He would never have a better chance than this, he thought. Ashur normally did not allow himself the liberty of swimming with the other men. As their captain, he took his responsibilities very seriously.

Sabta doubted that the opportunity would present itself again. Sabta crouched down, keeping the rise between him and the men splashing in the cool water of the river. He was shaking as he crawled toward the hummock. His greed to own the ring was stronger now than his fear.

Sabta knew that for a second his arm and head would be exposed to the swimmers. He snatched the ring, crawled a short distance from the hummock, and ran toward the buck-thorn thicket. He fell to his knees behind the trunk of a tamarisk tree and watched nervously to see if anyone had seen him take the ring. There was no shout or pursuit.

Quickly he dug a small hole with his knife and buried the signet ring at the base of the tree. He returned the knife to his belt and made his way through the underbrush to the camp. As he emerged from the thicket, he encountered Malta.

"You are supposed to be at the stables, caring for the horses," Malta scolded. Sabta, his face guilt ridden, ran immediately toward the stables.

***

Ashur waded through the shallow water to the bank, laughing as he dodged a handful of sand Dekar threw at him. He shook the water from his hair and stepped out of the puddle of water forming at his feet in the sand. The relaxing swim had been enjoyable, but now it was time to return to his duties. Taking up his tunic, he cautiously searched for his signet ring. His loss did not register for a moment. Possibly one of the other men had tripped over the string, causing the ring to be kicked down the bank. No, he thought. He had been the last one into the water. His signet ring was missing. Someone had taken it. Could one of the men be playing a joke on him?

"What is wrong, Ashur?" Dekar asked, watching Ashur search anxiously along the ground.

"My ring's missing," Ashur declared.

Dekar and the other men scattered out, looking along the ground as they combed the area. Ashur could see from their sober expressions that they were not part of a scheme. He ran up to the camp to enlist the assistance of Malta and the captain of the Gibore Hail.

***

When Malta heard that Ashur's signet ring was missing, he immediately suspected Sabta. He said nothing of his suspicion to the other men, however, because the code forbade accusing a man without sufficient proof. After he fully understood the details of the ring's disappearance, he went to the spot where he had encountered Sabta emerging from the undergrowth.

Backtracking along the game trail, he carefully searched any likely place where the ring might be hidden. He must find the ring before Sabta had the opportunity to return for it. Malta was certain that Sabta was the guilty one. Sabta's emerging from the buckthorn thicket was not coincidence.

At first, Malta had thought him guilty only of shirking his duties. Thinking back to the moment when he had confronted Sabta, he did not remember seeing anything in his hand. However, he could have concealed the ring under his tunic. Malta glanced over at two of the young men who had followed him into the buckthorn thicket. They halfheartedly poked through the underbrush. He would like to take hold of Sabta and shake him until he confessed. He pressed on, determined to find his friend's ring. The ring was precious to Ashur.

Malta came to the tamarisk tree where Sabta had hidden the ring. His hunter's eye caught sight of the freshly dug dirt at the base of the tree. At first, he dismissed it as the work of a ground squirrel or another small animal. He raked through the loose dirt with his foot and then kicked the trunk of the tamarisk tree to get the dirt out of his sandal.

Nothing!

***

Dusk was settling about the camp when Ashur called off the search. Ashur thanked the men who had helped him look for the ring and made his way back to the tent he and Malta shared.

He entered the tent and slumped down onto his sleeping mat, his emotions churning. The loss of the signet ring severed the only link he had with his past. Without it, he would never learn the identity of his father and mother or why they had abandoned him.

Malta entered and sat beside his unhappy tent mate. Ashur was unable to conceal the deep disappointment of his loss. Malta reached quickly into his tunic and tossed the signet ring to Ashur. Malta had returned to the freshly turned dirt beneath the tamarisk tree. The thought had occurred to him that Sabta might have buried the ring with his knife. When he dug more deeply into the ground with his own knife, he uncovered the ring. He had intended on making some sort of joke of finding it, but the obvious pain on his friend's face caused him to abandon the idea. The jubilant look that appeared on Ashur's face was reward enough.

Ashur struggled for words to express his gratitude. "I am fortunate to have a friend such as you, Malta," Ashur said, very seriously.

Malta stood and pushed Ashur's head down roughly. "It is not a great thing. I thought I knew who took the ring. Next time we will catch him in the act."

***

Ashur was ordered to report to Jair, the commander of the fortress near the city of Jerusalem. Jair was a distinguished officer whose grandfather and namesake was lauded in the Book of the Heroes.

"Well, young Ashur, I have heard some interesting things about you. You are Machir's son, are you not?"

"Yes, Commander," replied Ashur.

"Tell me about this famous chariot horse of yours. What is his name?" questioned the commander. "I have heard that he is very fast and that no one can beat him. I suppose old Machir has taught you well, too."

"His name is Tirsah, Commander," Ashur said proudly. Apparently, Tirsah's local fame had spread.

"We have some very good chariot drivers and some fast horses here at the fortress. You may get to test your Tirsah against them before your training is over," Jair said. He relished the thought of his regulars putting this young upstart in his place.

As time passed, more positive reports came to Commander Jair's attention. Not only was Ashur an

expert in driving the chariot, but
he also excelled with bow and sword.
Word of Ashur's prowess spread
throughout the militia and regular army at the Fortress of the
Heroes. The only criticism directed
toward the young man by officers of
his training cadre was that he was
too peaceable. A couple of the officers thought Ashur lacked the cocky
demeanor necessary to lead his comrades into battle.

The regulars at the Fortress of the
Heroes promoted their own champion.
Ashur was about to be reintroduced
to him. Pithon had grown up in Solem,
and his chariot horses were from
the same bloodline as Tirsah. Ashur
learned that Pithon was a descendant
of one of their country's most famous
warriors. More feared than revered,
this giant of a man possessed great
strength. He had trained from childhood in the skills of war and become
known as a hunter—a hunter of men,
an avenger for the king. This designation did not originate from any
special ability in taking wild game.
The label came from an incident in
which Pithon tracked two mercenaries

who had deserted to return to their native country of Libya. He overtook them and killed both. Pithon then returned with their ears and presented them to the king.

***

As Ashur's prowess and reputation grew, Pithon became jealous of Ashur. In the past, the distance separating Ashur's father's lands from the village of Solem kept the two from confrontation. The more recognition Ashur received, the more Pithon increased his harassment of the young man. Ashur patiently withstood the taunting and thinly veiled threats. Now he understood the opinion that the people of Solem held of the man. Pithon was considered somewhat deranged—and mean besides.

"He is not known for his intelligence," Malta observed. "Rumor has it that he was once kicked in the head by a horse."

"There is a wise saying of our people," Dekar said. "'Never weary of making friends. Consider a single enemy as one too many. He who turns his enemy into a friend is the bravest hero.'"

Malta spat on the ground. "Yes, Dekar, but you do not know him. Remember also this saying: 'Fear only these two: Elohim and the man who has no fear of Elohim.'"

"I have heard nothing good about Pithon. Nothing," Dekar admitted.

Ashur came to consider the evil Pithon a special demon assigned to him by Satan to make life miserable. Reared in the loving environment of Machir's household, Ashur was unprepared to deal with hatred and bullying. He heard the rumors about Pithon and saw the sidewise looks at the mention of his name. However, he was totally unprepared for savage attacks on his person without cause.

He accepted the hard but fair treatment of the regular army captains. His father had prepared him for some abuse from the regulars. Ashur obeyed orders without hesitation, fulfilling every command to the letter. No matter how trivial or demeaning the order appeared, Ashur obeyed.

In trying to deal with Pithon, however, he failed to comprehend how a man could hate him when he had committed no transgression.

"You must try to ignore him," Dekar said. "He is an evil man. I tried to talk to our captain, but he refused to listen to me. I will go to Commander Jair."

"No, you will only get yourself in trouble," Ashur said. "I can handle him. The Gibore Hail allows harsh treatment of the militia."

"Yes, but Pithon takes this jealousy toward you beyond the bounds of reason. Commander Jair will not allow this vendetta to continue if he knows about it. He is a great man. I know he will put a stop to it if he knows about the abuse you are suffering at the hands of this man. Let me go to him," Dekar begged.

"No!" Ashur said emphatically. "Pithon can threaten and abuse me, but he cannot harm me. I see now why he has been doing these things. He knows about Tirsah, and he must have guessed that we would be matched in the chariot race. He is trying to intimidate me even before the race begins."

"That, together with the insane jealousy he has for Shoshanna," Malta added. "When Shoshanna's brother told him how Shoshanna talked about you all of the time and how she admired you, Pithon went into a rage. I thought he would strike her brother."

The young militiamen looked forward to completing their training on festival day. The commander of the fortress designated certain of the newly trained men to compete against the professionals. As expected, Commander Jair chose Ashur to represent the militia in the chariot races.

An arena outside the fortress would be the location of the contests. Tradition called for the militia to match their own champions against the heroes of the fortress. Practically the entire garrison turned out as audience for the event. The warriors stationed there wanted to see the two champions and their steeds in head-to-head competition.

Ashur and his young friends
cheered heartily for their mates,
but none of them fared well against
the seasoned veterans. First they
were beaten on the archery range and
then in wrestling and the strength
events. A subdued group of young men
looked to Ashur to recapture some
measure of self-respect for them.

"My bow was crooked today," Dekar
lamented. "It is up to you, Ashur.
Only the chariot races remain."

The dirt track for the chariot
races bordered an irregular wall
constructed of broken rock and
small boulders. The object of the
race was to determine which of the
chariots could complete six laps
around the extended circle in the
shortest length of time. The danger
of striking the rock boundary or
overturning increased with the speed
of the chariot.

Greatly complicating things for
Ashur was the ruling by the fortress
commander that required the use of
two horses by each contestant. Ashur
could choose any of the chariot
horses as mate for Tirsah. The
choice was difficult, for any horse

harnessed with Tirsah would slow him down. He had no time to prepare them to race together. The horses needed to know each other, and both needed to be familiar with their driver. This practically assured the success of the army chariots.

"Belshaz is the only horse in the stables that can run with Tirsah. He is the obvious choice," argued Malta.

"He can run like the wind without the chariot," admitted Dekar, "but he has very little experience with the chariot."

Ashur had not considered Malta's Mitannian stallion, Belshaz, at first, for he did not do well pulling the chariot alone. Belshaz was a horse with a long, sinewy build, a bony head, and mottled color. He was not a beautiful horse, for he lacked the normal flesh that would give him proportion. At first, his fragile build and unimpressive looks had caused Ashur to overlook him. He was an unknown quantity. However, Ashur had seen him run, and he knew when a horse was fast. He assessed the horse's wide and well-muscled withers and powerful legs. "What Malta says is true. There is no other choice if we want to win," Ashur said.

"Belshaz could get you killed if he takes your chariot into the rocks," interjected Dekar. "You will prove wise to take a horse with more experience. You might even beat the other army chariot."

"Finishing second will not satisfy me. Belshaz is the only hope we have of beating Pithon. We have to take the chance," Ashur retorted with quiet determination. "I have a better reason than most for risking my life, is it not true?"

"Yes," Dekar said eagerly, caught up in Ashur's bravado.

Malta shook his head. "Elohim save us. The most exciting thing about being young is that you do not have good sense."

"This is something I have to do. Pithon has to be beaten." Months of maltreatment at the hands of Pithon had left Ashur bitter.

Since Pithon owned the more experienced team of horses, the commander felt assured that his champions would prevail. Four chariots entered the race, two from the army; Pithon's team and a pair of bays. There were also two from the militia; Ashur's team and a matched pair of blacks.

Men stretched a rope between two ashlars at the starting line. Behind this rope, the four teams of prancing horses and the chariots gathered. As luck would have it, Ashur drew the fourth and most outside position. Pithon held the inside or rail position.

"Ashur must battle his way from the outside," Dekar offered, fidgeting nervously.

"Yes, but he will not have to worry about being forced against the rocks," Malta responded.

"True," said Dekar, gaining some measure of encouragement from these words. "He can either try to race to the front or hang back and make his move when the opportunity presents itself. I'm sure Ashur knows this."

The four chariots lined up behind the rope. The horns blared and the four teams charged off down the track. Belshaz and Tirsah, having only a short time together as a team, got off to a poor start and immediately fell behind the pack. Belshaz shied away from the noise of the trumpet, and he veered toward the inside of the track. This threw Tirsah off stride and sent the left wheel of the chariot crashing into one of the ashlars. Ashur fell forward and all but lost the reins. Regaining control, he slapped Belshaz sharply on the left flank with the reins.

He shouted words of encouragement to Tirsah. "On Tirsah, on great one! Steady—steady. Now we can run." Tirsah's great strength and the power of his stride started to pull the other horse along, and the chariot began to run true down the track. Miraculously, the wheel of the chariot held together. Ashur's father had built it well.

As they came around the curve completing the first lap, Pithon was leading, the bays were in second place, and the other militiaman's team was third. Ashur's chariot was last.

As they passed the crowd again, Belshaz tried to shy away from the shouting warriors. This time Ashur and Tirsah were ready for him. Ashur smiled wryly as he saw the great stallion lean into Belshaz to force him away from the wall. Ashur slapped Belshaz again on the left flank to make sure he did not crowd to the inside.

Halfway around the second lap, Ashur's team passed the militiaman's chariot and managed to make up some distance between him and the blacks. As they charged around the curve to complete the second lap, Tirsah strained to push his nose by them.

"Run, Tirsah!" Dekar yelled as the chariot roared by the starting line. The noise of the crowd drowned out his shout. Far in front, Pithon was already using his whip. The race was rapidly turning into a runaway.

Midway into the third lap, Ashur's Tirsah and Belshaz fell into a rhythm and began to gain on the bays. The chariots charged past the starting line in a cloud of dust. The men of the militia were all on their feet, shouting encouragement. Belshaz now seemed to be running free and unencumbered. With the strength and stamina of Tirsah, the chariot began to fairly fly down the track, passing the bays as if they were standing still. With Ashur's chariot striking the rocks and the resulting horrible start, the crowd had considered Ashur eliminated from the race. Now, from his vantage point above the track, the fortress commander leaned forward, anxiously measuring the distance between Ashur's team and Pithon's chariot. If Ashur came in first, outrunning both of the army chariots, it would be a major embarrassment.

Ashur's heart sank as he saw clearly the great distance between his chariot and that of the leader. He started to pull back on Tirsah's reins and ease up, fearing that the great horse's heart might burst with such an effort. Even Tirsah could not overcome the gap between the two chariots in the remaining two laps. But Tirsah defied the bit in his mouth and seemed to lengthen his stride at the suggestion that they might give up. Ashur gave Tirsah his head and turned his attention to Belshaz. He wondered if the other horse could keep up the blistering pace.

Malta's words proved prophetic, though, as the Mitannian stallion matched Tirsah stride for stride. Now Ashur had the feeling that the chariot was truly flying. They began to cut into Pithon's lead. Pithon began to look back frequently as his lead narrowed. He whipped his team mercilessly. The sting of the lash served only to discourage the tired steeds, for they were already giving their best for their cruel master. White lather covered their sides.

Ashur reluctantly applied the whip to Tirsah. The magnificent beast responded with every ounce of muscle and heart, propelling the chariot alongside Pithon. For a moment, Ashur's eyes met those of Pithon. Ashur could see the hatred in his eyes. Pithon knew he was beaten as Tirsah and Belshaz moved around his chariot.

Unpredictably, Pithon pulled sharply on the reins, causing his chariot to swerve into Ashur's.

"A madman," Ashur thought, utterly dismayed.

The wheels on the two chariots locked together, grating and screeching. Then they jerked apart. The left wheel to Pithon's chariot broke loose, sending his chariot careening along the boulders at the edge of the track. Then it flipped over, throwing Pithon end over end into the dusty rock-strewn track.

Alone now, Ashur charged across the finish line. Tirsah finally slowed, and Ashur was able to bring the horses under control and to a halt. He saw that Tirsah's flanks were heaving. Ashur leaped from the chariot and ran to the exhausted horse. When he saw Tirsah's nostrils full of foam and flecked with blood, he groaned aloud and hugged the great stallion's neck. Then Dekar and Malta and the other jubilant militiamen mobbed him.

As the young men converged on him and led him away, Ashur stopped momentarily to watch as Pithon was carried from the track. His anger toward the man drained away. Nonetheless, he knew that it would be useless to offer him sympathy.

***

Inside the arena, the men deposited Pithon's battered and bruised body on a table. He cursed as the royal physician dug at the slivers of rock embedded in his hip and side. The physician drew back in fear and dodged aside as Pithon flung an empty wine goblet, narrowly missing him. He motioned to his assistant to bring more arak. "Make haste," he urged, annoyed at the servant's own fear and slow response.

Pithon continued to rage and vowed openly to avenge himself on Ashur for the indignities he had suffered. "I will wait for him in some dark alley. I'll come up be-behind him and decapitate him with my b-battle axe. His head will roll down the street, and . . . and I will dismember his flopping body, hacking limb from limb."

Finally, Pithon had consumed enough of the strong drink that he lost consciousness, and the physician resumed washing his wounds. "He is consumed with hate," the physician remarked to the assistant.

"I would not want to walk along the street with this Ashur. Pithon will most certainly kill him," the assistant observed.

"Or be killed," the physician added. He was not willing to concede Pithon the victor in a fair fight.

CHAPTER 6

Carchemish and the Piles of Bones

*T*he assassination of King Solomon's district prefect in the city of Ekron began a series of events that eventually drew Ashur into the conflict.

The Philistines inhabited Israel's west coastline on the Great Sea. King Solomon's father had defeated them in long and bloody wars. In the peak of their power, they had formed a confederacy of five great cities: Ekron, Gaza, Ashdod, Gath, and Ashkelon. In one fierce battle, before their subjugation by the king's father, they had killed thirty thousand Israeli warriors.

King Solomon had stabilized much of this area. Ekron was the only city that remained rebellious. Now, all the people opposing Solomon's rule had gathered and fortified the city. The situation had deteriorated until Solomon called his counselors together. After hearing from each at length, he dismissed them. Now only Zabud remained to help him make the final decision.

"This boil must be lanced," Zabud urged.

"My mother's vision for me was one of peace," Solomon said regretfully. "We found peace with Egypt without our people going to war. Let it be the same with Ekron. I have offered them my hand in peace, but again they have rejected it. They have hardened their hearts against me. Let the sword of Israel remain sheathed, but the disdain of Ekron I must answer with the judgment of my father. That judgment will be executed by our Assyrian mercenaries."

"Your wisdom is from above, and your judgment is that of righteous anger, my lord king," concluded Zabud devoutly.

The mercenaries, under the command of the *rabshakeh,* the military ruler of Carchemish, marched against Ekron. Three hundred chariots and three thousand foot soldiers formed the force. The people of Ekron were warned of the approaching army and prepared an ambush in a deep valley outside the city. In turn, Assyrian scouts discovered the ambush that awaited them. The rabshakeh, the Assyrian commander, sent part of his warriors marching into the valley, while the remainder attacked the enemy on the heights from the rear. The soldiers of the rebellious city were so surprised that many leaped from the mountain rim to their deaths on the rocks below. A great slaughter followed. So complete was the destruction of the army that the first rush on the city itself resulted in complete victory for King Solomon's mercenaries.

Ober, King Solomon's own general, reluctantly fulfilled the most difficult part of the king's judgment. He ordered Tiglar, the Assyrian

commander, to execute all the captured men, women, and children.

***

King Solomon's hopes for peace
were quickly shattered again. The
king's friend, Zabud, came into
the garden and walked hurriedly to
Solomon. "Master, we have received
word that the Assyrian army has surrounded the station and garrison
at Carchemish. They threaten to
slaughter every man. We must ready
the army and march at once if we are
to save them. We will teach these
treacherous Assyrians a lesson they
will never forget. Let us annihilate
them!" cried the angry counselor.

"Let us calm ourselves, Zabud,"
Solomon reproved his counselor.
But Zabud had little patience with
any of their neighbors who did not
embrace Elohim.

Solomon was surprised that the
Assyrians would revolt. They had
remained in subjection to him for
some time. The Assyrians were cruel
and barbaric and not his favorite
allies, but they understood strength.

They had been intensely loyal subjects out of respect for his military might.

"Something is not right here," he
thought. Why would Tiglar lead his
army in revolt? The obvious response
was to send an army to remove the
rabshakeh and place his own officers
in command of their military units.
The Assyrian warriors were fiercely
proud. Gaining the fealty of the
rabshakeh was the right way to deal
with them.

The friend of the king interrupted
his thoughts again, urging a rescue
column at once. Solomon dismissed
him so he could study the situation without distraction. Alone in
the privacy of his inner chambers,
Solomon reviewed the events pre-
ceding the revolt.

The original inhabitants of
Assyria were Sumerians who were
not of pure blood. They mingled
with other invading peoples. The
Sumerians were overrun by Shinar, a
neighboring country to the south. At
this point, the Assyrians stopped
the intermixture with other peoples. Now the proud city-states

of Assyria boasted that they were of purer blood than the people of Shinar. They kept careful records of their royal lineage.

Assyria and Shinar were weakened by these fierce internal wars. Solomon isolated and subjugated them. He knew, though, that they were of one family blood. Should they ever become united, they would become a formidable enemy. There was no threat of this occurring in the near future, and he dismissed this possibility for the present.

King Solomon had ordered Tiglar and his Assyrian warriors, under Ober's watchful eye, to besiege Ekron and to destroy its inhabitants, every one. They burned the city and leveled the walls stone by stone. The king had granted the Assyrian leader his request to return to Carchemish, supposedly to rest his wounds. This new rebellion by Tiglar could not be ignored.

Finally, he arrived at what he felt would be the proper response. He recalled the counselor. "Send to me a fearless young officer, one of the finest chariot warriors in my

army. I will send him to the rabshakeh to resolve this problem."

Zabud was dumbfounded. "If we send
one man to Carchemish, they will flay
him alive and send his skeleton back
with all the meat carved from it.
Surely you jest, my lord king."

"I do not jest," the king replied.
"He will travel under my own royal
standard. I will send a personal
message to the rabshakeh. The officer
can take a translator with him."

Zabud opened his mouth to object
or to argue for at least a division
or a company but thought better of
it. He had learned the futility of
arguing with Solomon once the king
had decided. Solomon's decisions
usually turned out well, no matter
how far-fetched they seemed. Zabud
shrugged. The king usually asked his
opinion when he wanted it, anyway.
He left immediately and issued the
order to the fortress commander.

The order worked its way through
the chain of command, and soon two
young officers were standing before
Solomon. One was Eliel, son of
Hashen. The other was Ashur, son of
Machir. Ashur had expected to return

home but now found himself standing before the king.

"These two young officers are both highly regarded by Jair," said Zabud. "He considers them highly intelligent. Master, young Ashur defeated Pithon in the chariot races." Zabud pointed to the other young man. "This one's name is Eliel. He is the finest archer produced by the mothers of men in many years." He went on to extol their qualifications at length.

The king was surprised to see that the fortress commander had sent him a young officer in the uniform of the militia. When he heard that this was the exceptional young man who had defeated Pithon in the chariot races, he listened with great interest to the description of his qualifications.

Solomon regarded the two young men thoughtfully. "Old Jair has covered himself again. The clever old fox has sent me two young men. If the chosen one fails, he can say that he probably would have sent the other," he thought to himself.

Solomon patiently explained the situation to the two young men. Then he questioned each of them how to

handle the situation if he were
chosen. Through the entire interrogation, he was most impressed by
one unique quality of young Ashur.
He had serene but unwavering eyes
that met his fearlessly throughout
the questioning.

***

Ashur and his guide followed the
caravan route northward to Hamath.
Tirsah patiently plodded after the
interpreter's mule. From Hamath,
they continued north to Arpad. Then
they journeyed northeast, leaving
the caravan trails.

Ashur had traveled the caravan
route farther before, to Kue with
his father. However, when they left
the familiar trails he had traveled on the horse-buying trips with
Machir, he had to depend on his
Assyrian guide. Ashur licked his
chapped lips and turned to look back
toward Solem. The sun was sinking in
the west behind them.

The guide led him across the low-
lands toward the mountains. The only
sign of life was an occasional lizard

or snake slithering out of their path. There was little shade along the way. They pressed on toward the hills on the horizon, resting only during the hottest part of the day. On and on they went, but the mountains seemed to come no closer.

Through Ashur's sun-weary eyes, the hills trembled in the shimmering heat. Dust and sweat stained his clothes. He drank from their precious water supply only when his guide did and gained the man's grudging respect.

"Here water is life," the guide said.

"In our country, too," Ashur replied.

Finally, the mountains began to take distinct form, looming larger on the horizon. Ashur and his guide followed a dry wadi to its end. They made camp on the side of a hill for the night.

Ammi constantly invaded his mind now. The need to be with her had turned into an intense flame. He dreaded the confrontation with her brothers and her mother. He rehearsed his proposal often, and sometimes it even sounded convincing to him. The time must be right. He considered having his father talk to her mother, knowing she respected his father.

Miraculously, a few desert flowers grew among the rocks bordering their camp. Ammi was very much like them, he thought, the delicate beauty and her love, both constant and enduring in the harsh land. His traveling companion advised him they were only a day's march from Carchemish. "Today was difficult, but tomorrow the ride will be easier."

Ashur noticed that Tirsah was staring intently toward the distant hills. His ears stood pointedly alert. Straining his own tired eyes to search along the skyline intensified their discomfort. "What's wrong, big fellow?"

His father had cautioned him to expect a visitor or an attack when he observed such behavior in a horse. He was relieved to see Tirsah relax his vigil and attempt to graze on the short, almost nonexistent grass around their campsite. Despite the empty landscape, Ashur no longer felt they were alone. His eyelids were now so heavy, he was beyond caring. His head barely touched his sleeping mat before he drifted away.

When morning light permitted, they resumed their mission. Throughout the day, Ashur's apprehension grew. He continually searched the rock-strewn slopes for signs of life and often looked over his shoulder to see if they were being followed.

Despite his best efforts, Ashur failed to establish any rapport with his guide. He wondered how the man felt about the subjugation of his native land. How did he feel about the rabshakeh and the present situation? Although he tried to get him to discuss the subject, the man was noncommittal. He avoided giving direct replies to his questions.

Ashur caught a glimpse of movement ahead and reigned in Tirsah. An old wolf stood for a second beside the road and then melted away into some white rocks.

"Satan," Ashur murmured to himself. A bad omen, he thought grimly. He remembered his earlier encounter with the giant wolves while protecting his father's flock. The hair on the back of his neck started crawling at the sight of his old enemy. He began to calm, and the muscles in his abdomen relaxed when he saw no other evidence of danger. Perhaps the wolf was what had caused Tirsah concern the previous evening.

A long-tailed hawk circled in the hot, cloudless sky, searching for something to kill. He marveled at the ability of the great birds of prey to stay aloft seemingly endlessly. Ashur wished he might fly away to some mountaintop. On the sheer cliffs, he would be as safe as the hawk.

He shook the reins to signal Tirsah forward again, and the chariot rolled up the road for another fifty yards. Something was unusual about the white rocks, he thought, as they got closer.

When he was near enough to make them out, he realized with revulsion that what he had thought were white rocks were piles of human skeletons. Some of the mounds of bones were three times a man's height. Human skulls were impaled on stakes. They were obviously entering the rabshakeh's territory.

He now saw for himself evidence of the cruelty of these people. Machir had related to him stories of their savagery, and his father was not given to exaggeration. Ashur glanced up at the hills around him and then looked over at the interpreter beside him. The man's face was expressionless. If the Assyrians placed the skulls there to put fear into strangers entering their territory, they had succeeded with him. He wondered if someone observed them from the peaks.

When he went over the hill, he found the road blocked by half a dozen horsemen. A glance to either side revealed other men on foot with bows and arrows already drawn. "Now we will find out if they will kill us on the spot or skin us alive later," Ashur thought to himself helplessly. The men on horseback quickly closed on them. "I will find out now if my guide is one of them and will betray me," he thought.

Ashur reigned in Tirsah and stood quietly in the chariot while his guide chattered away in the language of Carchemish. At close quarters, the men of Carchemish were seen to be of average height, dark in complexion with bushy eyebrows and beards. Their noses were large, and they had powerful builds; however, they did not look as fierce as their reputations. This offered some measure of encouragement.

Strangely, part of a discussion he had once heard came to him. The question had been something like, "Why are the people of Shinar so round-headed?"

"Because they are delivered by unskilled midwives" had been the reply. He failed to find any humor in the story now and was quite thankful the men could not read his mind.

When he saw the guide point to King Solomon's standard on the chariot, he interrupted the chattering and gesturing of the men. "Tell them we want an audience with the rabshakeh of Carchemish at once. Tell them I am a special envoy from King Solomon with an urgent message for the rabshakeh."

His guide relayed his words to the Carchemish horsemen. When he stopped speaking and before the men could reply, Ashur shook Tirsah's reins and set the chariot in motion. The horsemen were startled for a moment by the chariot's movement. Their leader shouted once for Ashur to stop, but when Ashur ignored him, he began to shout orders to his own men. A man detached himself from the others and headed down the road at a hard gallop, Ashur assumed, to alert the rabshakeh at Carchemish.

The fortifications of the city loomed on the horizon. The imposing scarp or glacis-type fortress survived from the days of the Hyksos reign. The steeply sloped and plastered earthwork ran thirty or forty feet above the first wall on the steep incline. To attack the scarp fortress, the enemy must cross a deep moat from the river. The first stone wall had its base in the moat and was some ten feet high. Atop the earthen mound stood another high wall of brick.

A small escort came out to meet them. The leader of the group that had intercepted them and the captain of the new escort exchanged greetings. Their original escort wheeled about and headed down the road the way they had come.

Riding into the strange and sinister city of Carchemish brought back Ashur's uncomfortable feeling of fear. He was now completely in the hands of evil men. What fate would befall him, he could not know. He followed his escort through the narrow streets. The inhabitants lined the streets, obviously alerted to his arrival. Young warriors in the crowd milled about, looking sullen. Others stared at him from windows and doorways, some with open hostility. A chant began to come from voices all about him. "Tiglar, Tiglar, Tiglar," they chanted. Ashur could understand that the crowd was shouting Tiglar's name, but he could not know the meaning of the other words they were shouting.

"What do they chant?" Ashur asked the guide uneasily.

"They chant the name of Tiglar to show their support for him. He is their leader, the rabshakeh," the guide replied.

Ashur felt some relief because he had thought they were already chanting for his death. The king had requested a fearless young officer, thought Ashur wryly. He was glad that no one knew his thoughts now.

They dismounted before the group of men who gathered to receive him. The men led him up the steps and into a large building. There were no rooms. The building was open and well lighted. The great hall's finely ordered mosaics of blue and green had an odd effect on Ashur, giving his surroundings a dreamy, surrealistic atmosphere.

His eyes went to a man seated on a throne at the opposite end of the great hall. As he approached, he observed that the man fidgeted nervously and seemed unsure whether he should rise. Nevertheless, from the deference shown by the men and by his interpreter, he knew that this was the rabshakeh. Ashur sensed that the name of this game was bluff. The rabshakeh had no way of knowing that he was a lowly captain of the militia or that King Solomon no doubt considered him expendable. He adopted his best swagger and went boldly forward to address the rabshakeh.

Some words his father had taught him came to him, although he could not recall whether they were words of the prophets or from the Book of the Heroes.

"I will not fear what man can do to me on this earth, for my final resting place is with Elohim," thought Ashur.

Ashur addressed the rabshakeh through his translator. He then observed an animated exchange between them. Finally, the translator turned to Ashur.

"I will explain the problem," he said. "King Solomon commanded Tiglar to destroy the city of Ekron and every inhabitant. Commander Ober, with Tiglar and his Assyrians, marched against Ekron and burned the city, killing every living person, except one. Tiglar spared one beautiful young woman of the city. He has claimed her for his own, and he has sworn to marry her day after tomorrow.

"Ober marched against Carchemish to order her destroyed. Tiglar's warriors blocked the road. When Ober discovered he was against insurmountable odds, he was forced to return to the fortress. The fortress is under siege. No one is allowed to enter or to leave.

"Tiglar absolutely refuses to give up the young woman. All of the populace and the army stand with him. The situation is a disaster. Even if Solomon himself were here, it would be a hopeless situation. No one can countermand an order of the king, not even the king himself. The king will lose one of his most valuable allies, and many fine young warriors will die before this crisis is solved."

After Ashur counseled with Tiglar at length, he was thoroughly convinced that his thinly veiled threats of Solomon's army leveling the city did not intimidate Tiglar. His officers seemed to expect the worst. To the man, they appeared ready to die to defend Tiglar's stand on the matter.

They met the young woman and listened to the entreaties of the rabshakeh. Ashur could understand why this dilemma had become a cause for all the citizens of Carchemish. The young woman had lost her entire family. Beauty and grace endeared her to all her captors, and her charm preyed on his sympathy. From his questioning, he learned that the girl's loyalties now lay with her savior, Lord Tiglar. Ashur asked if she would return to Jerusalem with him to be turned over to King Solomon. However, she said that she would do that which her benefactor, Lord Tiglar, commanded her to do.

"My life is in his hands, master," she said timorously.

"All of our lives are in the balance," Ashur said to the translator as the servant led him back to Lord Tiglar. There seemed no possible way to defuse the situation.

They met with Tiglar again, and the rabshakeh demanded to know Ashur's decision. "Will you interfere with the marriage ceremony?"

"I will give you my answer tomorrow," Ashur said with the firmest voice he could muster under the circumstances. He had no idea how to resolve the predicament.

"When will you meet with us again, young representative of Solomon?" demanded Tiglar. Ashur detected some hint of hope in his voice. The rabshakeh obviously hoped that Ashur would miraculously find a way to spare the young Philistine woman. This would counteract Solomon's judgment that Tiglar's rebellion would bring on him and the people of Carchemish. The rabshakeh knew they could not hope to succeed against the army that Solomon would send in his wrath. King Solomon had expressed concern that the rabshakeh's martyred death would provoke long-term repercussions. Ashur must convince him that there was an alternative other than the suicidal course he had chosen.

"I will come again unto you in the morning." Ashur bowed stiffly and strode out of the great hall.

At midmorning the next day, Ashur secured approval to send for the commander of the fortress. He could accomplish nothing without the agreement of Ober and Tiglar on some mutual disposition of the problem. He had remained awake through most of the night. Through the early morning hours, he had remained alone, except during a small breakfast brought to him by a servant. Ashur had considered and discarded many ideas. The small garrison in the fortress was bottled up and useless to them. He was certain that Tiglar would take the fortress and eradicate the station if a solution could not be found.

When the fortress commander arrived, Ashur consulted with him for a short time. He hoped Ober might make some suggestion that would hold some promise of working. However, the commander proved to be as unimaginative as he was haughty and unbending. When the guards came to usher them in to the rabshakeh, Ashur still had no notion of what he might do to prevent the worst from taking place.

As they strode into the great hall, he absently asked Commander Ober, "Sir, do you have a daughter?"

"Yes, I have a son, who is age twelve, and a daughter of sixteen years," replied the commander. "Do you have any children yourself, young officer?"

"No. I have no wife yet, Commander," Ashur replied. "And probably never will," he thought, as they faced the hostile rabshakeh in the great house.

"Lord Tiglar, as you know, I came here as an emissary of King Solomon. I have requested Commander Ober to come here to attempt a settlement of this issue. We must stay here until we resolve this matter," Ashur stated simply and in what he hoped was translated into the most positive and conciliatory tone.

Prolonged negotiations throughout the day brought absolutely no movement. Tiglar proved to be as obstinate and pigheaded as Ober was tactless and stubborn. Ashur could think of nothing further to propose. They reached utter and hopeless stalemate, the principals dangerously close to ending the discussion. Ashur then suggested that Tiglar give the young woman to Solomon as a gift or let him purchase her for a large sum of money. Tiglar turned a deaf ear to this, too.

Ashur looked over at Tiglar and in a low voice said to the translator, who had gained his confidence, "The rabshakeh is like the stag in the rut season. He is very wise and prudent, except in the rut, when he charges in where normally he would not and the hunter takes him." Ashur motioned toward the commander of the fortress. "His pride will allow no compromise. Elohim, save us," Ashur said, "for we are about to die."

Time had run out, and the only possible solution that would save them would be gone the next morning when the young virgin was married to the rabshakeh. Solomon would not accept any woman who had been with another man. Ashur did not think that Solomon would or could countermand his own order, anyway.

All at once, a light of thought and glimmer of hope came to him. Commander Ober started to rise to his feet to end the discussion and would have retired to the fortress. Ashur reached across and almost physically restrained him from rising. Addressing Lord Tiglar, he said loudly, "Lord Tiglar, I believe I know a solution to this perplexing problem. May I have the holy man, the reader of the code, brought here? Please bring the young virgin of the sea people, too."

The rabshakeh's face was inscrutable. For what seemed like an interminable period of time, Ashur held his breath. Tiglar signaled tiredly to one of his men. The man hurriedly left the great hall. A short time later, the old holy man and the young virgin entered.

Ashur, observing the appearance of the old man, was sure that he had the confident look of someone who knew well his office and had mastered his subject. The old man looked very much like the old one who read the code by the gates of Solem.

"O holy one, noble reader of the code, what does the code say in this matter? If a warrior wants to spare a young virgin from a conquered city and would take her as his wife, what says the code?"

The old man did not hesitate. The words began to roll off his lips as readily as if read from a parchment. "At Jahaz, the warriors of Elohim captured all the cities of Sihon and destroyed every man, woman, and child of every city. They left no survivor."

He felt the blood drain from his face. He was white and ashen, for his plan had backfired. This was not as he had remembered the code.

However, the holy man paused only a moment and then continued. "But if a warrior sees among the captives a beautiful young virgin and desires her and wants to take her for his wife, then he can bring her into his house. She must shave her head and trim her nails. She must also remove the clothes of her captivity and remain in that warrior's house and mourn her father and mother a full month. After that, the warrior may go in to her and be her husband, and she may be his wife."

The old man hesitated as if to go on, but then he bowed and stepped back. Ashur's heart had begun to beat again as the old man spoke the words the way he had remembered them. He stepped forward quickly to carry out the rest of his plan.

Ashur and Commander Ober had been relieved of their swords and searched before the meeting with Tiglar. This only aided the element of surprise for Ashur's actions. Ashur snatched the sword of the nearest guard and handed it immediately to the startled Commander Ober. He ordered the frightened interpreter, who had fallen silent, to continue and walked over to the young woman and dragged her in front of the commander. Ashur thrust her down before him. "Now, Commander, you pass sentence on this child. Her life is in your hand."

The young woman attempted to rise to her feet, but Ashur shoved her back to her knees, where she remained, sobbing. The guards drew their swords and formed quickly in front of Tiglar. They would have interfered with Ashur's handling of the girl, but Tiglar raised his hand to stay them.

"Now, Commander, what say you? Will you execute the young woman, or will she live?"

Ashur watched as Commander Ober hefted the Assyrian sword and unconsciously tested it for balance. The commander turned his attention to the young woman sobbing at his feet, her head bowed before him. For a long period, he studied her. He gazed around the room at the men held spellbound by the events they were watching. Then the commander laughed, as though he suddenly realized that he indeed held the judgment of life or death for all of them.

Would his colossal pride cause him to pronounce the death sentence on the girl and them as well? Ashur watched in horrified disbelief as the commander raised the sword to shoulder height. He was going to strike her, but the sobbing girl heard the laugh and raised her head to see who it was that could laugh at her misery. For a moment, her eyes met those of Commander Ober. In that ghost of a moment, as Ashur had hoped, Ober saw the face of his own daughter. The fortress commander tossed the sword aside. The blade clanked noisily on the stone floor, jarring the participants out of their reveries.

"I do not execute women," decided the commander. "I order the woman's head shaved. The wedding must be postponed for a month while the young woman mourns her father and mother. Then she will be given to the rabshakeh in marriage. The wisdom of the mighty Solomon has spoken from afar through the code. As it has been spoken, so let it be."

Sighs of relief arose from all present. Tiglar nodded and spoke a word of acquiescence. He was visibly relieved and elated at the words of Commander Ober. As they left the great hall, Ashur filled his lungs with a deep breath and cast his eyes to the heavens. A change was coming. He could smell it in the air.

Light rain fell on the fortress of Carchemish as Ashur said his farewells to Commander Ober. He promised to carry a message to his family of the commander's safety. With a tenuous peace reestablished, he returned to Jerusalem to report to King Solomon. There he received a well-deserved commendation and left to visit his home. The king offered him a very liberal commission in the regular army. Ashur declined, however. "The military is an honorable profession, but I prefer to live a peaceful life, sire, as you do."

CHAPTER 7

The Signet Ring

Ammi and Ashur met by the pond in the little valley. She felt as though her heart went out to meet his coming. Ashur took Ammi's hand and led her to a shaded glen off the main trail, where they rested under the large terebinth tree beside the pool. A gentle breeze mixed the faint scent of hyacinths with the fragrance of the field. White-blossomed almond trees bloomed on the hillside. Sounds of the lark and other birds singing merrily gave the two young people a feeling of well-being and extreme happiness.

The tree they leaned against had stood as a landmark for the area for many years, and the upper extremities were dying. Part of the old tree was rotten and hollow inside. Ashur knew that it was home for many a bird and small animal. He loved to sit and study nature in motion around him. A pair of turtledoves cooed in the tamarisk grove, prompting Ammi to comment, "I love the sounds the doves make, don't you? It is so peaceful."

"Yes, it is. Their calls are so different. My father says the doves, unlike other birds, only mate once, for life." Their eyes met. The smiles they exchanged made it obvious that both were thinking of the implications and meaning of the word *mate,* and the wondrous and mysterious intimacy of marriage.

"What will happen if his mate dies?" Ammi asked.

"I don't know. I guess he dies of a broken heart."

"No! You're terrible," Ammi reacted, punching his arm. "I missed you so much," she said, turning serious. She leaned forward and brushed her face and hair against his shoulder.

"How much did you miss me?"

"I cried for a week when you went away. I thought of you all the time." She sighed, making the same sound she made when they kissed.

Ashur, unable to bear the ecstasy of the moment, moved to lighten the intense nature of their conversation.

"Let me tell you a story of the tortoise."

"A story about a turtle?"

"Yes, a tortoise. Tortoises live on land. Put your hands out." He took her hands in his, turning her palms toward the sky.

"There once was a boy tortoise that lived on an island." Ashur released one hand and placed his index finger in the palm of her other hand to indicate the location of the tortoise on the island. "The island was beautiful with an abundance of nice trees and leaves and bugs to eat. The tortoise's island was perfect, except for one thing. No young female tortoises lived on his island." Ashur scowled, getting into his impromptu tale.

Ammi smiled. "How terrible! What did he do?"

"There was another island nearby. He purposed on swimming to the other island to see if any female tortoises inhabited it."

"Tortoises," Ammi accused. "You mean more than one female turtle?" She withdrew her hands from his.

"No, wait. Let me complete the story." He took her hands again.

"He was searching for only one girl tortoise," Ashur corrected himself, pleased with the suggestion of her imagined jealousy. "Our little tortoise hero waded into the water and tried to swim to the other island. Alas, tortoises do not swim well. He was forced to turn back. From the safety of the shore he looked across to the other island, and what do you suppose he saw?"

"*One* little female turtle," Ammi smiled.

"Yes, *one*," Ashur agreed. "There were no more little girl tortoises around, anywhere, only this special one."

"So, what did he do?" Ammi asked, her curiosity piqued.

"In despair, he looked all around for a boat or shallow place to cross."

"Turtles do not have boats."

"I mean, a log, a stick, or something," Ashur recovered. "The tortoise was in such despair, he considered throwing himself into the water to drown." At this point, Ashur wondered where the story was going.

"What did he do?" Ammi squeezed his hands, feigning exasperation.

"He searched for anything that would take him to his turtle love. He entered some trees—in the Black Forest," Ashur embellished from his experience. "Our little boy tortoise discovered that he was not on an island after all, but a peninsula. With hopes rising, he struggled through the forest." Ashur traced his fingers up her arms, across her shoulders, and behind her neck. "The girl tortoise came to meet him. They kissed and found everlasting happiness together."

With that, Ashur joined his hands together behind her neck and brought his face close to hers until their lips came together in a warm kiss. Her audible sigh and response signaled to him that the humor and story pleased her immeasurably.

Ashur spoke softly to Ammi of his love for her and their plans for the future. He took her in his arms and kissed her again. Ammi was the first to take her lips away, pulling back from the warmth of Ashur's mouth. She sat back with her heart pounding and something inside crying for more. Nothing, she thought, could possibly feel that good. "Oh, Ashur, I am so happy. I love you with all my heart. I'll love you like this every day for the rest of my life."

The two young lovers noticed a field mouse by the pond. Suddenly a hawk swooped from the top of the tree. Iron-like talons fastened on the unsuspecting mouse. Ammi watched in horror as the hawk began to tear it apart with its beak. The mouse squeaked pitifully. The incident destroyed the beauty and peacefulness of the moment. Oddly, Ammi's mind flashed to the loss of her father.

"Why does Elohim allow so much cruelty in this world?" Ammi asked, more as a statement than as a question directed at Ashur.

Ashur stood as if to try to do something to bring back the precious minutes they had shared. The hawk had forgotten their presence, but Ashur startled him by rising to his feet. The bird dropped his prey. Several powerful beats of his wings took him deep into the tamarisk grove.

Ammi walked to the torn and lifeless form of the mouse and bent down to examine it. "The poor little thing," she sobbed, her tears and pain returning easily when reminded of the death of her father.

Ashur followed her. He took her by the wrists, pulling her into his arms. He raised her arm and kissed the back of her hand. "You will be all right, Katan-Ammi," he said, using for the first time her father's endearment for her.

She burrowed her face into his chest, finding comfort in the strength and warmth of his arms. He caressed her hair. When the tears had ceased, he lifted her head and kissed her forehead and her eyes. The salty taste of her tears and the perfume of her hair mingled in his senses. Her emotion touched him, but he was more accustomed to the cruelty of nature. A rustling sound in the hollow tree behind him suggested that at least one more mouse hid there. They probably made their trips down to the water at night. The dead mouse had paid the ultimate price for his daylight thirst.

Ashur recalled the incident that had shocked him so when he found vultures devouring the newborn lamb and the still-living mother. He had remained sickened for some time by the experience but had learned to accept such events as commonplace.

***

Ashur traveled the next day to the village of Nahal to visit a silversmith known for his great skill. He had gone there once before in his quest to identify the signet ring. He found the silversmith working outside. Dekar's father greeted Ashur warmly. "Have you come to Nahal to trade horses?" he asked, motioning to the second horse tied by a rope to the back of the chariot.

"Greetings, good and noble craftsman. Where is that great horseman, your son, who could not ride a donkey?" His friend Dekar owned the sorriest mount in all the land. Dekar had taken a terrible teasing after he had somehow managed to get thrown by the beast. His friend admired Ashur's beautiful and powerful Tirsah.

Inside the silversmith's shop, he explained the purpose for his visit. "Great craftsman, I would like to strike a bargain with you. I would like to trade this worthless stallion, the brother of Tirsah, for a ring, a clever duplicate of my ring, but in miniature. But you must promise never to let a certain clumsy son of yours ride him," said Ashur, smiling, noticing Dekar, who appeared at the door.

Dekar listened to the conversation from the doorway. A look of bewilderment spread across his face. He entered the building and embraced his friend. "Ashur, it is too much," Dekar said incredulously as he grabbed his friend in a wrestling hold, the way the young men displayed their affection. "You are crazy; the brother of Tirsah is worth much more than the cost of the ring.

Father, tell this young fool that he is mad."

The two powerful young men wrestled around the room, threatening to upset the tables laden with the craftsman's tools. Ashur struggled halfheartedly to break the arm lock that Dekar had on him. Finally, they stopped to catch their breath, and Ashur shared with his friends the reason for his visit.

"Have you asked the Solemite to marry you yet?" Dekar queried, guessing that Ammi had something to do with the miniature ring.

"Not yet," Ashur replied.

"Well, when?" Dekar pressed.

"I do not know. Her brothers are not very fond of me. I want to give Ammi a meaningful token of my love. Since I cannot bear to part with my ring, I want your father to make a miniature replica for Ammi, then create a special ribbon so that she may wear it around her neck."

The older man's wink and nod sealed the bargain. "Here," he said, removing the leather string from the ring and returning it to Ashur. "You should continue wearing this, or else Ammi may suspect that something is going on."

"You have a wonderful idea," Dekar said approvingly. "One day I will find a woman as fair as your Ammi. I will do the same, if it is all right with you," he added, not wanting to infringe on the uniqueness of his friend's idea.

"Of course you will," Ashur said heartily.

***

More than a month had passed since his visit to Nahal. Ashur was sitting at the table in the house, fashioning a new harness for Tirsah. His mother was working in her garden, and his father was helping some workmen repair the front gate to his estate.

"Yee-ee-ha-ah!" The shout and sound of thundering hoofs came from the courtyard. Chariot wheels rumbled near the front of the house. Ashur rushed to the door and outside, where he was met with a cloud of dust. He jumped back as the chariot rumbled by. Dekar was driving Tirsah's brother wildly around the well in the courtyard.

The next time around, the chariot came dangerously close to striking the well. Wild-eyed, Dekar reined the horse in, then leaped down from the chariot to calm the excited animal. Ashur coughed loudly and excessively. "Who is stirring up all this dust?" he laughed as his father joined them. A smug smile said that Machir was a party to this fun and had opened the gate to give Dekar entrance. His father was pleased to see Dekar's newfound skill with the chariot and the horse that he had helped Ashur train.

When things calmed down, Dekar took Ashur's ring, the miniature ring, and the delicate ribbon from a pouch. He handed over the contents to his friend. "I hope you will be pleased with my father's work."

Ashur examined the gold band carefully. "It is even better than I hoped. How did your father make it so smooth?" he asked, delighted at the definition of the symbol. "The ring is a masterwork."

"My father said Ammi's ring was a challenge because it was so small."

Finally, Dekar took leave of Machir and Nelmaah and set out for Nahal, proudly driving the war chariot. Ashur seized on the earliest opportunity to meet with Ammi.

***

Ashur found her, as he hoped he might—alone in her father's garden. They sat on the stone bench beneath an apple tree. "I have a gift for you, Ammi. It is important to me for you to have a part of me with you always." He allowed her to look at the ring for a moment, then placed the ribbon and gold ring around her neck. "Take this ring and set me as a seal upon your heart," he said, as he brushed her lips with a kiss.

Uncontrollably, she threw her arms around his neck. Their lips crushed together in a rapturous, burning kiss. Her hair fell softly across his chest and face. The passionate response threatened to topple them off the bench. A bee dropped from a blossom above them and buzzed dangerously close to their faces. They broke away from their embrace and laughed at their looks of alarm.

Ammi tucked the ring inside her tunic. "I will wear the ring, here, near my heart, always."

"If you ever need me when we are apart, send me the signet ring," he instructed gallantly. He kissed her again.

They left the village and walked together to the terebinth tree. Ashur adopted the bee from the incident, and it became an integral part of his courtship of Ammi. "Bzz, bzzz, watch out! Here comes that pesky bee again." He tickled the inside of her ear with his fingertip, trailed along her hairline, and down her neck. "Watch out! Do not let the bee sting you."

"He had better not sting me," Ammi threatened, brushing his hand aside, pretending irritation. "I am about to swat this bee into never-to-be-seen-again land," she said. Nevertheless, she loved his touch and loved the way he made her laugh.

"I cannot believe you want to kill this innocent bee. He only wants to taste the beautiful, sweet-smelling flower." He kissed her again, first on the mouth, and then he savored the bare, warm skin along her neck. "Sweet. Yes, intoxicating," he whispered. The ever-present scent of the desert gardenia perfumed her hair. The warmth of that kiss burned a permanent memory in his mind.

Ammi broke away from him. "Grandmother was right. The more you kiss, the more you want." She grabbed his arm and dragged him to his feet. "We must find something to do. I love to be close to you, but this is too much."

"You are right," Ashur replied, nodding his head in agreement. They spent the rest of their time together skipping flat rocks across the pool by the terebinth tree. From that day forward, they considered their betrothal sealed, a promise that one day they would unite in marriage.

***

When Ammi showed Shoshanna the signet ring Ashur had given her, her reaction was not what she had anticipated. She had expected Shoshanna to share her happiness. The look on her friend's face was one of disappointment.

"You love Ashur, too, don't you?" Ammi asked Shoshanna quietly.

When directly confronted with the question, Shoshanna's lip quivered, and she burst into tears. She felt that she had somehow betrayed Ammi. "Oh, Ammi, I am sorry; it is true. I always thought that if something happened . . . " She hesitated, unable to express herself without fear of further offending Ammi. Then the words came tumbling out. "I should have told you. I thought that if I did not tell you, I could be around him, too; and if it did not work out that you and Ashur married, that I . . . that we . . . ."

"It is all right," Ammi said. "I think I have known for a long time. You have not done anything wrong. I love Ashur, and he loves me. Ashur is very fond of you, and if something happened to me, I would want you to have him."

Shoshanna could tell that there was nothing condescending about Ammi's words, and she knew that her friend meant what she said. For Ashur's sake, she would want Shoshanna to love Ashur in her absence.

Shoshanna went on to explain her distress. Partly, she was upset with Pithon. Ammi knew about the man and could understand Shoshanna's fears. "Ammi, I am deathly afraid of him," Shoshanna said despairingly. "He will not leave me alone. None of the young men will come near me. I have heard that Pithon threatens them."

"Have you had your father speak to him?" Ammi asked.

"Yes, but Pithon ignores him. You know my father. He is a peaceful man. He would not say a hard word to any man except as a last resort. He hasn't seen the things Pithon has done around me. He thinks I am exaggerating. But Ammi, I am terrified of him. Some people say he's crazy. They say that he has killed several men. That man, Sabta, who hangs around Pithon all the time, he has the look of evil. He sends chills down my spine."

"Mine too," Ammi said sympathetically. "What if your father told the elders or possibly the district prefect?" Ammi suggested, trying to find a solution that would console Shoshanna. "I will ask Ashur what to do. Maybe he will talk to his father."

"Thank you, Ammi. You are a true friend." When Shoshanna was ready to leave, Ammi offered to walk her part of the way home. Shoshanna refused, since this would put Ammi at risk when she returned alone.

"Enough light remains. He would not try anything in the daylight. Nevertheless, I cannot come again to visit in the cool of the evening," Shoshanna said unhappily.

The two young women embraced, and Shoshanna hurried down the street. Ammi cast a nervous eye at the gathering dusk. She wished one of her brothers was there to see Shoshanna home, but they were away. "The watchmen of the city are already out," she tried to reassure herself.

Shoshanna almost made it home. She heard steps, and a shadowy figure suddenly appeared. Without speaking, the man grabbed her. He tried to get a hand over her mouth as he dragged her down a dark alley. Shoshanna's bloodcurdling scream pierced the night. Pithon threw her to the ground and smothered her cries.

"Over there," the watchman said, "I saw someone go into that alley." The two watchmen rushed forward with drawn swords.

Pithon, kneeling over the crumpled young woman, heard the guards coming. His eyes were glazed with lascivious desire, and he cursed the interruption. He ran across the street, vaulted a low wall, and fled into the night. The guards found Shoshanna in the alley, lying in a pool of blood.

They immediately transported her to her nearby home, where her parents anxiously examined the injury to her head and eye. The watchmen returned to search the area, and word of the incident circulated through the village.

When Ammi arrived at Shoshanna's bedside, she lay lifeless, except for her shallow breathing. "Is she going to be all right?" Ammi asked anxiously.

"I cannot say. She is breathing, but she makes no movement," her father said huskily, his voice choked with emotion.

Shoshanna's mother and father, along with Ammi, took turns sitting with her through the night. They were all beside her the next morning when she first moved and moaned. All three rushed to take her hand. When she cried out, it was for her father. "Father, it was Pithon. He attacked me," she sobbed.

"You will be all right now, daughter. I am here."

"I am here beside you, too, Shoshanna," her mother said.

"Mother, what is wrong with my eye?" She felt around with her hand. "I cannot see out of this side," Shoshanna cried, turning her head trying to see her mother.

"The eye is injured. We must wait for it to heal," her mother told her, trying to comfort her.

Ammi left the room, for she could no longer control her emotions. She could not bear to look at the terrible wound any longer. The sharp cornerstone had gashed and blackened the eye socket. The eye had sustained broken blood vessels. She was sure that her friend would lose the sight in that eye. Shoshanna's father followed Ammi outside. He left to meet with the elders of the village.

Later, when confronted by the watchmen, Pithon shrugged indifferently at the accusations. "I did not attack the woman. Pithon does not have to force women," he snarled, when accused of attacking Shoshanna.

"Let us send for the district prefect," said Shoshanna's father, justly incensed. "Keep this man under guard."

"Where are my accusers? Who are these liars?" demanded the unrepentant Pithon.

"Shoshanna has named you as her attacker. Everyone knows you have wanted her. You tried to get her every way you knew how and she rejected you," her father raged.

"It is her word against mine. There are no witnesses because it did not happen," Pithon lied again.

Shoshanna's father went to one side and conferred with the elders, urging them to have Pithon held.

"Pithon is right," said the head elder. "There are no witnesses. We have only your daughter's word against his. The night was dark. She could be mistaken."

"There is no mistake. That lying jackal attacked my precious one. And you do nothing. You, my *friends*. You have daughters of your own. Who will be next if this outrage goes unpunished?"

"Pithon is the grandson of a famous warrior. You cannot formally accuse him without witnesses. Our women enjoy much freedom and protection, but our land is not totally free from violence," the elder said, implying that nothing could be done in this case.

* * *

Pithon returned to Jerusalem and remained unpunished for the attack. The watchmen had seen but a glimpse of her assailant. The alley where the assault took place was dark. This made a positive identification impossible and left family and friends filled with anger and frustration.

"We could not make out the face or form of the man in the poor light," the watchman said honestly, regretting his inability to implicate an attacker.

Although Pithon had not spoken to her, there was no question in Shoshanna's mind that it was Pithon who had struck her. She had to admit to the elders, though, that her attacker had not spoken. Pithon insisted that he had been with Sabta in another part of the village when the attack occurred. Sabta falsely corroborated his story.

Ammi came daily to sit beside Shoshanna, holding her friend's hand. Shoshanna struggled with fear in the night, unable to sleep. She struggled during the day, too. Each day she had to deal with the unnatural feeling of seeing out of only one eye.

"I think I may go mad, Ammi," Shoshanna said, overwhelmed with fear and dread. "I hate being so afraid. He stalks me as a leopard hunts his prey." She was afraid to be left alone in her own home and refused to leave her bed.

CHAPTER 8

Shields of Gold

One day King Solomon was at work in a museum he had built. He was busy with one of his scribes, cataloging the different birds and their eggs and nests, when a messenger arrived from Ezion-geber.

"Sire, the station at Ezion-geber has been destroyed by the Sukkiim," reported the messenger. "The garrison warriors and the shipmen are all dead. I and two others were all that escaped."

Solomon tossed aside the bird nest he was studying and motioned to the scribe attending him. "Bring Zabud and my military advisors to me." While he waited for his counselors, he carefully considered this new problem presented by these unique people.

The Sukkiim, cave dwellers who lived on both shores of the sea of Elath, were serpent eaters. Their language was more shrieks or whistles rather than articulate speech. Their food was principally meat, their drink a mixture of blood and milk. They were said to be so fleet of foot they were able to run down their prey. Their large tribes, for the most part, occupied themselves with tribal wars.

Under careful questioning by Solomon, the survivors reported that the suddenness of the attack had caused the downfall of the garrison. The warriors were adequately armed and trained, but they had received no warning of the attack.

Solomon formed a new partnership with King Hurom of the kingdom of Tyre. With tales of gold from Ophir and Havilah, Solomon convinced King Hurom to help him fortify Ezion-geber. "Give me Hiram-abi and Kedarus, your captains of the ships, and we will build a great city of the sea," entreated King Solomon. "Around this city of more than two and one-half square miles, we will build a wall twenty-six feet high and thirteen feet wide."

"Is there no gold to mine in Israel?" King Hurom asked.

"Israel has no gold to mine, although there are traces in the Eilat Mountains. The lands rich in gold lay to the south of Israel. Ezion-geber, on the southernmost coast of Israel, is the gateway to these gold-rich areas. The caravan routes from Ezion-geber south to Marib are extremely hazardous, though. The caravans pass through a hostile land inhabited by fierce tribesmen and bandits."

King Hurom became convinced of the importance of the venture and returned to Tyre with a promise to send the men needed to build the city.

***

"Father," King Solomon greeted Hiram-abi when he arrived. He used the same expression of respect as did King Hurom in addressing the skilled craftsman. "I have sent for you because I have a new project for you, one that may prove to be most difficult work and dangerous as well. This is what we are about to undertake."

He continued to describe the walls of the city. The gleam in the eye of the great builder did not catch fire until Solomon spoke of what he would create inside the city. "Inside the city of Ezion-geber, beyond the great desert, we will construct the greatest smelting furnace the world has known."

Solomon's excitement increased as he described his plans to Hiram-abi. "As you know, most of what we know about the furnaces and casting, we learned from the sea peoples when my father subdued them. I have sent the best from Israel and a couple of your countrymen to Ezion-geber to select a site for the smelting furnace. While you stayed in Tyre with your family, they studied the land. The men have returned, and what you see before you are the reports they have made to me.

"They have found that the winds almost incessantly blow down the valley from the north. They propose to build the furnace in the middle of the valley. Here!"—he stabbed at the map—"not here, in the shelter of the hills where springs flow with water. I want you to go to see if their findings are plausible. If they are, you will build the hottest smelting furnace made by man—a furnace fanned by the winds to cast the purest metals."

Solomon planned a fleet of ships to sail south with the prevailing winds. The ships could bring back much larger loads of trade goods than the slow-moving caravans. He was tempted to go with the ships to Marib, where gardens of spices perfumed the air for miles around the city. There he could see for himself the beautiful queen of Marib he had heard so much about. He could see the temple of the moon.

Perhaps in Marib he could question the shipmen and learn what lay beyond the Great Sea. But so many things remained to finish in Jerusalem and in the north. Solomon decided to send Zabud to Ezion-geber to oversee the building of the city of the sea.

Months later, Zabud returned to report to the king. "Fuel for the furnaces will soon be a problem. We are cutting all the trees in the area. With its new walls, the city is now safe from surprise attack," he said. "However, the construction is costing many lives. Hundreds of men have died," Zabud complained. "It is the quarries all over again. We must do something about the working conditions. Will you speak to the Minister of the Mas? He is responsible for the forced labor. The climate and terrain at Ezion-geber are harsh, and the Sukkim take a heavy toll on the workers, too."

Solomon was in no mood, however, to have his conscience prodded by the *melek reeh*, the friend of the king. "More lives may be saved in the long run if we complete the walls in Ezion-geber and the walls of the fortress cities," the king countered.

***

A schism was developing between the two men, primarily caused by the increasing number of marriages to foreign women and the resulting compromises brought about in every quarter. Solomon pushed on with the building of the city, ignoring the working conditions of the slave laborers.

In one part of the city, the workers crushed copper and iron ore. In another stood the foundry in which the ore was smelted. Providing the necessary wood to fuel the furnaces for smelting the ore and for lumber for the ships was a tremendous undertaking.

The prevailing winds at Ezion-geber blew for six months in one direction and six months in another. When a fleet had been assembled and the winds were right, they sailed toward Ophir and Havilah. Laden with copper, iron, and goods from the caravans, the ships' captains sailed to the south. Solomon instructed them to secure lasting markets for his merchant ships.

War galleys accompanied the fleet as protection against the pirates who sailed the South Seas. The ships returned with gold, silver, ivory, exotic animals, and other trade goods of every imaginable sort. Caravans transported the goods to the city of Jerusalem, where they were displayed for the king.

The kings and governors of surrounding countries brought gold and silver to Solomon. Craftsmen made two hundred shields of beaten gold for the king. Twenty-two pounds of gold went into each. He also had three hundred smaller ones, made about one-third of the weight of the others. Together the golden shields weighed 6,600 pounds. The king put them in the Yaar Hallebanon, a separate building where they were displayed.

***

Solomon heard voices, arguing in the Hall of Pillars.When he went outside, he heard Zabud arguing with his prefect, who had just returned from Ezion-geber with Zabud and one of the caravans. "I know the king will want to see her," he heard Ben-hesed say as he entered the hall.

"What is going on out here?" Solomon demanded. He could tell from the defeated look on Zabud's face that he had again been trying to protect him on some moral issue.

The prefect hastened to make his case before the king. "We have captured a woman of the Sukkiim. We thought you would want to see her, my lord king. She is a princess of her people."

"You mean, you thought the king would want to see this heathen woman?" Zabud tried to intimidate the prefect.

"You have brought the woman to the palace?" the king asked, his curiosity aroused.

"Yes, sire," he replied, as though admitting some guilt. "She is the daughter of a tribal chieftain," he added again, defensively.

"You have done well, prefect. I am pleased that you thought of me when you have been so busy with the affairs of your new city," the king said, putting his arm around the shoulder of his prefect and guiding him toward his chambers. He ignored Zabud, who followed them inside. It irritated the king to have Zabud make decisions without consulting him.

"Come in and tell me of Ezion-geber. Does all still go well? We will talk of the Sukkiim woman later."

They discussed the fortifications of the city at great length. Solomon asked about the ships and their trade goods, the accommodations of the men, and the trade agreements.

Zabud became sufficiently bored that he asked the king's leave to retire. After Zabud left the king's chambers, Solomon asked the prefect about the Sukkiim.

"The fortification of the city is a complete success," he said. The walls have allowed our warriors to repel the attacks of all enemies of the kingdom."

Again the prefect brought the conversation around to the young woman. "We captured her on a raid. Her village lies in a wilderness area southwest of the city. The chieftain of this war tribe causes us the most grief. She is very wild, sire. It took three powerful men to subdue her. She is very statuesque, beautiful in an exotic way. At least, she is interesting to me," he hastened to add. "The women of the Sukkiim wear no covering on their breasts."

"Bring her to me. I will look upon this woman of the Sukkiim," the king said, intrigued by the prefect's description.

When she was led in bound before the king, she certainly lived up to her captor's description. The princess stood erect, her eyes meeting his for a moment before she turned her body sideward to stare toward the wall. Her eyes held no fear, nor was fear present in her bearing.

"She has done remarkably well after her capture, compared to the men, sire. She eats well. The men refused to eat, and several died. We released those who were alive to return to their people. She knows nothing of their fate. I brought her to you, sire, because of her standing among her people. Her father escaped us in the raid. He has sent men to Ezion-geber, offering all kinds of ransom for her. I will do with her as you command me."

"The woman is obviously impressed with the throne room," said King Solomon. The young woman stared at the tables laden with the golden serving vessels and at the rich luxury of the room.

"Has the girl eaten?" Solomon asked the prefect.

"No, my lord king. I will have her fed when she returns to her holding room."

"Bring food," he ordered the servants. When the table was laden with food, he ordered her released.

"But, sire!"

"Release her! I will be responsible for her. Bid the girl to eat. You may leave, prefect. You have done well. I want to study her, alone."

"Yes, sire." The prefect did not argue. He released the girl's bonds and bid her seat herself on a couch beside the low table.

"Oh, prefect, has the girl seen a mirror?" Solomon asked, another thought coming to mind.

"No, sire, I do not believe she has," replied the prefect.

"Have the servants bring one of the golden shields from the Yaar Hallebanon, and tell them to bring a mirror," the king ordered. As the prefect left the room, he saw the king seat himself across the table from the woman of the Sukkiim. The hungry woman began to eat immediately.

* * *

While King Solomon dallied with his latest conquest, an ominous plot was developing in Egypt to the south. Siamun, ruler of Egypt, formed an alliance with Hadad, a prince of Edom, and Rezon, the robber baron, to undertake the invasion of Israel. Rezon targeted King Solomon's hoard of gold.

King Solomon's father had subjugated Rezon's homeland. He had placed a garrison in the little oasis city to guard the trade routes. Those of Aram who could not accept the rule of the old king had fled to the east into the desert, where they roamed for years.

When Solomon's father died, Rezon returned to Aram, drove out the garrison, and proclaimed himself king. King Solomon sent an army to retake the city, but Rezon fled into the desert and again drove out the garrison troops after the army departed. For Solomon, Rezon was merely a distant troublemaker and no real threat. He had tabled action for the moment until some future time when he could decide how to eliminate the rebellious Rezon.

At Pharaoh's court lived a prince of Edom, who as a child had fled with some of his father's faithful followers to Egypt. Hadad's father and his followers had petitioned Pharaoh Siamun for asylum. Siamun had gladly offered them protection since they might prove useful to him in his future dealings with Solomon's father. He had given Hadad's father and his followers land and houses, which the young prince eventually inherited.

Hadad also found favor at court. Pharaoh gave him the sister of his first-ranking wife in marriage. A son was born of this union. Hadad, the man whose name meant "thunderer," hated the people of Israel. When he heard that Solomon's father had died, he asked Siamun for permission to return to his own country.

"Tell me what thing you lack here in Egypt," Pharaoh demanded. "You have everything a man could want." Pharaoh grieved to learn that Hadad planned to take his son away with him, since he was a great favorite of the monarch. Nevertheless, Hadad left Egypt. In Aram, he met the cunning robber baron, Rezon. Rezon shared Hadad's abhorrence of Israel. From this vengeful alliance came a sinister plot.

Pharaoh Siamun had watched nervously from afar as Solomon's power grew. Rezon and Hadad persuaded Siamun to launch an invasion of Israel. Pharaoh hoped to regain Israel and control of the trade routes.

"He who controls the trade routes controls all the wealth that travels them," Hadad said, tantalizing Siamun. "First, we will attack Gezer. Then, if Solomon does not advance to meet us, we will march on the city of Jerusalem."

Further complicating the political situation was Solomon's marriage to Osoris, a princess of Egypt. King Solomon had elevated her over his other wives. The addition of more wives and concubines had strained their relationship. Nevertheless, he had no reason to expect an invasion from Egypt.

Solomon's father had attacked Gezer several times, but lacking siege weapons, he had been unable to take the city. Gezer remained unconquered, and the people exacted heavy tolls from caravans traveling through its territory. Thus it remained an extreme source of irritation to Solomon and to Pharaoh Siamun of Egypt, because the caravans were beneficial to both.

Further, if Solomon's armies left Jerusalem to meet the advancing army of Egypt, Rezon's bandits, posing as refugees from the south, would gain entry to the city. They were to overwhelm the gatekeepers just before dawn on the appointed day, and Hadad's men would storm the garrison of the Yaar Hallebanon. The cunning Hadad reasoned that Solomon and most of the army would go to Gezer to confront Pharaoh Siamun and the army of Egypt. He was certain that Siamun's large army would be discovered and reported to Solomon as soon as the army entered Israel.

Hadad's success would depend on his being able to surprise the defenders at Jerusalem. Therefore, part of his men would land by sea and march overland. The chariots and wagons that would be used to transport the golden shields to the ships would have to come from Egypt by land. The drivers would not be told about the attack on Jerusalem. If discovered, these wagons were carrying rations for the main army as it advanced to the north. News of the attack on Jerusalem would reach Solomon as he marched to Gezer and so discomfort the army as to aid Pharaoh Siamun in winning a great victory.

"My spies report that Solomon takes a few of the golden shields into battle with the army. However, I believe most of them will be left in the Yaar Hallebanon," Hadad said with a diabolical smile on his face.

When word came to Solomon that Siamun was attacking Gezer, he seized on a bold countermove. He decided to take the army to meet Pharaoh at Gezer.

"The warriors of Gezer will present the army of Egypt with a formidable opponent," King Solomon said, addressing Zabud, his most trusted counselor. "They will defend their citadel. If our warriors attack at the end of the day, we might strike the enemy while the warriors of Egypt are exhausted. Siamun will expect us to be preparing for a siege."

Solomon considered the poorly fortified Jerusalem incapable of withstanding the siege weapons of Egypt. Marching against Pharaoh Siamun with the army left the city largely unprotected. He left the Millo, the Yaar Hallebanon, and the new Fortress of the Heroes with only a few units of the Gibore Hail and militia. By engaging Siamun at Gezer, Solomon hoped to gain time to provision the city and time for other units of the army to arrive from the north. They could be used to reinforce the defenses of the city, or they could join the army with him at Gezer, as circumstances dictated. He gave orders to this effect to the commander he left behind in Jerusalem.

"I do not understand Siamun's attack on Gezer," Solomon said to Zabud. "If his ultimate goal is to take Jerusalem, he should bypass Gezer. Gezer will not come to Jerusalem's aid. Siamun has no way of knowing this, however. He probably feels that he could not leave an enemy behind him on his exposed flanks. Perhaps the hated toll extorted from his caravans has something to do with his attack on Gezer."

Even with Egypt's siege weapons, Solomon thought Gezer could withstand a siege for several days. This would weaken the army of Egypt. He wished the Yaar Hallebanon was enclosed within the walls and that Jerusalem itself was better fortified. Time had not allowed him the luxury of fortifying the city.

When King Solomon's army arrived at Gezer, the city lay in smoking ruins. The Egyptians had destroyed Solomon's garrison at the station nearby. No survivors could be found.

The Egyptian warriors were arrayed in formation before Solomon and poised to do battle. Under the banners of their companies stood foot soldiers, chariots, and archers. Solomon stood quietly in his chariot, breathless with the magnificence of the moment. Around him, horns were blowing and captains shouted orders as his army formed for the conflict.

Solomon immediately moved to avoid the battle. He sent emissaries to the king of Egypt under a flag of truce. To his relief, his offer of a conference was accepted. The two great rulers met outside Gezer.

"Great Pharaoh Siamun," Solomon said, "let us hold council. You are a powerful monarch and a wise ruler of men. You are master of all the lands of the Great River. All that observe Pharaoh bow at the mention of his name. The splendor of Pharaoh Siamun is known throughout the earth. Only the men of Shishak make war against the mighty king of Egypt, and they are of no consequence to the great and noble Siamun."

Siamun shifted uneasily on his seat at the mention of Shishak, his old enemy. Pharaoh suddenly remembered the long distance to his capital city of Bubastis. Suddenly he did not feel quite so powerful. He admitted to himself that he felt uneasy leaving Bubastis with such a thin army of defenders. He had unconsciously been so uneasy he had brought his family with him on his campaign against Gezer. Ram-siaman wondered if Solomon could have formed an alliance with Shishak. Shishak might now be launching an attack on the unprotected Bubastis.

Actually, Solomon considered Egypt an excellent buffer between his kingdom and the wild and vacillating Shishak. He did not covet Egypt, and besides, he thought Egypt to be an isolated land. Great deserts and mountains bound Egypt on either side. The Great Sea lay to the north, and the river and impassable waterfalls protected the southern region.

Solomon knew that an invasion launched against a resident army entrenched in that long and narrow valley of Egypt would be so costly as to be prohibitive. As long as Siamun and Shishak battled each other, they would not trouble him.

The Egyptian king and Solomon had four lengthy meetings. Each time Pharaoh marveled at the persuasiveness of this man. Pharaoh stalled for time and for word of the success of Hadad and Rezon or word from Bubastis. He began to become more conscious of the difficulty of maintaining supply lines. His army was too large. Even if he defeated Solomon in a great battle, his capital city of Bubastis lay unprotected. His archenemy Shishak might take advantage of the situation. He would be reluctant to advance on Jerusalem even with a great victory over Solomon's army. Solomon also continually reminded him of the great friendship between Israel and King Hurom of Tyre. This left Siamun to wonder if an army was marching from Tyre to Jerusalem at that very moment.

Another thing that worried Pharaoh was reports from his captains who had engaged Solomon's warriors from the station. Solomon's men had fought to the last man. Each fallen

warrior had killed several Egyptian
soldiers. The objects of Pharaoh's
anger were Hadad and Rezon, who had
talked him into this ill-conceived
expedition.

As his servant prepared him for
sleep, the Egyptian king actually
found himself considering an alliance. Solomon had offered him a protected land route so his caravans
of goods could travel safely from
Egypt to Tyre.

The actual war truce turned into
a banquet. Solomon summoned servants
who brought forth delicacies from
his royal storehouse: choice wines,
honey, breads made from fine flour,
succulent meats basted and marinated
in his favorite sauces. The separation of their tables and other
restraints and prejudices were gradually broken down by the powerful
presence of King Solomon.

CHAPTER 9

A Sinister Plot and the Battle at the River

*I*n the absence of the regular army, Ashur was left in command of the militia. He was responsible for the men who remained at the Fortress of the Heroes. However, the duties of leadership equaled the stress of having the regular officers about. He and his militiamen at the fortress patrolled the roads to the north and east of Jerusalem. They waited uneasily for word of the army, unaware of the events taking place at Gezer.

Ashur flicked Tirsah with his reins, and the horse immediately increased his gait. They drove through the gate and took the road to the north, away from the fortress and away from Jerusalem. Other units of cavalry and chariots patrolled against possible raiders to the west and south. An ominous cloud hovered over those left behind. Jerusalem and the Yaar Hallebanon were woefully undermanned until the northern armies arrived.

"Whoa, Tirsah," Ashur said, as he reined in and turned the horse around. He had gone a short distance, planning only to give Tirsah some exercise and then return to the fortress. As they turned about, he caught sight of riders from the fortress coming down the road. He recognized one of the men as Elkai, who had accompanied him as servant and aide.

"*Saha badnu*," Elkai said breathlessly, wishing Ashur health. "I bring an urgent order by way of this soldier from Jerusalem."

"*Badnu salmo*," Ashur replied, answering with the standard "Peace to your body." The young soldier saluted and handed the order to him. "What has happened?" Ashur asked, knowing instantly that something terrible had occurred. The soldier wore a Jerusalem guard's uniform. Obviously, he had recently been in combat. A sword or other sharp object had scored his chin. Blood mixed with sweat and dust stained his uniform. His lathered horse spoke equally of the urgent mission.

"What is it, Elkai?" he asked. The unexplained situation sent a number of fears through his mind. "Is Jerusalem under attack?" Ashur leaned against the wheel of his chariot and read the orders.

"Yes," Elkai answered. "Nevertheless, the city is secure. The robber baron, Rezon, attacked the Yaar Hallebanon. The host of the army was away with Solomon at Gezer. Rezon's men gained entry into the city by posing as refugees. Warriors breached the outer door to the city. They overwhelmed the small garrison of the Yaar Hallebanon."

The young soldier continued the story, pouring out his tale to Ashur. "A blade struck me a glancing blow that knocked me unconscious. The blood from the wound on my face streamed onto my neck, causing the invaders to overlook me.

"When I gained consciousness, I crawled behind a wall, where I watched the enemy load the shields of gold on chariots and wagons and make their escape. I could hear everything that happened inside the compound. They called the leader Rezon. I heard them say that if they could make it to the ships, they would make their escape. They are headed for the coast.

"Reinforcements came down from the Millo as I washed away the blood. The subaltern of the royal guard immediately sent a messenger to Solomon and dispatched me to the fortress to give this order to you. Your militia is the only unit of chariots and horsemen of any consequence in the area. The nearest unit of any size is at Lakhish. We sent messengers there, too. I am sure the contingent of chariots at Lakhish will be on the way after the messenger gets there."

When the soldier finished his report, Ashur mounted his chariot. Elkai shouted to him. "The men of

Solem, Nahal, and the other villages are assembling. The horses and chariots are ready."

Ashur glanced again at the order before stuffing it in his belt. There was no mistaking the meaning of the short message. It read: "The men of Rezon have fled to the west. Pursue Rezon and delay his retreat to the sea, no matter what the sacrifice."

A subaltern of the royal guard had signed the order. Ashur did not know this commander. Nevertheless, he was sure the man knew the chariots of the militia would have the only chance of catching Rezon. They must catch Rezon before he reached the sea.

When they reached the fortress, Ashur requested a few tools that he felt might be useful. Elkai found a fresh mount for the young soldier. Ashur immediately dispatched his own messengers to summon militia scattered around the countryside. He left Elkai behind to guide the men that would follow. They were soon riding at a full gallop toward the sea with the few men who could handle the chariots and were of fighting age.

Ashur immediately began to assess the logistics of the situation. Loaded with the heavy gold shields, Rezon's chariots would not make very good time. It was possible that the chariots and horsemen of Ashur's militia could overtake them. However, they would not have a sufficient force to do much damage. Only in one place could a few men have any chance at all against overwhelming numbers.

As they traveled, his plan began to come together. He stationed messengers behind for the men that would follow. "Where the river runs into the mountain," was the message, "there we will make our stand." He knew the river would be swollen with the heavy rains. The only place the raiders could cross was where the river had changed course and left a natural ford. He halted the men once along the way in the shade of a canyon.

"Wake up, man!" The sound of Ashur's voice awakened the young soldier as he was about to topple off his mount. The attack had occurred at the end of his watch, and he was exhausted.

"Here you will wait for the main company of militia that follows. Bring them to me where the river strikes the mountain. Elkai knows the place of which I speak."

Though the young man was out on his feet, he protested being left behind. "I can stay awake. Let me go with you. I must avenge the death of the royal guard, my friends."

"I must leave someone for a messenger. You will be in no shape to fight even if you make it there. You are exhausted. Get some rest, and bring the militia to me at the river." The young warrior could not argue with this logic.

Ashur allowed a few minutes for rest. Before they could get underway again, Benhail had stretched out on the ground and snored loudly. A ripple of laughter spread through the band as a couple of the men made humorous reference to his snoring. Ashur took heart from this. He glanced around at the group of men who followed him. They were undaunted by the task that lay ahead. Although they had not received the extensive training of those in the regular army, they were not unfamiliar with their bows, swords, and spears. Every man in Solomon's kingdom was required to have military training. Ashur had entered many competitions himself and knew that these men were proficient with their weapons. They would acquit themselves well, if they could get to the river before Rezon.

When they arrived at the river, Ashur galloped Tirsah forward eagerly and then reined him harshly to a walk. Tirsah shied from this unusual treatment. "Steady, Tirsah, steady." Ashur tried to calm him, straining his eyes ahead for the telltale ruts that would signal passage of the heavily laden chariots.

Ruts already marked the area. Ashur leaped to the ground to examine them. Ruts, yes, but not deep ruts made by heavily laden chariots or wagons. The enemy had crossed here on the way to the city of Jerusalem. However, they had not crossed again.

Ashur knelt in the sand a moment to survey his chosen battlefield. The heavy chariots, loaded with the golden shields, could not cross the rain-swollen river. The river had begun to withdraw and shrink away from the mountain, leaving a little narrow flat between the river and the foot of the mountain.

"Here we will stop them," Ashur shouted, as he began giving orders. "Hattil, put your best archers on that ridge and anywhere on the side of the mountain they can find a place to stand. Get some archers up above the range of the enemy's arrows. Take as much equipment up there as possible. Hurry! Every second is critical.

"Nahass, take the tools and try to start a rockslide to block the way. Miklot, make a barricade of the chariots. Break off the wheels so they will be difficult to move. Form two rows. Put your strongest men of the sword behind the first row of chariots. Have them keep their heads down until the enemy reaches the barricade and the battle becomes hand to hand.

"Malta, you will be in charge of the horsemen. Send some men to hide Tirsah and the other chariot horses. Your men must see that no one crosses the river below. You will reinforce us if they breach the barricades."

Ashur hesitated a moment to try to visualize the battle. Again he turned to Hattil. "Hattil, station the other archers behind the swordsmen at the first barricade. Place a second line of men behind the second row of chariots. Put another row of archers behind them. Take the rest of the men behind those rocks over there. When the enemy archers cannot fire without fear of hitting their own men, bring them into the fight."

They had almost finished the first row of barricades when Nahass signaled Ashur to get the men out of the way. His men dislodged rocks and boulders until they blocked the flat below.

"Back to the chariots!" Ashur shouted, as Nahass signaled that they could begin work again. The first barricade was completed. They had almost completed the second one when a loud rush of stone and boulders came crashing down in front of the first row of chariots. The second slide was extremely successful. This halted all the workers, and a shout of triumph rose as they surveyed the narrow pass that Hadad's men would now have to traverse.

***

"What was that?" Hadad halted the column and shouted for the lieutenant in charge of the chariot brigade nearest him. "Find out what raised all of that noise and dust."

The officer charged off in the direction Hadad indicated. He was near the pass when the two point riders came back to meet him. Hadad watched the interchange, which took place well out of earshot. He fidgeted nervously as Rezon rode up to him.

"What is wrong? Why are we halting? We must not stop; we must get to the boats," he chided.

"I do not know yet, you fool," Hadad replied. "We will rest the horses until the point riders and my lieutenant report to me. Bring up a company of archers in case the enemy attacks the head of the column."

Rezon walked down the row of chariots and ran his hands over the golden shields. He stared nervously behind the column toward the city of Jerusalem. When he saw the point riders return, he rejoined Hadad at the head of the column. He blurted out his own feelings before they could finish telling Hadad of the men blocking their retreat to the sea. "Hadad, we must not tarry here! There cannot be many men at the river. I fear pursuit from Jerusalem. Let us push on immediately."

Hadad was cautious. Like most military commanders, he hesitated to attack an enemy without knowing its strength. Seizing an opportunity from the boldness of Rezon's words, he said, "Rezon, most of your men avoided the conflict at Jerusalem, yet you will all share in the treasure. Now let your men overcome this small band. We must be on our way to the ships." In this manner, Hadad thought, he could avoid further loss of his own troops and test the enemy's strength. Stung by this accusation, Rezon prepared his men for an immediate assault on the barricaded defenders.

***

Ashur watched the enemy preparing to attack his positions. He wondered how he would acquit himself in armed conflict. He thought of himself as courageous. In the forest, he had killed wild animals as fierce as any man. To kill an animal was one thing. To take the life of another human being was something altogether different. He did not know if he could do it. Oddly enough, he found that he feared being reported a coward more than he feared death. He wished this fight could be avoided. He had tried to picture himself bravely engaged in battle with hundreds of angry men trying to kill him. Then he imagined himself immobilized by fear, as one of the warriors of Egypt ran up to him and plunged a spear deep into his side.

A swishing sound and cry startled him out of these thoughts. An arrow passed by his head. He instinctively crouched, turning to look at the man who had cried out behind him. He watched a young man from Solem fall at his feet, an arrow embedded in his chest. Ashur turned to face the enemy charging toward the narrow pass that he defended. He shouted at two of the young men who were frozen with shock. Anger welled up inside him. The blood of his countrymen stained their hands. These robbers and murderers had defied and stolen from his king. These evil men threatened the very freedom they enjoyed in this land. Fear gone now, Ashur rushed forward with the men to join in the battle.

Rezon led the first charge. They ran a gauntlet of arrows from men concealed above and behind the barricades. Many attacking warriors fell before they reached the defenders. The fallen bodies littered the narrow gap so that those behind stumbled and fell over the bodies of their comrades.

"Back! Back!" Rezon shouted when he surveyed the carnage around him. The robber baron and his fierce band were soon in full retreat.

Ashur and his men shouted and brandished their weapons at the fleeing enemy. Looking around, he observed that his own force had suffered few casualties and had held the pass. This greatly encouraged him.

When Rezon reached safety, he turned toward the defenders and shouted curses. Crestfallen, he made his way to where Hadad stood watching the debacle.

"We must have your archers." Rezon gasped the words as he gulped in air. "They have the advantage of the heights."

"You sounded so confident. I did not think you wanted any help from me," Hadad said sarcastically. Hadad now understood the situation and shouted orders to different officers. Archers marched forward to take up position just outside the range of Ashur's bowmen. Chariots that were free from carrying the golden shields were sent upriver to look for another crossing.

With the archers in position, Hadad signaled the captains of his infantry. A phalanx of men moved forward to the attack. Hattil's archers on the cliffs began raining arrows from above, but they had less effect on the copper-and-bronze-protected shields of Hadad's soldiers.

Now, too, the archers were under fire from Hadad's bowmen. Many of Hattil's brave defenders fell from the heights. Bodies of attackers and defenders stacked at the narrow slide. The fierce battle became hand to hand. Sword and axe crashed on shield and armor. The failing light of dusk made it impossible to distinguish friend from foe. The enemy withdrew again.

Ashur gathered his depleted group of warriors around him. Gone now was the face of the brave Hattil. After being struck in the chest by an arrow, Hattil had plummeted to his death. Miklot had died under the crush of bodies between the slide and the river.

Following an ancient custom, Ashur divided the night watch between his two remaining captains. Malta took the star-rise watch, Sadoc took charge of the middle watch, and Ashur stood the dawn watch. Malta reported it was almost impossible for the enemy to cross the swollen river at any other location. Small bands of reinforcements trickled in, greatly encouraging the defenders.

At dawn, the remaining remnants of the militia took their positions at the narrow gap. The first rush overran the depleted and weakened warriors. Ashur found himself hurled back by the crush of charging men. Sweat ran into his eyes and threatened to blind him. He could not parry all of the swords and axes thrusting and swinging at him.

"Long live King Solomon!" he shouted in defiance.

One of the great axes crashed down on his shield, which struck his head. He lost consciousness. His last thoughts were not ones of fear, but of what would lie beyond.

Beyond this life.

CHAPTER 10

The Fortress
of the Heroes

Ashur awakened to the buzzing of a fly in his face. Immediately aware of a terrible dryness in his throat, he tried to sit, but a splitting pain in his head forced him to lie back. Ashur had the sensation that Chazad was licking his face. A hazy figure appeared over him, and he heard a familiar voice. Dekar wiped his face with cool water.

"We thought you were going to sleep forever," Dekar quipped, as he helped Ashur drink from a gourd. Dekar's voice reflected great relief that his friend had regained consciousness.

Elkai was also hovering over him, an anxious look on his face. "Our God, Elohim, is merciful," he said.

"What of the shields, and Tirsah?" Ashur asked, wiping water from the edge of his mouth after he had assuaged his burning thirst.

"We caught up with the enemy shortly after they overran you. They fled when they saw us coming with chariots from the northern army. They ran like dogs into the hills, but they abandoned their wagons and the golden shields. We found Tirsah and the other horses where you left them. Tirsah is safe. You must have taken all the fight out of them," Dekar said scornfully of Hadad and Rezon.

"What of Malta?" Ashur asked, remembering that he had been one of the last men standing with him as they were overrun.

"Malta survived. They knocked him into the river. He drifted into some bushes and played the corpse until Hadad crossed the river. When we arrived, he and Sadoc had dragged you up here in the shade. Malta went back to Jerusalem to report to the king when he returns from Gezer.

Word is that King Solomon has made a truce with Pharaoh Siamun. You are probably some kind of hero," Dekar allowed, admiringly.

Ashur continued asking about the other men that had fought with him at the river. However, at some of the names, Dekar shook his head to indicate their deaths. Many were wounded. The delaying action had been a success, but a costly one to the young militiamen.

When Ashur sufficiently recovered, Dekar and Elkai helped him aboard a wagon that Hadad's men had abandoned. Ashur shared the ride back to the Fortress of the Heroes with some of the king's golden shields. Except for a headache that lasted two full days, a gash above his hairline, and a sizeable lump on his head, Ashur had suffered no permanent damage. A few days later, he resumed his duties. Then he began a long and tedious period of time at the Fortress of the Heroes.

He became acutely aware of his lonely separation from Ammi and his family. Finally, the king ordered the militia to return to the north country, to Megiddon. King Solomon planned to honor them for their part in the battle at the river. The men of his village and those of Nahal were excited at the prospect of being honored by the king.

Ashur was more excited at the prospect of returning to Solem. Surely now that peace reigned in the land, the king would release them from service in the Gibore Hail and allow them to return to their homes.

"Do you miss her?" Dekar asked, catching Ashur with a desert gardenia in his hand while staring off toward Solem.

"Like the strength of my right arm," he said, gripping the back of his forearm with his hand.

"I guess you will have to settle for my unmatched company," Dekar offered.

"A poor consolation," Ashur said, flinging a small stone at Dekar, which struck him on the back of his leg. He retreated, feigning great injury.

While Ashur and the men of the militia awaited the arrival of the king in Megiddon, his father's old friend Iddon visited Ashur. The old oracle traveled around the country, ministering to the unfortunate. He had just come from Solem, where he had visited with Ashur's father. Iddon enjoyed no official recognition by the king. Nevertheless, many people held him in high esteem. Ashur's father honored him. As a young boy, Ashur had found favor in Iddon's eyes. The old man had praised him for studying at the feet of the reader of the code. Iddon spent more time with him now, questioning him about the battle at the river. Ashur found himself responding to the old man's warmth and wisdom. He shared his personal life with the kindly man. He told Iddon the story of his beginnings and showed him the mysterious ring found with him in the cave.

Iddon studied the signet ring carefully as Ashur waited impatiently for him to respond. After an interminable time, the old oracle said, "I believe I have seen a signet ring such as this. However, it was a long, long time ago. I am not sure. The man who owned that signet ring said that he was the last of the shepherd kings. He said that his people had lived in Egypt until King Ahmose drove them out.

"When I met this shepherd king, he and his tribesmen lived with the sea people in the city of Ekron. If they stood with the Philistines in the wars against our country, they probably died there," Iddon added, disappointingly. "You see, the tribes of the shepherd kings were great horsemen and chariot warriors. Many years ago they ruled all the lands that are now Israel and Egypt. You could be a descendant of the shepherd kings," the old man mused. "Perhaps even a prince of their people, judging by the ring. Only Elohim knows the truth now, my son.

"Do not be discouraged. A natural way of life is that your search may lead you to new beginnings, new ways. You must forget the past. This is a sad story of a people who have no homeland and now have no identity. Their blood stains the ground across the entire breadth of this land, as it was with our people. Those who survived have assimilated with the Philistines, and Hurri, and Assyria, and Egypt, and our people. You are now a spiritual son of Israel."

This was true. His love for Elohim, for Nelmaah and Machir, and now his love for Ammi had given him a new identity. He was now part of this fierce national pride and heritage.

Iddon had told him that he was possibly a child of the shepherd kings, a descendant of great chariot warriors, perhaps even a prince. Machir had never mentioned Ekron in his war tales. Ashur vowed to bring up the subject at his earliest opportunity. He would have to be careful, for Nelmaah had forbidden him to mention his lost origins. Machir preferred to think of Ashur as his own son.

Iddon continued. "There was another man who had no beginning, Melchizedek, the first king of Salem, a shadow of one who will come in the future. This king will reign forever. He broke bread and took wine with the warriors in the valley of Shaveh. He bestowed a blessing on our patriarch when he defeated the king of Elam. You must not despair. Perhaps you, too, will in some way foreshadow the one who is to come.

You must remember that nothing is beyond the knowledge of the Almighty. We are all part of his plan and purpose."

***

That night, old Iddon the prophet had a dream. Relating that vision to Ashur the next morning, he said, "I saw heaven opened and beheld a white horse. He that sat on the white horse judges and makes war. His eyes were as a flame of fire. On his head were many crowns, and he had a name written that no man knew but he himself."

"Who was that man?" Ashur asked in wonder. "What does the dream mean? Was the man my father?" he guessed, thinking of their conversation the previous night. "Was the man on the white horse the Lord Elohim, the living God? Was he Solomon, the king?"

Iddon continued, ignoring the questions. "Total blackness covered the earth. Out of the darkness came bright clouds from heaven. Then one arrived whose face shone as a blazing light, bright as the sun. His hair was white as snow, and he came with many angels. A voice came out of the cloud, like thunder, and a two-edged sword came out of his mouth."

"Is this the Messiah?"

"Yes, but when he comes to judge and rule, his eyes will penetrate like flames of fire."

"Like the eyes of the great wolf," Ashur interjected.

"His eyes are not like the wolf. They are like nothing you or I have seen before. His eyes will be the eyes of judgment. Every knee will bow to him.

"Then I saw a city of great beauty. The walls of the city were like a transparent diamond. The city itself is pure gold, but like clear glass. Precious stones cover the foundation. Pearls cover twelve gates, and the streets are pure gold, but translucent.

"Then Solomon appeared in my dream, but he had two heads, like two spirits. One spirit was clean, and the other unclean. You were in the dream, too, but your spirit was clean. I recognized you because the woman called your name, and she said the name of the king."

"Who was the woman? What does all this mean, holy one?" Ashur asked confusedly. "I do not understand what all this has to do with me. What does the dream mean?"

The old prophet shrugged his shoulders. "The revelation is not given to me now. But this was given: Let your spirit seek that of the Lord Elohim, your heavenly father. Be not concerned with things of this earth, for our lives are even a vapor that appears for a little time and then vanishes away. As a flower of the field, so we flourish. For then the wind passes over it, and it withers away."

CHAPTER 11

King Solomon's Harem

Solomon brought increasing numbers of women into the palace. His wives and their fathers besieged him with petitions to allow his foreign wives to worship their own gods. Many of the marriages were for the sake of alliances. He found it increasingly difficult to refuse them. Finally, Solomon gave in to one particularly distraught young bride who went on a hunger strike. He could no longer bear to see her waste away. He allowed her servants to bring in a statue of Chemosh, the god of Moab.

These events and others that followed led Zabud to confront the king.

"Queen Osoris sought permission to bring her own altars and statues from Egypt," he said, recounting some of the circumstances that had occurred. "She threatened to leave the palace and return to her native home. This forced you to build Osoris a temple of her own. These concessions led to others, and now we have gods of all shapes and forms present in a myriad of altars throughout the city. The king's own priests predict dire catastrophes for the kingdom because of these permitted blasphemies. They want the king to explain the presence of the altars to these strange gods. They have asked me to come to you."

"The foreign gods were to accept the sacrifices in their distant homes," Solomon replied, gesturing weakly. He paused and then added. "My enemy will not attack the city if his daughter lies within the ramparts."

Encouraged that he had not incurred the king's wrath to this point, Zabud continued, carefully choosing his words. "King Solomon rules all the kingdoms from the river Euphrates to the border of Egypt. The conquered peoples bring tribute and taxes in food, gold, silver, barley, and straw for the king's horses. Your palace and court have grown so that one day's menu for your table includes ten grain-fed oxen, twenty oxen from the fields, and a hundred sheep, besides deer, gazelle, roebuck, and fattened fowl.

"You have forty thousand stalls of horses for chariots and twelve thousand horsemen. You have dominion over all the kings west of the Great River, and peace on all sides. Yet I fear the kingdom will be destroyed from within." Zabud paused, aware that the king's jaw muscles were grinding in telltale anger.

"I think your services are required in the kitchens—to oversee the evening meal," King Solomon said. He dismissed his spiritual advisor abruptly.

***

King Solomon had launched an extensive building program to secure Israel's boundaries. With the Great Sea on the west and the impassable desert on the east, only a narrow northern boundary and a narrow southern boundary remained to protect.

The fortification of his capital city, Jerusalem, was nearing completion. His southern border was relatively safe, with Pharaoh Siamun as ally. His friend, King Hurom of Tyre, dominated the Great Sea to the west and the lands to the northwest. To the east, Rabbah was a buffer between Israel and the desert tribes. Solomon could now turn his efforts to the north, to the strategic pass at Megiddon and the great plain.

King Solomon traveled to the north for two purposes. First, he planned to honor the young men who had fought the battle at the river, and second, to fortify the pass controlling the Megiddon plain. The surviving warriors of Solem, Nahal, and the other villages assembled in Megiddon. The townspeople and people from all over the countryside came to observe King Solomon honor the young warriors.

Through the middle of the Carmel Range, the most magnificent mountain

range in Israel, was a narrow gap.
Solomon realized that whoever held
this valley controlled the entire
area. This pass was the most natural connection between central
and northern Israel, and therefore
between the great river in the north
all the way to Egypt in the south.
He began construction of the fortress of Megiddon in the fall.

Behind the natural mountain barrier lay the fertile plain of Jezreel,
so called after a place that was the
winter retreat of the king. The strategic location and ideal terrain for
warfare led to the use of the valley
as a battlefield. Megiddon was built
above underground springs. These
waters were named Kishon, meaning
"river of slaughter."

Solomon could not rest until the
fortification of Megiddon was completed. "When I have finished the
fortress, I can finally relax. Then
I will know the mountain barrier
is secure," he thought, driving the
workers relentlessly.

"The brave warriors who died in
battle and the survivors must be
honored, as we honored the men of the

royal guard who defended Jerusalem. It is fitting that we do this here at Megiddon. The people of this area have much pride in their warriors," the king said.

Ashur's father attended the ceremony and watched with great pride as his son was honored. "Always remember, my son," he had often said, "fathers judge their sons for their strong moments, never their weak ones."

When the fortress was completed in the spring, Solomon stood atop the walls and surveyed the valley of Jezreel that the fortress commanded. He filled his lungs with a deep breath and let it out slowly. He tried to free himself of the drive that had so feverishly compelled him to complete the fortress. Perhaps now he could fully enjoy the pleasurable rewards of life that he had ignored in his passion to complete the fortifications.

The beauty of the valley of Jezreel in the spring was breathtaking. Shades of green mixed with gold were predominant, and here and there were white and gray sandy areas without vegetation. Beyond lay low mountain ranges, and then the straight line of the horizon bordered blue skies.

The pass at Megiddon had been the scene of a great battle more than five hundred years earlier. The army of Thutmoses III of Egypt defeated a combined army of thirty-two of the shepherd kings at the entrance to the great valley. In this valley, in yet another conflict, the first king of Israel had died in a battle called Gilboa. Solomon dismissed this dissonant thought.

Solomon felt good to be away from the duties of his capital city of Jerusalem. The daily responsibilities of his court had become drudgery. He had enjoyed the building of the fortress, but its completion left him in a reflective mood. The delights he once found in the harem at the palace had now diminished to the point that the women no longer pleased him. The king had changed over the years. As he tired of the women, he sent them away or relegated them to lower rank.

"I find more bitter than death the women whose hearts are snares and nets, whose hands are bands. One good man I find in a thousand, but not one woman," he said to Zabud.

Solomon was disgusted with his wives' constant scheming, all striving for preeminence, practicing every means of deception toward that end. The king became afraid to show deep affection toward any of the women of the harem because of their demands on him.

In his loneliness, Solomon embraced the gods of his wives. However, this brought him only frustration and guilt. "All of my works and estates will be left to the son of a foolish woman. Who knows whether he will be a wise man or a fool?"

It was not easy being so renowned a king. His greatness had spread throughout the land. People came to him with all types of petitions. Some were impossible to solve. His people expected healing from disease and crippling injuries. "Am I a god that I can heal the sick and make whole the crippled?" he demanded angrily of Zabud. "Who has begun these rumors of magic and healing?"

"They say, Lord Solomon, that you converse with the birds and animals, and that you are perhaps Moloch or El himself."

"I am no god. I feel terrible when I hear of the deaths of children sacrificed to the gods," he answered. "Most recently, a group of followers of Moloch burned their children on a pyre in the valley of Gehinnom in the very shadow of the palace. I ordered severe punishment for the members of this so-called religious group. However, when my ministers reported back, I learned that one of my wives was involved in the ceremonies." He threw up his hand to express his feeling of helplessness.

Zabud was tempted to say "I warned you," but the king had forbade him from ever addressing the subject of his foreign wives again. "The indulgent life of the harem has sapped his physical vitality," Zabud thought. "A cynical indolence has crept into his being. Their own selfish interests motivate the people surrounding him. Without me, the king would be totally alone."

CHAPTER 12

Ashur Fights
Pithon in the Ring

*A*fter completing their obliga-tions in Megiddon, the young warriors returned to Solem. When Ashur rode into the square, Ammi's heart began to beat almost as fast as thoughts flitted through her mind: "Maybe since Ashur has become a hero, he will no longer care for me. What if he no longer finds me attractive?" She feared that he might find her too young and immature, now that he was a captain of militia, the youngest ever appointed to that rank. How quickly fear and doubt could turn love into pain!

As a reward for his valor, Ashur, his house, and his father's house stood free of taxes. They no longer had to serve in the army. Should Ashur have sons, they would serve only if they chose to volunteer.

Friends and well-wishers surrounded and congratulated Ashur, but he broke free of the crowd. Clearly, he was looking for someone. "Ammi," he shouted as he spied her standing to one side with her brothers and mother. Ashur closed the distance between them with long strides. The young people moved to embrace, but then remembered the presence of her two brothers. Ashur was overcome with her appearance. Her hair was fashioned in a unique and elegant braid, making her appear more mature than he remembered.

Shyness froze Ammi as Ashur stood before her, smiling. When he removed his helmet, his hair was slicked back with perspiration, giving him a hawk-like appearance. His wavy locks had been cropped short with a sharp knife so that no enemy could gain an advantage by grabbing long strands. The lower part of his face was square, as to give a hint of ruggedness, but otherwise the same sensitive lines remained. A new piercing, authoritative look in his eyes had replaced the peaceful look of the shepherd. The bare arms that had always been powerful and muscular now had the appearance of chiseled iron. The boy that she loved had grown into a man. Her feelings were confused between the desire to be close to him and the new and exciting fear of being crushed in those powerful arms.

Ashur wore a *shiryon*, or breastplate of armor, but disdained protection for his midriff. His bare abdomen was wet with perspiration from the heat, and ropelike muscles rippled under glistening skin. Her eyes swept down his frame to take in his powerful legs. Blushing at her thoughts, she averted her glance.

"I am glad you have returned," she said, finally finding voice.

"It is good to be home. I thought of you often. The truth is, I thought of you constantly," Ashur replied.

The words spoken to Ammi by her old grandmother came to her as she looked on the man she loved. "My desire is unto my lord, my husband. He is my beloved and my friend." The old matriarch had died, but her wisdom about men and sexual instruction remained with Ammi. "Desire you feel for the man you love is normal and natural," the wise old woman had said, preparing her for these feelings. Ammi welcomed them now, eagerly and confidently.

"On his deathbed, your grandfather told me that he always remembered the first night we were together, when I shed my gown and came into his marriage bed. He said he remembered the breathless perfection of my body. That man! And me, I have always been too fat." She had flushed at the admission. "He said that with that memory and the children I gave him, he could die a happy and fulfilled man. Many are the times I have found comfort in those words."

Her grandmother had taught Ammi to groom herself, to walk erect, to hold her shoulders back, and to comb and plait her hair. "Yes, oh yes," her grandmother had exclaimed. "You look spellbinding with your hair like this. When you meet the man that you will marry, you must save this look for a special time, when he has been away or if you have a rival. Remember, where there is mystery, there is excitement."

The strength of Ammi's grandmother had compensated for her mother's weaknesses and had been valuable in Ammi's growth. She had praised Ammi for her character and taught her that a feeling of responsibility was its own reward.

Ammi's grandmother had often spoken of her passing as a homecoming, a natural event. She had prepared Ammi for her departure. As her health failed, she began to act strangely. Sometimes she could not remember things that had happened the day before. While in this confused state, she had made a statement that moved Ammi deeply. "I will go to him soon," she had said, referring to her departed husband. "I cannot go to him now. He has not finished our house."

"Do not speak such words, Grandmother," Ammi had replied. "I could not bear to be without you.

You make me sad when you say these things."

"Nonsense," she had said, her mind clearing. "I am old and worn away. We must face the reality of death without fear. Elohim will change me in the twinkling of an eye." Her words were to prove prophetic, for two days after the festival of the new moon, she died.

Later, when they were alone, Ashur shared with Ammi the story that old Iddon had told him of the shepherd kings and the mysterious Melchizedek, who had no beginning. "He said that I might even be a prince of the shepherd kings," Ashur said, fingering the signet ring. "I guess I will never know for sure. I do not care, now that I have you."

Ammi smiled and embraced him. She saw that he caught himself from slipping into the old habit of brooding. "You will always be my prince," Ammi promised with genuine devotion. Ashur also told her of the dream that Iddon had recounted to him of the powerful figure on the white horse.

"Iddon said our lives here on earth are like a flower of the field that appears for a short time and then is gone," Ashur repeated.

"When my father died, Iddon said something very odd to me." Ammi recalled the old prophet's parting words the day he had come to her home after her father died. "He said that all the rest of my life would be richer for the sorrow of my father's death. Now I think I understand what he meant. I would not have known how to love you as deeply as I do, had I not known that sorrow," she reflected.

Ammi and Ashur wandered around the village hand in hand. The young lovers basked in the glow of feeling that all was right in their world. They joined a crowd gathered around a ring where two young wrestlers sparred for an opening. Ashur realized that Ammi was probably not enjoying the wrestling as he was. He was about to lead her away when Pithon walked into the ring and shouted for the crowd's attention.

"Ashur, come join me in the ring. I challenge you. Come on, hero; let's see what you are made of."

The crowd instantly started chanting, "Ashur! Ashur! Ashur!"

His friend Malta appeared at his side and took him by the arm. "You have nothing to prove, Ashur. Let me speak for you." Malta turned to confront their common enemy. "Pithon, mind your tongue! Ashur has had enough fighting for a while. Let him enjoy his rest."

"He has been drinking, and his envy eats on him," Malta observed, turning back to Ashur. "The wine makes him meaner than a bull of Bashan."

Still Pithon continued taunting Ashur. The dislike Ashur felt for him and the encouragement of some of his friends to silence the braggart caused him to weaken. Pithon had challenged him in front of Ammi. He could not walk away.

"Ignore him. He is an animal," Ammi admonished Ashur. "I despise him. He is a loudmouthed boor. Do not dirty your hands with his kind." Ammi had wished for a confrontation between her champion and Pithon as a child, but now as a young woman in love, she dreaded what was about to take place.

"You have beaten him in the chariot races, Ashur," Malta said. "Don't fight him bare-handed in the ring. He is too strong. You would not have enough room to maneuver. Don't . . . " Malta's voice trailed off.

Ashur was already unbuckling his sword to accept the challenge. Flushed with his recent successes and driven by his repulsion for Pithon, Ashur allowed himself to be torn away from Ammi and carried forward by the crowd.

The two men circled each other warily. Despite his huge size, Pithon moved with the catlike grace of a leopard. His thick black hair was long and unkempt. Thick bushy eyebrows shielded nervous, beady eyes. Ashur had the same feeling as if looking into the predatory eyes of the great wolf. "Ah, but this man is more the embodiment of Satan than is the wolf," he thought to himself.

Pithon emitted a loud roar and charged forward. Ashur dodged to the side and grasped Pithon by his tunic and his long hair, propelling him forward and over his shoulder with every ounce of strength he could muster. Pithon flew through the air and came down heavily on the ground. The wind exploded out of him like a stomped wineskin. The crowd applauded wildly at the sight of their hero bringing down the bully, Pithon.

"Pin him!" screamed Malta. "Finish him. Do not let him get up!" Malta was beside himself, trying to urge Ashur to seize his advantage and end the contest as quickly as possible, but Ashur would not be denied the opportunity to vent his long-controlled rage. Several reasons compounded his anger: Pithon's attack on Shoshanna, the pain that Ammi had experienced for her friend, and the undeserved suffering Ashur had endured.

Ashur allowed the crowd to step in and lift Pithon to his feet. This gave Pithon a few precious seconds to regain his breath. The two combatants closed on each other again. Pithon unleashed a powerful swing, his huge fist missing Ashur's face by inches. Ashur smashed up and into the off-balanced Pithon's face with forearm and shoulder, driving him back against the crowd.

Pithon stood for a moment wiping his bloody mouth with a burly arm. The look he gave Ashur then was the promise of death. They fought on.

Pithon aimed a kick at Ashur's face, designed to break his jaw, but again found his target to be too quick for this strategy. Ashur found that his hardest blows had no lasting effect on the huge man. The first time he had thrown him, Pithon's huge build hurt him more than any blow Ashur had landed on his now-bloodied face. Although Ashur fought like a madman, he found himself tiring, and Pithon's own fists were now beginning to find their mark.

Malta groaned, "I knew he should have finished him." His words proved prophetic, for the crowd pressed in tighter, leaving Ashur no room to avoid the slower but ever-oncoming Pithon. One of Ammi's brothers led Ammi away.

Pithon finally grabbed Ashur, crushing him in a bear-like hug and falling on top of him. Ashur felt as if he would smother with his nose crushed into the foul smell of Pithon's chest. Struggling with every bit of courage and strength, he heaved mightily, trying to dislodge Pithon and get off his back. He continued to struggle until he had exhausted every reserve.

Pithon would have killed Ashur if the judge had not come forward and forced Pithon to let him breathe. He sat up but still maintained his humiliating position atop Ashur, holding his arms by the wrists. Leaning forward, he allowed spittle from his mouth to hang down. Just before it would drip down into Ashur's face, he would suck it back up. He did this twice before the judge pronounced Pithon the victor and again tried to pull Pithon off Ashur. This time, before releasing him, Pithon let the spittle drip into Ashur's face. The crowd expressed revulsion at the unmanly conduct and slowly melted away. Many of them had hoped to see the obnoxious bully taught a lesson. Instead, they had seen their champion humbled. Only Malta remained to wipe away the blood, sweat, and dirt from Ashur's face, and the ultimate indignity, the filthy mucus of Pithon's saliva.

Crushed and crestfallen, Ashur slipped quietly between two houses and left the scene of his disgrace. He paused on the side street to clear the blood from his nose. A man stepped into the street and went to the side of his house to retrieve some item. Ashur turned his head, hoping the man would not recognize him. This might appear suspicious, however, he thought. He wished the man would quickly complete his task so he might pass by. The man he watched out of the corner of his eye was the father of Miklot, who had died in the battle of the river. Ashur turned his face toward him, raising his hand in awkward greeting. Miklot's father turned away without acknowledging him and reentered the house. This compounded Ashur's despair.

Finally, he reached his father's estate. He went first to the house of Elkai to wash his face and borrow a clean tunic. Elkai did not question him, only expressed concern for his well-being.

That evening, at home with Machir and Nelmaah, Ashur tried to recapture the happy feelings of seeing Ammi again. He always felt close to his father as Machir related stories of his own service in the Gibore Hail. Ashur did not tell him of the defeat he had suffered at the hands of Pithon. He described his part in the battle at the river and the honor the king had bestowed on him, offering him a commission in the Gibore Hail. He knew his father would soon learn of his humbling, and this greatly dampened his homecoming.

Surprisingly, Ashur had sustained few obvious physical wounds. Nevertheless, he was crestfallen, to say the least. His nose had stopped bleeding. If his eye blackened, it would not show until the next day. He had been humiliated in the sight of Ammi and practically the entire village.

Ashur began to praise the exploits of King Solomon to his father. "They say that the queen of Marib fainted when she came to Jerusalem and saw the magnificence of Solomon."

His father swore an uncharacteristic oath and turned away. "Solomon has turned his back on the faith of his fathers. He has embraced the gods of his heathen wives. The oracle, my friend Iddon, relates to me that Solomon now has more than sixty wives. Most of these women are from foreign lands. He says that Solomon has more than eighty other women that he has not married, and that his lusts have no restraint. He pays homage to their gods."

"I do not understand, Father. I thought Solomon the king to be a wise and godly man," said Ashur, utterly dismayed.

"This is true, my son," said Machir. "However, Satan knows the weakness of man and uses the woman to cause his fall, as he did in the garden. Satan caused the fall of the first man by deceiving the woman. Elohim's plan for us is for one man to love one woman and to cherish her as a gift from him."

"Yes, Solomon is very wise in affairs of the world," Machir said.

"However, he has no feeling for the poor of the land. Maintaining his lavish court, the chariot cities, the army, and the palaces placed a heavy tax burden on the people. Iddon says hundreds, perhaps thousands, perished in the quarries while he was building his palace."

Ashur stood and walked to the hearth where Chazad slept on the floor. He knelt to pet the dog. "What does the *melek reeh* say to him?" Ashur ventured, confused, because before this, he had always been taught to revere the king.

"The 'king's friend' is all but banned from the palace, apparently for disturbing the king's conscience," Machir replied. "The king does not appreciate having such a wise and loyal counselor. Iddon is not allowed access to the palace. He treats Iddon and now Zabud with the same coldness that he seems to have for the Lord Elohim. He is a man who should bow down to the supreme ruler of the universe. As a powerful ruler himself, he offers praise more as a pretense.

"He has led our people to unsurpassed glory. We are free from the persecution suffered at the hand of Egypt and Hazor. Our people do not see war or hear the sound of the trumpet or hunger for bread. A proud nationalism and peace reign throughout our land. Yet his human achievements, apart from accountability to Elohim, are empty."

"One thing I do not understand, Father. Why does Elohim allow evil in our world?" The troubled young man asked several difficult questions. "Why does he allow so much suffering?"

"I have not studied the books of the code, like my friend Iddon. According to the prophet Iddon, Elohim has no beginning and no end. He is perfect. Elohim rules the universe from his chariot-like throne, the *merkibah*. He created angels to serve and praise him. An arch-prince called Lucifer guarded Elohim's throne. Lucifer's name meant 'bright and shining one.' However, his name changed to Satan when he tried to usurp Elohim's power. One-third of the angels joined Satan in his rebellion. Elohim sentenced Satan and the other fallen angels to a lake of fire. This sentence is not executed yet."

"Yes, I know, Father," Ashur said, frowning. "The elders teach us that only Elohim is perfect, but why are we here on earth?"

"Into this conflict between God and Satan entered an inferior creature called man," Machir explained. "This lesser creature proved the sentence given Satan to be just by choosing Elohim. Iddon calls the fallen angels 'sons of perverseness' or 'sons of darkness.' They are in warfare against Elohim's elect."

"So man is important in this struggle?" Ashur questioned.

"Yes. We are warriors involved in a great conflict." His father paused a moment as if to gather his thoughts, then went on.

"Elohim created the first man and woman, and they lived in a place called Eden. Satan's deception and lies led to their removal from this perfect place. Iddon calls those of us who are faithful to Elohim 'sons of light' or 'sons of righteousness.'

Many people will follow Satan and his unseen demons. They are mistakenly convinced that he is more powerful than Elohim."

"How will this struggle end, Father?"

"Finally, in a great apocalyptic battle, Elohim will defeat Satan and his fallen angels. He will cast all who follow Satan into the lake of fire. Then he will carry all his elect to the heavens, where we will live forever and ever."

"Thanks for helping me get things back in perspective, Father," Ashur said. Never before had Machir stated his personal beliefs in such detail, and never had there been a better time.

***

Ashur and Ammi met again under the terebinth tree. The gnarled tree stood as a silent sentinel, guarding their special haven. Leafy branches spread over them, like wings of a mother hen over her chicks. Nevertheless, the beauty and peacefulness of the pool and tamarisk grove had changed for the sensitive Ammi. The awful attack on her friend Shoshanna, coupled with the cruel killing of the little mouse by the hawk on this spot, filled her mind with uneasy thoughts.

Ammi was not occupied with Ashur this day as she usually was. Ashur's thoughts were filled with the humiliation of being beaten and spit upon by Pithon. The two unhappy young lovers were sitting quietly, trying to find the words to express their thoughts to each other.

Ashur needed desperately to be assured by Ammi that she still loved and respected him as she had before. He raised his arm, touching the back of his hand to her lips. She grasped his hand in hers and kissed the back of his hand. This had become a kind of ritual between them. The first time he did it, she thought it odd. However, she came to realize that he offered his hand because he did not trust the passion that holding her and kissing her lips aroused in him. Although she yearned for Ashur to hold and kiss her, she loved him more for his restraint.

"Are you angry with me?" Ashur asked.

"No! You misunderstand me," Ammi responded. "I want to comfort you. I love you. I cherish you. You are my hero. I got great satisfaction seeing Pithon tossed on his back after what he did to Shoshanna. You were winning when my brothers took me away. I cannot believe how you threw him up in the air like you did. He is so huge. Malta says you would have won had the crowd not pressed in on you."

Ashur smiled at the praise. She did not understand how he had used Pithon's momentum and his own strength to launch him skyward. He felt better to learn that she had not witnessed his defeat. "I wanted to teach Pithon a lesson, to humiliate him. I succeeded in humiliating myself and embarrassing you."

"No! That is not true. You did nothing wrong. You tried to stop him from hurting people. Too many people are afraid of him, afraid to stand up to his bullying. I pray he does not lay an ambush for you as he did for Shoshanna. He hates you. I am frightened that he will try to hurt you again."

"Do not worry. Next time there may
be a different ending. The ring didn't
give me enough room to maneuver.
Malta tried to warn me. No harm is
done. My pride is hurt, but that is
of little consequence."

"Someone has to worry about you,"
she said, as she leaned over to put
her head against his. "He will taste
justice one day."

Ammi was moved with compassion by
the unhappiness she saw in Ashur's
eyes. She responded to his deep-
seated needs by moving into his arms,
caressing his face, embracing him,
kissing his face and lips. Her inhibitions were overcome by her own
desire to please him, wanting to
make him forget his unhappiness. Her
unrestrained passion surprised Ashur.

Ammi shyly and delicately expressed
her desire for love's fulfillment.
Curiously, she adopted a symbolism
similar to the metaphor-like speech
popular in the land—apples being
a familiar symbol of love. "I am
faint with love," Ammi said. "Stay
me with raisins and apples; wake not
my love until love pleases—and now
she pleases." The sensual effect of

her words were as strong on her as they were on Ashur. Indirectly she expressed her deepest feelings in a way possible only to those of the purest of spirits. The words gave expression to long-repressed desire. In this way, the young lovers shared a sensual intimacy without shame, longing for the fulfillment of their marriage.

She stepped away from him, thinking to lessen the fire of his embrace, hungering again to be the object of his eyes, basking in the warmth. The longing she saw in his eyes was unbearable.

"I love you," Ashur responded. "I need you in every way that a man needs a woman." He kissed the top of her head, enjoying the clean natural odor of her hair. He drew her hands to his lips and kissed the backs of her hands. Then the sensitive palms, her eyes, down the side of her neck, the silken skin under her neck. She thought she would swoon. His hands caressed her face, her hands, and arms, touching her very soul. "You are more beautiful to me than all of the flowers of the desert. I love

you more than the air I breathe,"
Ashur murmured, brushing her ear
with his lips.

"I love every word that falls from
your lips," Ammi responded." I love
you. Oh, how I love you!" She wanted
him to tell her again and again how
much he loved her, but she was afraid
she would in some way diminish the
heady thrill unless he volunteered
the words. Her thoughts were consumed with him, with their marriage.
She could not bear to look into his
eyes. When they were married, she
would lie beside him and watch him
in his sleep. He would be vulnerable
to her and would not see how desperately and shamelessly she loved him.

She began to kiss away the hurt in
his eyes. "See, I can kiss even better
than Chazad," she said, applying a
wet tongue to his eye and panting
like the dog. Chazad, until now, had
stood guard nearby. He took hearing
his name as an excuse to come and
push between them. They laughed and
broke apart. She climbed onto a low
limb on the ancient tree. The limb
grew almost parallel with the ground.

Ashur wiped his eye with the back of his arm. Life with her as his wife would never be dull. He put his hands around her waist and swung her back to the ground. She clasped her arms around his neck. Never before had she kissed him with such passion.

They broke apart, embarrassed that they had held the kiss for so long. He gazed at her for a long moment, then caressed her face. She moved toward him to again be in his arms.

"Let us go to your mother and brothers tomorrow," he said. "We will ask for their blessing on our marriage."

***

The young lovers were in a semireclining position against the trunk of the old tree when a warning bark from Chazad alerted them. Sabta arrived on the scene with Ammi's two brothers. "There! There they are!" shouted Sabta. "I told you that he was seducing her. He has been meeting her here. I saw him forcing himself on her." Before Ashur could defend himself, they took Ammi away from him.

"Mother will hear of this. How would our father feel if he could see you lying with this uncouth barbarian?" her brother accused her.

"I did not lie with him as you accuse me," protested Ammi. "My father would not allow you to follow me around and spy on us if he were alive." Ammi was furious. Her brothers practically dragged her home.

***

Ashur's forced separation from Ammi was even more difficult under the circumstances. He was certain, however, that Ammi would explain the incident to her mother. He flicked Tirsah on the rump with the reins. The stallion responded immediately, sprinting down the road as darkness closed in around them. As he walked Tirsah into the courtyard, he could smell his mother's cooking. "It is good to be home," he thought, even considering his recent turn of fortune.

He made sure Tirsah was comfortable in the stable and then walked to the house. He took off his sandals and washed his feet and hands, anticipating another meal prepared by his mother.

***

Two days later, Ashur's world was turned upside down again.

"This message came for you while you were gone," Machir said, casually passing it to his son.

"Who brought the note?" Ashur asked.

"Shoshanna's brother brought it. The boy said Shoshanna sent it to you."

Ashur's face paled as he read the short letter. Shoshanna wrote that Ammi was being sent to the north country early the next morning. The note explained that Ammi could not see Ashur again and that she had asked Shoshanna to let him know why she was leaving without saying good-bye.

"I must leave at once," Ashur said, rising. "I must go to the house of the king's merchant tonight."

"What are you going to do, my son?" Machir asked. "You cannot ride into Solem this late at night. I forbid you to take Tirsah or any of the horses. If you go to Solem tonight, you will walk. Now sit and eat your food."

Ashur sat down, obeying his father. His rebellious thoughts remained unspoken. Ashur knew that he must go to Ammi regardless. To discuss the issue further would only make matters worse. His father was sincere. He was only trying to keep Ashur from further alienating Ammi's mother and brothers. Nevertheless, Ashur considered himself a man now and felt that he must make his own decisions regarding Ammi. He was prepared to accept the consequences of his actions.

He toyed with his meal for a short time and excused himself. When he kissed his mother warmly on the cheek, she gave her permission. She glanced hopefully at her husband. She was usually submissive, but the look was an auspicious one that prevented Machir from further stern action.

***

Ammi shut and locked the lattice-
work to the windows, washed her feet,
and prepared herself for bed. She
lay down and soon drifted off to a
troubled and fitful sleep. Memories
of the warmth of Ashur's kisses on
her face and lips caused her to toss
about. She sought him in her dreams,
wishing he were the cachet of myrrh
that lay between her breasts.

***

Ashur ran through the night. With
eyes sharpened by many nights in
the wilderness, he ran without fear
through the mountains, leaping over
the occasional obstacle with sure-
footed and unbroken stride. Heat
lightning flashed in the western sky.
In the moonlight, he saw two startled deer crash through a thicket
and into the forest.

The guards at the gate knew him
and did not challenge him when he
entered the village. The low wall
around her father's villa caused
only a momentary delay as he vaulted

over it into the courtyard. He saw the old gatekeeper nodding beside the entry. Leaping the stairs two at a time, he made his way to the window and softly rapped on the lattice. The second more urgent knock roused Ammi from a deep sleep.

"Rise, my love, my fair one, and come away with me," Ashur implored. Half-asleep, Ammi could not tell dream from reality. Was it really Ashur's voice she heard at the door?

"Open the lattice, my sister, my love. My head is damp with the dew. I am wet and cold from the night," Ashur persisted.

Ammi crossed the room to the window. However, having Ashur appear at her bedroom window destroyed her composure. She had hungrily sought him in her dreams, and now he was here, in the flesh. "It is not convenient; I have already retired," she said. "My brothers will be beside themselves if they find you here. Please go. My mother is already very angry with me."

Her excuses were like blows to Ashur, who was exhausted from the long run in the night. He turned to

leave. She returned to her bed, wondering how he could have gotten there.
Her head cleared, and she realized
he must have traveled throughout the
night. She had reacted more out of
guilt and fear than from the way she
truly felt. "What is wrong with me?"
she wondered aloud.

Bounding across the room, she
unbarred the door and opened the
latch. He was gone. Immediately she
was aware of the fragrance of the
desert gardenia. She lifted her hand
to inhale the delicate scent. Ashur
had obviously reached through the
hole in the door and crushed the
desert flowers on the latch. In the
moonlight, she saw the bruised blos-
soms and petals lying scattered on
the floor. Her heart shrank in her
breast. Had he crushed the flowers
in anger that she had refused to
see him? A well-known custom of her
people was for a daring young man to
visit his betrothed secretly in the
night. The prospective bridegroom
left a sweet fragrance on the door
latch. However, it was beyond the
bounds of propriety to demand that
she open to him.

Ammi put on her robe and veil and ran through the courtyard, past the sleeping gatekeeper, and opened the gate. As she went into the city, she caught a glimpse of a man walking around the corner of a building, and she ran after him, calling Ashur's name. She ran to where she had seen him, but he was another street away. This continued until she was well into the interior of the city. When the man could finally hear her calls, he turned. She gasped when she realized that she was not following Ashur at all.

Her shouts attracted another of the watchmen assigned to sentry duty for the city. The first guard turned and came back to her. Before she could explain her predicament, he snatched away her veil. He mistook her for a prostitute, and what he then suggested shocked her so that she became almost incoherent with fear. Running to the other watchman, she grabbed his arm with such force that he slapped her and shook her.

"What is wrong with you, woman? Did you not get paid for your services?" the second guard said.

"I am trying to find my friend. He came to my home, but before I could receive him, he went away. You must have seen him. He came down the street just ahead of me. Please, if you will ask my mother—she is the wife of Dedan. My father was the king's merchant," Ammi begged tearfully. She had never in her life been struck in the face by anyone in anger. "My friend, Ashur, stays with the stonemason. His son's name is Malta," said Ammi, hoping that the watchmen would know one of the names.

"I do not know any of these people," replied the first watchman defensively. The way he said it made Ammi think otherwise.

"I know Malta. I know Ashur, the son of Machir, too," said the second man. "His father is a friend of my father."

"Yes, he is the one. He is the son of Machir. He will tell you who I am," Ammi said, relieved that now they would not believe her to be a prostitute.

Finally, the first watchman took Ammi home while the other went to the home of the stonemason to summon

Ashur. Her brothers were furious when the guard awakened the household. They were still berating her for her foolishness in going out alone at night when Ashur arrived. When she saw him, she ran to him and held him. He saw Ammi in tears and grew angry at the way they were treating her. Ashur and Ammi's brothers immediately clashed.

"Back away," Ashur demanded, grabbing one of the brothers by the arm and forcefully removing his hand from Ammi's arm. Ammi tearfully led Ashur away from her angry brothers and into the bedchamber of her mother. Her brothers followed her and continued their verbal assault.

"Mother, Ashur and I are deeply in love," Ammi said to her mother. "We want to be married. Tell her, Ashur."

"Yes, it is true. I love your daughter as I love my own life," Ashur confirmed. "I want to marry her."

"Our sister is too young to marry," her brothers countered, indignant at the challenge to their newly acquired authority.

"We will continue these discussions at a more sensible hour,"

Ammi's mother said. "See that you remove yourself from this house," she said, addressing Ashur coolly.

Ashur bowed submissively to Ammi's mother. However, the bow sharply contradicted the expression on his face.

"Ashur, it is best for you to go. I will speak to them in the morning," Ammi soothed, fearing further conflict between her brothers and Ashur.

When the morning arrived, however, Ammi's angry brothers refused to discuss the matter with her. To avoid a possible scandal from her frequent meetings with Ashur, they agreed to send Ammi to Baal-Hamon in the north country. Their father had once threatened to send her brothers to work in the vineyards there "to learn discipline and obedience." The vineyard at Baal-Hamon was rented to her family by the king.

Ammi was appalled to learn that the previous night's appeal was all for naught. Her mother refused to argue against the decision made by her brothers. She would be sent to Baal-Hamon, where she would be forced to work in the vineyards under the family's overseer.

***

A few days later, Ashur and his friend Malta were walking down the street in Solem. Ashur saw Sabta beside the sheep pens. He immediately recognized him by his skulking stride. Sabta was looking the other way, so Ashur quickly crossed the street. He was standing right beside him before Sabta saw him. Sabta's mouth dropped open. He would have bolted like a scared rabbit, but Ashur's powerful arm reached out and grabbed him before he could escape.

"Get your hands off me! Let me loose," protested Sabta. "I haven't done anything to you. It was a mistake. Pithon will kill you if you hurt me."

"What are you doing here by the pens, Sabta? Are you going to steal one of the lambs? The mistake you made was not leaving the village when Pithon left," Ashur warned ominously.

Sabta's Adam's apple bulged as he swallowed nervously. He obviously had thought Pithon had intimidated Ashur so that he would not retaliate. Ashur reached down and grabbed him by the leg. Making a circular movement, he lifted Sabta into the air. Sabta let out a startled scream as he sailed over the fence. The scream came to an abrupt stop as Sabta landed face-down in the smelly muck of the pen.

"I probably should not have done that," Ashur said to Malta, feeling a slight pang of conscience as he observed the downfallen Sabta lying in the muck.

"He deserved what he got," Malta replied. "He needed to learn that he cannot hide under Pithon's coat-tail all of the time." He yelled at Sabta, "I'm warning you, Sabta, if you ever show your face around here again, I will break your skinny, lying neck. You must live with your conscience and with what you did to Ashur and Ammi."

"Perhaps they were right," Sabta thought to himself as he sat in the mud. Things had not gone well for him lately. He was just one step ahead of the village watchmen. Maybe it was time for him to move on to new horizons where he could ply his

trade upon those who were uninformed
of his thieving nature.

CHAPTER 13

The Vineyards
of Baal-Hamon

The first days of work in the vineyards of Baal-Hamon were nightmarish for Ammi. Every joint ached. Nevertheless, after a few weeks of this routine, her muscles became accustomed to the new rigors forced upon them. The relentless rays of the sun darkened her naturally white skin. Rejection by her mother and brothers was difficult, but the separation from Ashur was almost too much for her to bear. Heart-withered, she trudged to the vineyards each day.

"The girl is very depressed," one of the women said to the overseer.

"She will get over it," the man replied.

Ammi awoke before dawn and prepared herself a small breakfast of bread and milk. She gulped the last bites as the sound of the horn summoned the workers. The overseer led her to the vineyard where he assigned her to work, then returned to the stand or leafy watch booth where he sat and guarded against thieves.

An ancient brick tower, neglected and too hazardous for use, overlooked the area. She walked through the rows of grapevines, gathering a small sack of stones. She took stones, her jar of water and her staff, and set up camp at one end of the vineyard. Ammi could sit, provided she stayed on the raised mound that the workers had built of stones and dirt. The mound provided a vantage point and allowed a better view.

One of her duties was to keep the foxes out of the vineyards or to trap them. The task was particularly repugnant to her because she hated to see them suffer. They would gnaw off their own legs to escape the traps. She was glad none of the little vixens were in the vineyards this morning.

The men worked at night during the full of the moon when the animals were particularly active. The foxes loved the succulent grapes and were persistent and cunning in their pursuit. The overseer had instructed her how to prepare snares to trap the animals. He assigned Solomon's expert archers to exterminate particularly persistent ones that learned to avoid the traps.

The vineyard was pleasant early in the morning. The vines gave off an earthy smell, and field larks sang merrily in the cool air. Her thoughts turned to Ashur. She remembered the first time they met. Her parents had taken her to the banquet house for the festival of Pessah. She had prepared for hours and had worn her best dress of fine blue linen. Oh, how she loved blue; even God must love blue, she thought, glancing up at the vastness of the sky, which was clear except for a few fleecy white clouds.

Her fanciful thoughts imagined riding beside Ashur in a chariot. The memory was a delightful one. His banner over me is love, she thought whimsically, picturing the two of them riding away together into the clouds. She was as a bride arrayed in all her splendor, adorned as a princess, with a *sefirah*, a royal diadem, on her head, beside her prince forever.

A flash of movement down one row of the vineyard interrupted her day-dreaming. She rose and immediately went to the spot where she had seen the fox enter. She shouted and struck the ground with her staff. Her plan was to try to drive the fox out the side where the traps were set on the trails.

The foxes were less cautious when startled and often stumbled into the snares when fleeing. She hated to see them caught, but after chasing the particularly stubborn ones during the heat of the day, it was better for her when they did get trapped. At least she did not have to kill them. The overseer would do so at the end of the day.

Ammi passed from row to row in the vineyard, looking first to the left and then to the right. She had almost reached the end row when she heard a low growl behind her. She whirled about to face the sound. A fox, a large male, was coming toward her. She backed away, raising the staff to defend herself, but terror gripped her. The fox stumbled toward her, snapping at a vine in its way. Her eyes went instantly to the animal's mouth. It was white and wet with saliva, foaming at the mouth. The words of the overseer leaped into recollection. The recipient of a bite from a rabid fox went mad and usually died.

Normally, the foxes were not considered dangerous. They were cunning hunters and valued for keeping down the mouse population, which was especially troublesome in grain-growing areas. The balance of their diets consisted of birds and other small animals. Rabies in the foxes, however, transformed them into objects of fear. Their fondness for the succulent grapes brought them into frequent encounters with those who tended the vineyards.

Ammi turned and raced for the only protection available to her, the old watchtower. Every step she ran, she expected to feel the sharp teeth of the fox pierce her leg, injecting the venomous saliva into her bloodstream. She heard his teeth gnash. Fortunately, the fox was partially paralyzed and did not overtake her. Ammi ran into the watchtower, then met with another obstacle. There was only one door. Trapped!

She heard growling and snapping again. She turned and saw the fox come into view at the doorway. He had followed her. It was as though the crazed animal blamed her for its pain and misery. The fox ravaged the side of the door, momentarily forgetting her.

Her mind raced with thoughts of escape, but the rabid animal had her cornered. The only window of the watchtower building was too high. She calculated whether she could somehow get up to the high window ledge. The fox seemed to steady himself, ready to make a determined rush at her.

Ammi tossed the staff at the fox, ran to the window, and attempted to leap through the window opening. The window ledge caught her waist high, but this left her legs dangling down where the fox could still reach her. Sheer terror gave her added strength. She threw one leg over the window ledge and toppled through, crashing to the ground outside. As she did, her knee struck a rock, sending pain searing through her leg.

Sobbing now, she clutched her leg to her. She heard the frustrated gnawing and snarling of the fox tearing at the inside wall. Then the noise stopped. Perhaps he was coming back outside, she thought, ter-ror-stricken. Now she was unable to run and unarmed besides. She strug-gled to her feet, searching desper-ately for another avenue of escape. She caught sight of the ladder to the loft. The watchmen had undoubt-edly slept in the attic.

Why had she not thought of that before? If she could make it up there, she did not think the fox

could get to her. Foxes did not
climb, did they? The loft offered
the only available safety she could
think of. Ignoring the pain, she
dragged herself to the ladder. She
managed to get into the loft. The
tired old timbers creaked under her
weight, threatening to let her crash
through the rotten floor. Later the
overseer found her huddling in the
loft, crying her heart out.

"Help me," she pleaded. "The fox
almost got me. I want to go home to
my mother—and to my brothers."

***

Rumors of trouble in the north
reached King Solomon in his palace
in Jerusalem. Continuing worry that
the Assyrian factions might some day
unite caused Solomon to turn his
attention to the cities in the north
that King Hurom had given him. Taking
personal command of the northern
army, including many craftsmen and
builders, Solomon journeyed to the
far north country. The king planned
to fortify the cities of Cabul and
then stock them with provisions for

the army. He sent his builders to Tadmor in the wilderness to build another fortress there. The people of upper and lower Bethhoran were subjugated and the cities fortified.

Then Solomon reinforced Baalath so that all the storage cities and all the villages for his chariots and horses were fortified. The kingdom was protected from Ezion-geber in the south to Hamath and Carchemish in the north. King Solomon ruled over all the kings from the river Euphrates even to the land of the sea peoples and as far as the border of Egypt.

Zabud watched nervously as Solomon shouted in anger at his purveyor from his fifth district. "He is not unlike a roaring lion pacing back and forth," said Zabud aside to the king's chief prefect. "Nothing seems to please him lately, and the slightest incident sends him into a rage."

"I want to inspect those vineyards at Baal-Hamon on the way back to Jerusalem. Make the arrangements," Solomon ordered Zabud, imperiously dismissing the purveyor with a wave of his royal hand. "And, Zabud, send to me the royal physicians."

The king's disposition was aggravated by the onset of a nagging toothache that refused to be healed by the best of his physicians. Even Queen Osoris's personal physician from Egypt was helpless. Their diagnosis that an invisible "tooth worm" caused the pain greatly irritated King Solomon. He sent them back to the palace and ordered them to find something that would kill this unseen worm by the time he returned. "If the pain becomes too severe, I will render the 'worm' insensible with arak," he vowed to Zabud.

"You will find sufficient patients with toothaches at the palace to practice upon," the king said to his physicians. He delivered the message in a tone meant to invoke their best efforts.

During the night, he strolled down among the workers' huts, sleepless and angry. The contented snoring of the men intensified the pain. "As long as they have a roof over their heads and a hot meal, they seem to find satisfaction in their wives and children. Elohim apparently gave the gift of love to sweeten the toil of the laborer. He denied it to the rich and powerful," he surmised.

Solomon's entourage set out to return to the palace at Jerusalem. They planned to stop at the vineyards of Baal-Hamon on the way. The king owned these vineyards and leased them to others. In return, each of the tenant farmers paid Solomon a thousand pieces of silver annually, leaving them with two hundred pieces for themselves. Yields were down. Solomon was angry at the purveyor's explanation of the cause for the decline and the request to renegotiate the payment.

"How can a pack of little foxes eat all the grapes and keep the workers from harvesting?" Solomon raged.

The king went to sleep that night with many thoughts in his head. He awakened with a start, a victim of fear in the night. He wiped the sweat from his neck, then pulled the clammy tunic over his head and hurled it into the corner of the room. The naked form beside him protested the movement by rolling away from him.

Leaning forward, he strained his eyes in the darkness to identify the nameless woman. He dreaded sleep. The nightmares might return, shadowy assassins or blackened phantom ships coming out of the mist.

* * *

The morning following her encounter with the rabid fox, Ammi dragged herself out of bed and limped to the gathering place of the workers. She sensed that something significant had taken place because everyone was buzzing with excitement.

The sounds of men and horses jolted her out of her depression. A procession was coming. First, the point men rode up and took position, motioning the workers back as the overseers shouted for everyone to be quiet. Then King Solomon rode into the camp. Ammi prostrated herself on the ground with the other workers and remained so. The overseers were the only ones allowed to stand in the presence of Solomon. They reported and received orders from the king.

The overseers continued their animated discussion with Solomon for a time. Then, much to her surprise, she heard her own name. The overseer called for her, as did some of the other workers. A woman beside her shouted, "Here, here, my lord. The girl is here." She turned to Ammi and said, "Go to him, child. They are calling for you."

Ammi limped to where the overseer beckoned to her. She did her obeisance before Solomon and faced the overseer. She wondered what wrong had been done to warrant the summons. Solomon warned the workers that the rabid foxes were showing up in other vineyards. The overseer apparently had bragged to Solomon about rescuing Ammi and had her brought to corroborate his story.

"Look here, child," Solomon commanded. "Come closer. Tell me about the fox. Don't be afraid." Ammi found herself thrust forward until she was looking up into the face of King Solomon. She related the story to her king. He seemed genuinely interested and encouraged her to go on describing the actions and condition of the fox. When she would have made the report brief, he asked more questions. Ammi was completely unaware of King Solomon's fascination with her soft voice and beautiful face.

Solomon, she observed, was everything that she had heard and more. Never had she seen a man as attractive and as commanding in presence as he. Not even her Ashur, she thought, would be seen by other people as she saw him. King Solomon's piercing eyes seemed to look inside her, giving him a wise and knowing look. She had heard it said that Solomon could read minds. She could now understand why people said that.

Ammi expected to be dismissed and sent back with the other workers. To her surprise, Solomon suggested to the overseer that she be placed with the daughters of Jerusalem, the ladies-in-waiting of the palace. Solomon turned to her and asked her directly, "Child, are you afraid of the foxes?"

"Yes, my lord," she replied without hesitation.

"Would you like to work in the palace with the daughters?" he asked.

"Yes, my lord."

"Then it is done," said Solomon to the overseer.

"But my lord, the girl's family has sent her to work in the vineyards to learn discipline," said the overseer, who hated to lose one of his workers.

"Go and retrieve your possessions, young woman." Solomon's tone left no room for discussion.

The overseer opened his mouth to say more but thought better of it. He bowed deeply to Solomon and stepped back.

Ammi hurried to retrieve her meager belongings. Solomon mounted his chariot, and at a slight signal of his hand, his guards moved forward. The king and his entire entourage followed. They were soon on their way to Jerusalem.

"My life has changed again," thought Ammi. She felt a deep sense of relief and gratitude toward King Solomon that she would not be going to the vineyards again.

* * *

In the king's palace, Ammi learned her new duties with the daughters of Jerusalem, the virgins of the harem. The daughters waited upon the queens of the harem. A distinct separation existed between the two groups of women. She also observed an obvious difference in status of the queens, the women whom the king married, and the concubines.

The king surrounded himself with beautiful women. Some were as young as twelve or thirteen. The mistress of the daughters taught her to comb the hair of the king's wives. Ammi's earlier experience at combing the hair of her unruly brothers proved useful now, as she carefully arranged the tresses of the beautiful Abishag. Ammi was completely awed by this woman. The beauty of Abishag was legendary in her home village of Solem.

When Ammi paused for a moment to rest her tired arm, Abishag examined her own image in a polished brass mirror. She smiled at Ammi, either to signal her approval of

Ammi's gentleness or proficiency, or to express welcome to a fellow villager. Whatever the reason, Ammi was grateful. She had received little more than cold looks and suspicious stares from most of the women.

Ammi watched curiously as a daughter of Jerusalem combed Queen Osoris's long hair into intricate tresses with an ivory comb. She bound the strands with rings of gold. Then, turning her attention to the queen's hands, she placed Osoris's fingers into a small vase. Each fingertip was stained a dark red. When she finished with the fingers, she dyed each toe, staining not only the nail, but also the entire toe.

"Osoris is the first-ranking queen," whispered another of the daughters, who noticed Ammi's fascination. "She is a princess of Egypt."

The daughter held a small palette in her hand. She dipped a short thin stick into the center of the palette and applied an ointment-like material to Osoris's eyes. First, the daughter lined the queen's eyelashes with a dark-green color. Then, changing ends of the stick, she dipped into a second color and lined the queen's eyebrows with it.

Osoris noticed Ammi watching and fixed her with a look that suggested Ammi mind her own business. Although Osoris did not convey open jealousy and contempt as did the other queens, she, too, was not very friendly.

"Do not let her bother you. I will show it to you when she leaves," whispered the daughter assigned to instruct Ammi in her duties as lady-in-waiting.

When the daughter finished grooming Queen Osoris, she attached two loose feathers to the queen's hair, a sign of her rank as the firstborn princess of Egypt. She carefully handed her the *waas*, a scepter with a straight shaft that split into two parts at the bottom and was topped by the head of a vulture. The scepter was the symbol of authority held only by Solomon's first-ranking queen. The people of Egypt revered the vulture, believing that it ate negative ideas. The daughter held up a bronze looking glass for the queen to inspect her work.

True to her word, when the queen left the room, the daughter scurried over and picked up the palette. "Here, I will paint your eyes now, Ammi. King Solomon will find you even more desirable then," said the daughter.

"No, please," Ammi said, alarmed at that prospect. "I only wanted to look at it."

Queen Osoris was, however, the most strikingly beautiful woman Ammi had ever seen, with those mysterious eyes, at least the equal of Abishag.

***

The mistress of the daughters noticed them examining the paints, causing her to come over and explain the preparation of the paints to Ammi. She picked up the palette. "They make green by grinding green malachite on slate palettes, and the black is made from antimony rock. Antimony, when ground, makes a black powder that shines like a mirror," explained the mistress of the daughters, handing the palette back to Ammi.

Ammi examined the intricately carved palette. Two sets of bull's horns decorated the top. A hole went through the center at a right angle to the flat portion. The little paint stick was crushed and softened on each end and was kept in the hole when not in use. On the front of the palette, there appeared figures of men marching, carrying standards. Below the men in the center were the bodies of two animal-like creatures with long, curved serpentine necks and heads. The necks of these monsters formed the cavities to hold the paints.

"You better return these to Queen Osoris's couch," warned the mistress of the daughters. "She is very possessive of them."

***

King Solomon dispatched men to Solem to investigate Ammi's background. His men returned to report to the king that Ammi was indeed the daughter of his late royal merchant of Solem. The most interesting news was of Ammi's mother. She was descended from old Hurrian royalty, long deposed. This made Ammi imminently qualified, in Solomon's eyes, to become queen of Israel. The news quickly circulated through the palace and reached the ears of the mistress of the daughters.

Solomon summoned the mistress to inquire about Ammi's character and demeanor. He asked many questions of her. The king was extremely interested in this young woman.

"What amazes me, my lord king, is the young woman's knowledge of the code of our people. With the proper training and experience, she might judge in your stead."

King Solomon's interest peaked the afternoon the mistress of the daughters staged a play. High-pitched and excited squeals punctuated the air as the king took his place on the dais. From his vantage point, he surveyed the group of young women gathered below. Taking their cues from the mistress, the women took their places.

King Solomon addressed the mistress. "I assume they are ready. Let the performance begin."

The young women imitated a marriage ceremony, accompanied by the king's female choir. The mistress had directed Ammi to assume the role of the imaginary bride. The tallest of the daughters reluctantly played the bridegroom. Ammi innocently entered into the part. She pirouetted and danced around the garden like a beautiful peacock, captivating King Solomon with the tilt of her head, the sway of her body.

"She is exquisite," the king said to the mistress of the daughters.

When the play concluded, Solomon summoned the young women one by one to express his appreciation for their performance. Ammi was the last.

"Thank you, Ammi. You have pleased me greatly," he said as Ammi bowed.

The king regarded her now at close range. Ammi was average in height but carried herself so erect that she appeared taller. The peach-colored gown brought out the rich glow of her cheeks and lips. Her eyes were large and luminous and had a frightened quality. Pouting lips looked as soft as rose petals. Where dark, silky hair met her forehead, it swirled uniquely before disappearing into smooth, creamy skin. Her arms were perfect in flesh and symmetry. King Solomon vowed to himself to have this woman.

***

Ammi roused from sleep the next morning to find herself face-to-face with two ladies-in-waiting. She did not know either of the women. Much to her embarrassment, right away they requested her to step out of her gown. They wanted to bathe her. Before she could object, they took her gown.

"Why are you doing this? I can wash myself," protested Ammi.

"You are a very beautiful young woman, and perfectly formed, too, I see," said the older of the women as she bathed Ammi in rose water and lemon to bleach her skin white. "You have found great favor in the eyes of King Solomon. You are being considered for entrance into the harem. You will never have to work again if you become one of King Solomon's concubines."

"But I am black from the sun," Ammi said, blushing under the appraising eyes of the women. "Solomon has many women much more beautiful than I am. I have seen them with my own eyes."

Ammi knew that for a woman of position to have her face, arms, and legs darkened by the sun ruined her beauty. At least, that was what she had heard from the women of the palace.

"The sun could not hide your beauty," said the second lady-in-waiting. "After all, black or white feels the same in the dark." The head of the daughters came into the room as this was said. Her frown sent the two ladies in retreat, but not before they cackled in laughter at the joke they shared at the expense of the humiliated Ammi.

"You must not let those two bother you, my daughter. I will have a talk with them later. I did not hear all of that. What did they say to you?"

"No, nothing, mistress; it is nothing. But I would like to return with the daughters. I am not worthy of this honor. I love another. If I cannot return to the daughters, please send me home to my mother and brothers. They sent me to the north country to tend the vineyards because my brothers were angry with me. Surely now they have forgiven me. Will there be no free will on my part?"

"Hush, child. It is not for you to say. That is a silly idea," responded the mistress.

"But I am betrothed to another." Ammi had maintained her composure while facing the unknown. Now that it was obvious she was to enter the sexual part of the harem, she began sobbing, and the words came tumbling out. "I love my betrothed with all my heart and ache to be with him. His name is Ashur. He lives near my village of Solem. I sit at his feet with great delight, and his words fall on me like dewdrops on the thirsty ground. He is my best friend. I am wounded with love for him. It is he my soul loves."

"Do not cry, Ammi," consoled the mistress of the daughters. The stern-ness disappeared, and she held the sobbing girl's head to her bosom and tried to comfort her. "You are not formally engaged, and no dowry was arranged. King Solomon has sent word to your mother, and she has given her permission and blessing for you to become one of King Solomon's wives."

Ammi wiped away the tears of frustration and tried to compose herself enough to argue the matter. "But mistress, what else could she do? She is alone now. My father is dead. My mother would not rebuff the mighty Solomon. If my father were alive, he would not turn away from me. He would know what to do."

She was sure that her brothers were delighted to learn that she was to become a wife of the king. This would mean much more influence for them. To appeal to her family would prove useless.

That night Ammi lay crying softly in the unfamiliar bed, caressing the signet ring Ashur had given to her. She found herself unreasonably angry and frustrated at Ashur for arousing deep sexual feelings within her. The threat remained that she would never be allowed the expression of those desires.

From outside, the strange call of a peacock startled her. She wished she were far from this strange place. She recalled the humiliation of being bathed and appraised by strangers and wondered what other indignities awaited her. What she missed most, besides Ashur, was her freedom. In the palace, she was a virtual prisoner.

She wished her father could come to her and hug her. She pictured him pulling the coverlet up over her arms the way he had done so often in her childhood. Then she imagined her heavenly Father holding her with the same warmth she felt when her father or Ashur held her.

CHAPTER 14

Jerusalem, the Palace and Riches Beyond Belief

$\mathcal{T}$he head mistress of the daughters of Jerusalem summoned Ammi out on the parapet as people gathered excitedly along the street below them. Soldiers began running to their stations along the wall. Others took up position along the street.

"Open the gates," shouted the captain of the guard. "King Solomon is coming into the city." The great iron-covered gates swung open. Below her and around her, people craned their necks to catch a glimpse of

Solomon. Ammi was curious enough to join them.

First, two horsemen rode through the gates; one peeled off to the left, the other to the right. A sense of drama and expectancy permeated the crowd. A trumpet sounded, and a lone chariot came through the gates. From the appearance of the horseman and the chariot and the reaction of the crowd, there was no mistaking the identity of the driver. Immediately following Solomon were the Giborim, sixty horsemen riding solid-black horses. Each man was clad in armor and carried a sword at his side.

"Those are Solomon's personal guard," said the mistress of the daughters. "They have dust of gold sprinkled on their heads; that is why the sunlight glistens in their hair. They are all expert in war, the strongest and most skilled horsemen in the kingdom."

Ammi admired the beauty of the sixty black horses, each ridden by a tall and handsome member of the king's guard. Every strong, young warrior was resplendent in his uniform of the royal guard.

"Here comes King Solomon," the mistress announced.

Solomon made his entrance in a chariot of war. The chariot was drawn by two matched white horses of flawless beauty. Solomon's chariot was directly below them, and Ammi now could observe the magnificent Solomon without his gaze on her. The king wore a garment of white trimmed in gold. She had to admit that she had never seen anything to compare with the splendor of Solomon. No other man commanded such physical presence. The lines of his face were perfect. He embodied everything that was physically attractive.

Many chariots followed closely after Solomon's royal bodyguard. Two black horses drew each of the chariots. Each had a driver, a shield bearer, and a ranking officer of the guard. The shield bearers carried highly polished gold shields that flashed in the sun. Unlike the king's bodyguard, each officer wore a helmet with a scarlet sash denoting his rank; this added more color to the procession.

Black basalt stones paved the streets leading into the palace. The horse's hooves and the iron-rimmed wheels of the chariots set up a roar of noise on the streets below. Ammi placed her palms over her ears. The mistress pulled a hand from Ammi's ear and practically shouted to her. "The war chariots are breathtaking, aren't they?"

"Yes, and loud," Ammi replied, wide-eyed at the majesty she witnessed.

The framework, wheels, pole, and yoke of the chariots were constructed of cedar and cypress. Polished gold and silver decorated the shield-like front of Solomon's chariot. On all the chariots, the axletrees ended in scythe-like projections designed to charge into, rend, and tear enemy foot soldiers. The bindings of the framework were of rawhide, while the floor was made of thick rope netting. Cases for bows, spears, and arrows were fastened on the sides.

Running along behind the war chariots were many Nubians carrying the empty palanquin, or carrying couch, of Solomon. These powerful young men were naked except for loincloths, and as they ran along, golden bands on their arms and legs jangled at each stride. The palanquin was constructed of cedar from Lebanon. The posts were made of silver and its back of gold. The seat of the chair was purple, woven with silver thread by the daughters of Jerusalem.

Solomon reined in his chariot horses in the courtyard off to their right, and his captains and personal guard took their places behind him. At the direction of the head mistress of the daughters, the waiting women began to descend to the courtyard, and soon Solomon's wives and other ranking dignitaries of the palace joined them. When everyone had gathered and all were standing quietly, Solomon signaled to the mistress of the daughters. She in turn spoke to those chosen for this occasion.

Four of the daughters began slowly walking toward Solomon. Two of them together carried an embroidered pillow on which sat an object covered with a white cloth. When the girls stood before Solomon, they knelt down. The other two young women took off the covering and folded

it, uncovering the marriage crown.
Solomon reached down, picked up the
crown, and placed it on his head.

Ammi had been curiously watching
this ceremony. Suddenly she became
aware that all eyes were turning on her.

"Solomon is stating his inten-
tion of marrying again," the head
mistress of the daughters told her.
"You have been chosen. There is no
greater honor for a woman."

Ammi stood frozen, stunned by this
revelation. Everyone assumed that
she would be as thrilled with the
king's declaration as had everyone
before her. She fought to maintain
her composure. The lessons she had
learned at her grandmother's knee
helped. The older woman had admonished her always to keep her wits
about her. Grandmother had maintained that a silly, hysterical girl
could not cope with the adversities
of life. She must gather herself and
draw upon her strength as a woman.

***

Ammi now found herself the center
of attention of the women of the

palace. But the sound of the heavy doors being bolted and unbolted served as a constant reminder that she was not free to come and go as she pleased. She could not share their excitement, for she waited in dread for King Solomon to announce their wedding day. Why had no one told her what could happen? She had only wanted to get away from the foxes. By entering the palace, she had probably ended her chances of ever seeing Ashur again.

As a member of the daughters of Jerusalem, Ammi worked for many hours with the other women on the tapestries and curtains that adorned the palace. "See, you pull the thread down like this," the mistress of the daughters instructed. "Then you come back through here."

Ammi enjoyed the delicate embroidery and for a moment managed to put her fears aside. She was completely engrossed in a difficult part of the needlework when one of the daughters of Jerusalem burst into the room.

"The caravan from Ezion-geber is here!" she blurted out to the mistress of the daughters. "It has finally arrived. The sari himself told me. He sent me to tell you, mistress," said the girl, literally bouncing with excitement. "I cannot wait to see what they have brought. Queen Osoris told me that there are beautiful gowns of a new material like nothing we have ever seen. She has already chosen hers, but she said that there are many others from which we may choose."

"Calm down, silly girl," replied the mistress, with her usual reserve. "We will have sufficient time to view the trade goods when the king summons us."

The mistress was quiet for a moment, reflecting on the girl's words. She continued speaking after the girl had left the room. "Now I know why Queen Osoris was preening herself so. As the first-ranking queen, she is the first to be summoned by the king to view the caravan's goods. She has first choice of the most beautiful and exotic items.

"You could be ruling queen, Ammi, if you follow my advice," confided the mistress in a more familiar tone than she had ever before used with

Ammi. "The king has told me that he is very impressed with your grace and beauty. Not since Queen Osoris has he been so taken with a woman.

"If you asked the king for the scepter before he marries you, I think he would give it to you. I have always believed that the scepter should bear the emblem of Israel, not that of Egypt. You must not tell the king I told you to ask for it. I would have to deny it," she said, now realizing that the king might interpret what she said to Ammi as being disloyal. For the mistress to risk such statements suggested deeper reasons. Perhaps Queen Osoris had mistreated her, or perhaps she suspected the queen of disloyalty to Israel or to the king.

"I am very loyal to the king, and I believe you would make him a fine queen," the mistress went on, carefully selecting her words. She served Queen Osoris without reservation, but she obviously favored one of her own people becoming preeminent. In her eyes, Ammi exhibited exceptional beauty, kindness and grace.

Unless the king took a new first-ranking queen from among his own people, there remained a distinct possibility that Pharaoh Siamun, by reasserting his claim over Gezer, might again invade Israel, declare Queen Osoris rightful ruler, and control the entire area. There must be some way to transfer Ammi's love and fierce loyalty from this Ashur to the king and to make the girl see the greater good that would come from it.

***

Solomon chose the royal gardens as the site where he would receive the caravan's cargo. The royal gardens lay outside the palace walls. He frequently went there when the hot east winds blew. Ammi had not seen the royal gardens. Their beauty would add to the occasion and were certain to impress her. He reasoned that they would compare favorably to the natural beauty of her home country to which she yearned to return.

"This is the most beautiful garden of all gardens," the mistress said to Ammi. "Perhaps here you will find love for King Solomon."

"The garden is a place of desolation to me," Ammi countered tonelessly. "My love needs no arousing from without. My desire is as natural and free as the gazelles and deer of the fields."

The mistress of the harem came to meet King Solomon as he entered the garden. She bowed low before him. "I have never seen the women so thrilled, my king," said the mistress of the harem. "All of the preparations have been made." Her own voice indicated her desire to please the king and the stress of preparing for the event.

Solomon looked around at the excited women gathered to view the treasure of Ophir. He saw Ammi beside the mistress of the daughters. For a moment, her eyes met his; then hers were downcast, supposedly occupied with her hands in her lap.

"Let it begin," Solomon ordered the captain of the royal guard, who had now appeared at his side. The captain of the guard walked a short distance from the king and shouted a command. Another distant command echoed his. Soon they heard the sounds of servants and drivers as they hurried to bring the wondrous cargo of Marib and Ophir before the king. The women of the harem strained their necks, standing on tiptoe for their first glimpse of the exotic treasures of the south.

Solomon stood on a dais beneath a huge mulberry tree surrounded by the women of the harem. At his feet lay treasures of the south, precious stones of the colors of the rainbow and gold and silver creations of every sort imaginable to man. Servants piled intricately carved pieces of ivory and sandalwood before them. The items that caused the greatest stir among his wives and concubines were the manlike apes and the beautiful peacocks. Spontaneous cries of wonder and delight came from the women as the beasts were brought into the garden and paraded before their eyes.

Other servants brought large jars of spices and ointments. Soon the air was filled with their fragrances. Solomon gave orders for the eunuchs to bring tiny bottles made of burned clay in to the women. Within these bottles were the costliest of perfumes and spices of the south. These were passed around for each of the women to sample.

"Oh, this is delightful," Ammi said to no one in particular. She made an exclamation of delight upon inhaling one particular fragrance. She was at first not inclined to give it up, so enchanted was she with the scent of the opobalsamum. The mistress of the daughters, noting Ammi's delight in the opobalsamum, reported it to the king. King Solomon made a gift of the perfume to Ammi. Yet when Ammi was alone again in her own quarters, the delicate scent only served to remind her of the fragrance of her memory of Ashur. To find out that her every move was being reported to the king frightened her.

One of the daughters of Jerusalem brought a gown to Ammi. The daughter held it out across her arm to display it to her. "Is it not beautiful?" the daughter asked enviously. "Look at the silver thread of the embroidery. It is wondrous! I would try to swim the Jordan River in the rainy season to wear such a gown for the king." Nonetheless, Ammi was aghast. She could see right through the gown. "I cannot wear this gown. Take it away. I would not leave this room wearing that gown. I would not offend you, Mahlah, but I am betrothed to Ashur."

The daughter was surprised at the outburst from the previously cooperative Ammi. The girl left the room with the gown. However, she soon returned. "The mistress of the daughters insists that this is the dress that you must wear." The girl did not seem to exult in this small victory. She said the words in a tone that indicated she was only trying to do her job.

"I am sorry, but I cannot wear that gown," Ammi insisted. She sat on the bed with her arms folded and her head down on her knees.

"Please, Ammi, do not cause a problem for me," the girl pleaded. "I am only trying to do as I am told." Ammi remained silent and continued her posture of noncompliance. After several more attempts at communicating with Ammi, the daughter again left the room to consult with the mistress of the daughters.

"Now they will probably send the eunuchs in to dress me," Ammi guessed. She was terrified at the thought of this new humiliation. Even if the men were neutered, who could know their thoughts? She had heard the whispered gossip of an affair taking place between one of the eunuchs and a certain woman of the harem.

"I will tear the gown to shreds before I will wear something that indecent," she muttered to herself. "Better to be naked before the eunuchs than to go in practically nude before the king," she thought, weighing her chances of maintaining her fidelity to Ashur. She determined to resist the wearing of this sensual gown, no matter what the punishment. To refuse to go before the king when summoned, though, was unthinkable.

When the daughter returned, the mistress and another of the daughters accompanied her. "What is this that Mahlah tells me?" the mistress asked of Ammi. "You do not like the gown that the king has selected for you to wear to the feast?"

Ammi looked up at the mistress when she heard her voice. "The gown is too immodest. You can see through it. May I wear something other than this?" Ammi pleaded. She doubted the busy king found time to select gowns for the women.

"No, I am sorry, my dear, but this is the usual dress of the daughters that are of special interest to the king," the mistress replied. "You will get accustomed to it. The gown is beautiful. Many of the other women will be wearing similar ones, but you will be the loveliest of all." Although the mistress was actually in sympathy with Ammi's modesty, there was nothing she could do without risking the king's disapproval.

"Please let me wear another gown. May I have a choice of gowns to wear before the king?" Ammi pleaded desperately.

The mistress could see that Ammi was far from voluntarily agreeing to wear the gown, and she wanted to avoid a direct conflict with her. The beautiful and intelligent young woman seemed destined to become a favorite of the king and would have great power as one of his ranking queens. Ammi might well remember an unpleasant incident and blame her for its occurrence. "Mahlah, come with me," she ordered. Ammi and the other daughter were left alone in Ammi's chambers.

The mistress selected two more gowns and sent Mahlah back to Ammi's chambers with them. "Take these gowns to Ammi, and you and Leeba return to me. Leave her alone with the gowns to make her decision." Mahlah could see no difference in the revealing nature of the gowns. Although she admired Ammi's stand on the issue, there was nothing for Ammi to do but cooperate and wear one of the beautiful gowns.

When the mistress finished her own preparation for the feast, she walked down the corridor again to Ammi's chambers. She would per- sonally escort Ammi to the feast. She was not surprised to find Ammi wearing the silver embroidered gown she had been asked to wear. Nor was she surprised to see that Ammi was wearing the silver embroidered gown over one of the other gowns. This is what she expected the modest and intelligent Ammi to do. The mistress rehearsed what she would say to the king if he commented on Ammi's gown.

The mistress led Ammi into the throne room and seated her on a couch at Solomon's feet. The eunuchs brought in beautiful ivory boxes carved with figures of cherubs and lions and placed them before her. At her feet lay a dazzling array of wealth, the likes of which few women would ever see. This implied that she would soon share this great wealth with her husband-to-be, the mighty King Solomon.

Solomon leaned forward and described the precious stones to her. "Here is topaz from the kingdom of Meroe, and these are from Sennar, and these from Hordofan."

He handed her a translucent diamond he identified as jasper. "This is a sapphire, the transparent blue one. Over there are emeralds and sardonyx; a clear red stone, sardius beryl; and amethyst."

Lotus and hyacinth blooms decorated the king's throne room. Wildflowers and the perfume of jasmine scented the air. Amazing mural paintings and artistic frescos adorned the walls of the room.

Servants brought forth dainty morsels of meat and cheese, fishes of the sea and other delicacies, breads and cakes made from fine flour, and honey, along with a myriad of recipes made with the plentiful olive oil.

The softest skins, pillows of down, and all the vanities and comforts known to man were brought and placed at Ammi's feet. Solomon signaled to the mistress of the daughters. She in turn called to men holding musical instruments, and they began to play. Two women behind them joined in, playing harps covered with leopard skins. Several women playing lutes followed. The haunting music had a heavy, sensual beat.

The eunuchs opened the curtains, and there emerged a strikingly beautiful woman clad in a long, flowing gown. She walked gracefully across the great-house floor with all eyes upon her. When she was in front of Solomon, she bowed deeply before the king and then walked to the first of the cushions at the king's left.

The curtains closed behind her, but now they reopened, allowing another equally beautiful Nubian girl to make her entrance through the curtains. Gold ankle bands made a tinkling sound as she walked. Tracing the steps of her predecessor, she, too, bowed deeply before Solomon and seated herself on a pillow at Solomon's right.

One by one, the lovely young women paraded before them, attired in every conceivable extravagance. They wore crescents, pendants, bracelets, and thin face veils. Others were adorned with head tiaras, armlets, sashes, amulets, rings, and nose jewels. This continued until a semicircle of beautiful young women were seated before them. Conspicuous by her absence was Queen Osoris, who had conveniently gone to Gezer to oversee enlargement of the gardens.

Ammi found herself wondering how all these women had found their way into the harem. She was interested in what actually happened in the harem, but she didn't want to be a part of it. From the moment she realized that Solomon had more than a fatherly interest in her, she had tried to devise a way to escape and to return to her first love, her only love.

After all the women were seated and the surroundings were to the king's satisfaction, he signaled for them to begin eating. Solomon reached with his hand to Ammi's bosom. He took the signet ring hanging from Ammi's neck in his hand and studied the inscription.

"Where did you get this ring?" he demanded.

"My betrothed gave me the ring. It is a duplicate of his own signet ring," Ammi volunteered, welcoming the opportunity to call attention again to the fact that she was betrothed to another. Nonetheless, she was somewhat alarmed at the king's tone of voice.

"Bring me the king's seal," Solomon ordered one of the servants.

The servant returned with the royal seal, which was kept under guard when not worn by Solomon. The king took the royal emblem and compared it to the little signet ring that he had taken from around Ammi's neck. To his astonishment, the rings bore the same symbol.

"The symbols on the two rings are identical," Solomon concluded. "They could have been fashioned by the same artisan. This could be a coincidence, but I do not believe this to be so," Solomon said, obviously chagrined. The king had declared the symbol to be his royal seal only days before. He had chosen the seal from among a number of rings left to him by his father from his many conquests. Having used his father's seal for many years, Solomon, in his pride, had decided to have one of his own.

"The ring is very unusual," he stated. Normally, the seals were engraved with a symbol or figure under which appeared the possessive *lamed,* "belonging to" Malchi/ son of Zaccur/the herder, or similar wording. There was no such identifying script on Ammi's ring or his own.

"Send for the royal silversmiths," he ordered the servant. The title referred only to the older, more experienced of the craftsmen, those who had received official designation by the king. Later, when they were assembled before him, he questioned each of them to see if there was one among them that had any knowledge of the signet rings.

"I think this signet ring was made for your father by old Jetur," offered one of the silversmiths.

"What happened to Jetur?" Solomon said hopefully.

"I do not know; he was very old," said the man who had known Jetur." He lived in a village near Rabbah." None of the other men knew anything about the ring, so he dismissed them. After he had questioned the only one of them who had any knowledge of the maker of the ring, he sent the man with two of his warriors to inquire into Jetur's whereabouts.

King Solomon considered sending for Ashur to question him about the ring. However, when Ammi told him the story of Ashur's discovery as a foundling with the signet ring attached to his leg, the king was bewildered.

"No one knew where this foundling came from?" Solomon asked skeptically of Ammi.

"No, my lord. My Ashur was obsessed with finding out the origin of the signet ring but was not able to learn anything about either the ring or his lost family. What do you think this means?" Ammi asked, equally puzzled.

"I do not know, but I will find out."

Solomon sent for two more of his elderly advisors. After he explained the situation to these men, he sent them out to make inquiry into the source of this mystery. He also sent for one of his old military advisors and again patiently explained the tale of the signet rings to him.

"Perhaps," he said, "the origin of the ring may be discovered through questioning my father's military officers. Arrange to have them come to me."

***

That night when Ammi retired to bed, thoughts of how it would be to be married to King Solomon swirled around in her head, muddled together with fear and memories of her love for Ashur. Then she began to think of her father. What she really wanted was someone who would love her like her father had loved her mother, that exclusive and all-consuming love of one man for one woman.

"Ha, I will gum you with the kisses of my toothless mouth," Dedan had joked, addressing her mother, a reference to their growing old together. Her mother and father had often said that their love for each other grew stronger as they grew older together. Something was basically wrong with the idea of so many women being kept for the sole pleasure of one man, Ammi thought.

Another thing disturbed her greatly. Solomon's children seemed to be everywhere.

Could she offer a total and exclusive love to a man who could not return such a love to her? Must she sacrifice herself so that she must share the man she loved with other women? In other cultures of the Orient, the wife called her husband *baal*, or lord. The wife was basically nothing more than a privileged slave whom the husband, by his own choice, freed from slavery. The symbol of marriage was the ring, which suggested the chain with which the slave was bound. Even the prophets spoke of the natural use of the woman by the man.

"The women of Israel, as a general rule, enjoy much better treatment than our sisters," she thought guiltily. Very few women in surrounding lands were not under the control of some man. This did not make her treatment just. "Must I accept the thinking of all the women who have gone before me, to be given at the whim of others more powerful than I, or do I have the same right as the man, to give myself to whom I please by my own free will? Shall I bow to the will of others, as did Merab, resigned to live my life as I am bidden? Must I forgo the love that I witnessed in my own father and mother and my grandmother for honor and riches and to placate my brothers and my mother?" Ammi thought with frustration and anger. "No!" she told herself determinedly.

This was her last thought as she drifted off to sleep.

***

Word of Ammi's avowed love for the young man from her village spread through the harem. When she emerged from her sleeping chamber, the curious women crowded around her. "Tell us more about this young man from your home," the daughters of Jerusalem urged. "What is he like?" At first, the women did not believe Ammi could prefer a man of the fields to the king.

"He stands out like the standard-bearer for ten thousand warriors," Ammi proclaimed. "His skin is smooth and tanned, and he has thick locks of hair as black as a raven, but his eyes are tender, like doves bathing beside rivers of water."

The simile brought exclamations of delight from the women. "Aie-eee! Where is this man that we can go to him?" one envious daughter blurted. Ammi ignored her, caught up in her memories. She could almost see his reflection in the pool by the terebinth tree. "The beard upon his cheeks is perfumed, and his lips are like blood-red anemones, dripping with liquid myrrh. His hands are like bands of gold. His abdomen is like carved ivory inlaid with sapphire, and he has strong legs like pillars of alabaster set on pedestals of pure gold. He is as magnificent as the cedars of Lebanon."

"I would like to see this man," a daughter exclaimed.

"Where does he live?" another questioned. "Is he from your village?"

"Oh, that he were here, that I might feel the warmth of his kisses," Ammi said, yearning for his love, remembering his tenderness.

"The man who wins your love will be very fortunate, Ammi," Ispah said, "for you are very beautiful. I have truly come to love and admire you."

"I feel the same, Ammi. You are very special. Almost all of the daughters admire you very much," said Mahlah. Many of the women of the palace had changed their attitude toward Ammi when they learned that she had found such favor in the eyes of the king.

"That is very kind of you. I have come to love you, too, but I wish I could leave the palace and go back to my home and to Ashur. Will you not help me?"

"Ammi, no. Do not speak foolishly. If you tried to run away, we would have to stop you," said Ispah.

"The king has brought me into the palace, and I am afraid of what will happen," Ammi cried, the fear becoming more real from having spoken the words.

"The king pays you a great honor. We will rejoice for you. All of the daughters are happy for you, except a few foolish ones," said Ispah.

"I am black from the sun, as black as the tents of Kedar. The queens stare at me, and I know I do not belong here," Ammi moaned. She was becoming increasingly uncomfortable from the jealous looks and contempt of some of the other women. She had not been able to care for her beauty, as did these pale, pampered women of the palace.

"My brothers were angry at me because I continued mourning my father. When they caught me alone with Ashur, that awful Sabta told a lie about us. All Ashur did was kiss me when I was leaning back against a tree. For a punishment, they sent me to Baal-Hamon, where they made me a keeper of the vineyards, and I have not been able to keep my own skin fair and soft."

"That is unfair, and it is not true that you do not belong." Mahlah and Ispah started speaking in unison and in dismay that Ammi truly did not realize how beautiful she was. "You have a natural beauty that goes beyond the color of your skin."

"You are darkened by the sun, but you become lighter each day. You will be as beautiful as the curtains of Solomon," Mahlah tried to reassure her, comparing her to the beautiful white curtains of the palace. "We think you are the most beautiful of all because your beauty goes both without and within."

"If I only knew where he was," Ammi said wistfully. "He must be back on the grassy plains, resting his flock somewhere beside still waters."

"If we let you go after him, then you would raise your children in a tent. You would follow your sheep-herder behind a bunch of smelly, dusty sheep," Mahlah added distastefully.

"Solem is not like that at all," Ammi said, thinking of the beautiful country around her village.

"You cannot be so naive that you would give up the luxury of the palace to return to the country," Mahlah said, the idea being ludicrous to her.

"You do not understand, Mahlah. My beloved is not just a simple man of the fields. His father is one of the king's royal purveyors. They raise the finest horses in all the land. Machir was a great warrior, as is his son, my beloved. My beloved Ashur is the youngest of the captains of the militia." The more she avowed her love for this young man, the more curious about him they became. "He is a warrior, yet he is a gentle, sensitive man. He walks among the flowers of the field and is at peace."

"My dear," said Ispah, "you must think what you are doing. No one has ever refused King Solomon. I would not want to imagine what he might do.

One word from the king and you will never find fulfillment. You are young. Solomon can keep you as one of the virgins forever. You will never have children. Would it not be better to have someone than never to know a man, especially if that man is one like King Solomon?"

"People say that King Solomon's father put his wife aside for disrespect. She ridiculed him for dancing in the street with the common people, and he never touched her again," Ispah said. "Solomon put his own brother to death over a woman." Her tone trailed off in fear, realizing she had uttered these words.

"What she says is true," echoed Mahlah. "You will be beautiful for many years and are sure to attract much of Solomon's attention. You must forget this young man, this Ashur."

The words that followed sent fear rushing through Ammi. "If you ever try to see the young man again, King Solomon will put him to death, and perhaps you, too," Ispah whispered.

Fear gripped Ammi so that she felt that even her heart bled tears. She made excuses so that she could be alone. Alone in her room, she took the miniature signet ring that Ashur had given her from around her neck. She held it tightly in her hand, wiping away the tears from her eyes with her closed hand. "I am destined to a different kind of slavery," she thought, remembering how as a young girl she had escaped the thieves and the slave market of Edom.

When she could control her emotions, she took a pen and the fine papyrus and wrote a short note to Ashur, telling him that she must never see him again. She accepted the inevitable and now must sacrifice her own happiness.

"Our love cannot be. You must find another. Shoshanna has always loved you," she wrote. "Let her love you now, and give to her all the love you have for me." This was the right thing to do, Ammi thought. She knew Ashur was very fond of Shoshanna, and the feeling could grow into love. Ashur had the power to return happiness to Shoshanna's life.

She also wrote to him of the incredible series of events that had led King Solomon to adopt the emblem on their rings as his own royal seal. She knew full well that Ashur would feel that the king had taken everything from him. There were so many things she wished she had said to him in person.

She called in her own special servant and gave him the little ring and note. "Take this ring to Ashur, of the house of Machir, near the village of Solem. Let no one see the note but Ashur," she instructed the servant.

"What shall I say to him, mistress?" the servant asked wearily, thinking of the long journey ahead. Ammi started to tell the servant to tell Ashur good-bye, but the words failed her.

"Just give him the letter and the ring," she instructed.

* * *

The mistress of the daughters intercepted the servant, but when she read the contents of the message, she nodded approvingly to herself and sent the servant on his way. She was mystified, however, by

450

the revelation that Ammi and Ashur bore rings identical to the king's royal seal. Why had the king not confiscated the ring? And what, if anything, should she tell the king? Would it not be better for the king to believe that Ammi came to him willingly?

* * *

Ashur received word that Ammi would marry King Solomon long before the servant arrived with Ammi's message. He was deeply distressed. He knew he could not conceal his pain, nor could he stand having his mother see him suffer. He quietly told his mother he was going hunting and prepared to leave for the oasis house on the eastern edge of his father's land.

"I am glad your father is away at Aram," she said, concern in her voice. "He would not like seeing you this way."

In the solitude of the oasis house, he could vent his anguish and frustration. He knew that there was no man on earth to whom he could appeal. No one could oppose the will of the king.

***

The evening of the next day found Ammi's servant resting beneath the terebinth tree near the village of Solem and drinking heavily from a wineskin. He planned to go into the village the next morning and inquire as to the whereabouts of Machir's lands and of Ashur. He staggered over to the pool, washed the dust from his face, and soaked his feet in the cool water. After he tethered the mule and prepared his bed, he took out of his pack the meager meal one of the kitchen servants had prepared for him.

In the gathering dusk, he did not notice the papyrus note as it fell to the ground. He paid no attention to the sounds of the night or to the faint rustling in the hollow tree behind him. In the middle of the night, the rustling became so loud that the old servant's mule paused from his grazing. A little pack rat emerged from the hole at the bottom of the tree.

As the night grew older, the mouse became bolder. Soon he was curiously investigating the ground around the sleeping man. The mouse found nothing to eat but a few crumbs of bread left over from the servant's evening meal. He was on the way back to the safety of his nest in the tree when he found the rolled papyrus note lying on the ground. After testing the fabric with his sharp teeth, he found that properly shredded, it would make excellent bedding material for his nest. With considerable effort, the pack rat dragged the small roll of papyrus to the hollow in the tree. The rat was still gnawing industriously at dawn as the servant was again on his way to Solem in search of Ashur.

* * *

"The melek reeh wishes an audience with King Solomon," the servant requested timorously. The servant was afraid to send the melek reeh away, even though he had been told that the king would receive no one.

"Send him away. Have I not told you that the king wishes to see no one?" Solomon responded angrily. The servant hurried away, relieved that he had received no stronger rebuke.

When the melek reeh learned that the king would not see him, he was both humiliated and hurt. "I am the melek reeh, the friend of the king," Zabud growled, emphasizing the full force and meaning of his title. "Surely the king will see me. He must have misunderstood. Go to him again. Make sure that he understands it is the friend of the king who requests an audience."

"I dare not, master," the servant said respectfully, but making it clear that he would not again risk the wrath of the king for anyone. When Zabud was convinced that no further appeal would help, he took his leave.

Each succeeding day deepened the rift between the king and the melek reeh. King Solomon decided he could no longer tolerate interference from Zabud. The spiritual leader of Israel, the king's most loyal friend was no longer allowed access. Solomon had now succeeded in isolating himself.

* * *

"Aaaaaaargh!" The primal roar reverberated through the house and outside. The sounds of wildlife fell silent, and Chazad took refuge under a bench, where he cowered.

In the seclusion of the oasis house, Ashur gave vent to the crushing grief of losing Ammi. Their friendship was even greater than the emotion and excitement of being man and woman. He agonized at the thought that he would no longer be able to see her, talk with her, touch her. He lay tossing on the bed. "I am so alone, so alone. My soul calls to her. Curses come to my lips. Ah, Elohim, why have you let this happen to me? What have I done to deserve this? Let me die. Oh, Elohim, the pain that burns my heart suffocates me. My skull feels as though it will fall in pieces. I am sick with love, Elohim, my God."

When he could sleep at all, Pithon was in his dreams. Pithon was holding him down, laughing and spitting in his face. He was mocked and humiliated. "Your woman belongs to the king now," he laughed. Sabta was there, too, and then the whole village was laughing and ridiculing him.

Ashur awakened from the half-sleep, half-nightmare and staggered from his bed. For days, he could not eat, and the severe headaches and nausea continued robbing him of his will to live and reduced the valiant young man to hopeless despair. He came to realize it was ineffectual to rage against Elohim. He could not strike him. He could not touch him. He could not even see him to know that he had disappointed or grieved him.

Doubts began to assail him. He questioned whether Ammi cared for him as deeply as she had professed. "Perhaps the king has truly won her love away from me," he thought, trying to stem a flood of guilt. He knew there were times when he had not fully appreciated the love she had for him. Ashur thought back to the time they had met as children, when Ammi left the desert gardenia on his knapsack. He thought of the times he had been with her as he had grown into a young man and she into a young woman. This beautiful flower, so delicately and wonderfully made, was a symbol of their love. The fragrance of these memories was forever burned into his mind.

Again and again he struggled to gain control of himself, only to dissolve into angry, sobbing defeat. Thoughts of Ammi with Solomon haunted his nights. "His hands on my beautiful Ammi," he moaned. Jealousy truly was as cruel as the grave. When he was rational, he tried to reason with himself. "I am not unique; others have suffered as I am suffering. Why am I so weak? I am not weak with other things," he raged. "Why am I so weak with this?" Without her, he felt he must shrivel up and die.

Finally, his mind-struggle reached far beyond himself to a new part of his spirit. "Gird up your loins, my son, like a man." The words came to him, but he did not know their source.

A new thought dawned on Ashur like a new day. "What is it that makes me different from Solomon?" he thought. "My spirit is different. Solomon wants her to satisfy his own lusts. I want her to love." A new resolve came to him. He knew that he must do something to avert this feeling of being suspended in time.

As if he were in a trance, he went down to the clear pool and washed himself. He stopped under a lone tree on the hillside to clear his eyes and wipe his face and brow. The tree was the first object he had focused on in days. This lone olive tree was as unique as the terebinth tree near Solem. Typically, it was in the process of resurrecting itself. From the same root grew a healthy and mature trunk, a young sapling springing forth, and a rotten, dying stump. He returned to his couch, where he collapsed into a deep sleep.

When he awakened, he left immediately for his home. There he found his mother anxiously waiting his return. He was relieved to learn that Machir had not yet come back from his trip to Aram to purchase new mares to breed.

Ammi's servant arrived shortly after Ashur returned from the old oasis house. "The lady Ammi sent me to give this ring to you," the servant reported unconcernedly. His eyes grew larger, though, as he groped unsuccessfully in the sack for the missing note.

"What did Ammi say? Did she tell you anything to say to me?" Ashur hurriedly demanded of the servant. He remembered telling Ammi that if she ever needed him, to send the signet ring to him.

"No, master, the lady spoke no message." The servant answered with a half-truth, avoiding mention of the note. "I asked the lady if she wanted me to tell you anything, but she told me only to give the ring to you."

The servant's mind raced ahead, trying to remember where he might have misplaced the note. "I must get out of view where I can search my clothes," he thought, so he quickly bid Ashur farewell. The look of extreme distress on the young man's face frightened the servant.

After a thorough search of his person, he hurried back toward the old terebinth tree by the pool. That was the only place he had opened his knapsack. "I must have lost the note when I stopped to rest," he thought. Perhaps he could find it and return to Ashur, saying that he had forgotten to give it to him. "If the mistress of the daughters finds out I have lost the note, she is sure to have me punished," he lamented to himself. He struck the old mule again on the flank, trying to urge the animal to greater speed.

***

Solomon conversed with his wisest officers and advisors. These men were most skillful at prompting the conversation to subjects on which he could demonstrate his vast knowledge to impress Ammi.

"What do you think, sweet maiden?" Solomon inquired of Ammi.

The question interrupted her daydreaming. Since it was obvious to Solomon that she had not heard the question, he repeated it to her.

"The fact is that all the rivers of the world appear to run into the sea, yet the sea is not full nor the lands flooded. How would you explain such a phenomenon, young maiden?"

"Well, my lord, I guess the Lord Elohim takes some water out of the sea so he can water the earth and trees and grass," Ammi stated without hesitation.

"Ha, har-rum," Solomon cleared his throat and grimaced slightly. The young woman had just stated quite simply his own conclusion, the conclusion he had reached after years of scientific study of the process of evaporation and precipitation. "Perhaps I have underestimated this young woman," thought Solomon. He would have to find other ways of impressing her than the ones that had worked on her predecessors.

Solomon had never met anyone like Ammi. She truly was not interested in the wealth, pomp, and ceremony of the palace. She exhibited no vanity and maintained a single-minded fidelity to Ashur, the son of Machir of Solem.

Solomon offered Ammi his favorite drink, the intoxicating arak. He began to drink heavily himself. "She will become much more cooperative," he thought, "if she will drink some of the arak, nibbling at her food the way she has." The possibility of the beautiful young woman losing her inhibitions intrigued him.

Ammi sipped from the cup obediently, then set it down and continued nibbling at the food before her. Despite further urging by Solomon, Ammi soberly refused to take any more of the liquid. Finally, the frustrated Solomon abruptly ended the celebration and withdrew to his private chambers.

In his bedchamber, Solomon continued drinking. He dismissed Telamai, his personal servant, and threw himself across his couch. He tried to sleep, but still the frustrations of the evening weighed heavily on his troubled mind. Who did this woman think she was? He was the king. He did not have to fawn over her. He could take her now and do whatever he wanted with her. "All the kingdoms of the earth are mine," Solomon grandly overstated as he stumbled to his feet.

Purpose now gave steadiness to his drink-clouded mind. He had cleverly designed the palace with a secret corridor that allowed him to visit any one of the women without the others knowing of it. When he reached Ammi's door, he swung it open with a crash. The noise brought guards with drawn swords and servants running, but the king angrily waved them away. He entered Ammi's bedchamber. In the dim lamplight, he could see the girl cowering in a corner of the room. Without hesitation, he strode across the room and dragged her to her feet. Her protests gave way to loud screams. As he held her, he saw through his drunken stupor that the girl was not Ammi. He cast her aside, left the bedchamber, and staggered back down the hallway. The guards exchanged nervous glances, then resumed walking their assigned corridors.

* * *

Solomon nursed his splitting head and listened unbelievingly to the report of the mistress of the daughters.

"Ammi was down in the garden when you burst into her bedchamber. The girl that you attacked was one of the daughters, one Iscah by name. I implore you not to punish her. She attempted to identify herself. She knew she was not the one you desired but was unable to get the king to listen to her pleas. I had assigned Iscah as lady-in-waiting to Ammi. She had entered Ammi's chambers at the precise moment the king entered."

"Assure the young woman that she will not be punished. See that she receives an honored position among the concubines," Solomon said to the mistress, embarrassed by the incident. "Does the maiden of Solem know what happened?" Solomon asked.

"No, master, I took Iscah to my own quarters while the maiden Ammi was in the garden. I told the maiden that Iscah had taken ill. No one knows but this faithful servant, sire," the mistress said devotedly.

The mistress did not mention the guards, for she knew they would never mention a word of the incident to anyone. She could tell from the king's expression that he was pleased with her handling of the situation, and he went on to tell her so.

"Well done. The king is grateful for your dedication.

"The maiden Ammi is exceptional, is she not?" Solomon said, wishing to change the subject and at the same time somehow justify his behavior.

"She is, sire. The woman of Solem has grace and beauty beyond all the others," replied the mistress without hesitation. "You will kill in her what you most desire, if you force her." Fearing that she had said too much, she took leave of the king and went at once to comfort Iscah. The girl would be consoled to learn that she would receive an honored position among the concubines.

* * *

Solomon could contain himself only one day short of a week before he continued his efforts to curry

favor with Ammi. His previous fail-
ures had served only to fuel his
determination.

"Have one of the peacocks brought
to me," he told one of the servants. The servant returned, leading
the beautiful creature on a string.
Solomon leaned near Ammi. "The tail
of the peacock has a thousand eyes to
observe your beauty." However, just
as he said this, the peacock chose
this particular moment to relieve
itself on the floor of the palace,
totally ruining the effect of the
compliment. Solomon observed Ammi
recoil involuntarily at this indiscretion on the part of the beautiful bird.

Muttering oaths under his breath,
Solomon took the servant aside.
"Have one of the axe men separate
the beast from its head, and let
the vultures have its carcass." He
returned to his seat beside Ammi as
though nothing had happened. Angrily
he thought, could nothing go right
with this maiden?

"I wish to show you something,"
he said smoothly, leading Ammi out
of the tainted room and into his

private bedchamber. "Sit here on the couch." The reluctant Ammi did as she was bidden. Perhaps he could use the fiasco of the peacock to his advantage.

The servant had sent one of the ladies-in-waiting ahead into his bed-chamber with instructions to light the incense lamps. When they entered the room, a strong, ambrosial odor pervaded the air. Musicians played from an adjoining room, unseen and unseeing.

"Master, I am grateful that you rescued me from the foxes, but I am promised to another," Ammi said.

"You have doves' eyes, my love," Solomon said, waxing poetic as he reclined on the couch beside her. With a short movement of his wrist, he dismissed the lady-in-waiting.

Leaning close to Ammi, he continued his words, describing aloud her beauty. His powerful nearness made his words unbidden caresses. "You are like a private garden, a spring that no one can have, a fountain for me alone. Your hair is like that of the black leopardess flashing in the sun, yet as soft as the loins of a lamb."

Trailing his fingertips lightly up her neck, he tilted her head back so he could admire the delicate beauty of her skin where it merged into chin and cheek.

Ignoring her protests that she was promised to another, he became bolder. That he assumed success was no accident, since he had been successful with countless women before. His magnificence was evident, but the cunning of his wooing of each individual woman bordered on witchcraft. Even the most unattainable had become weak and trembling under Solomon's touch.

Solomon's hand trailed down Ammi's neck again and paused just above her breasts. "Your breasts are like twin fawns that feed among the lilies," he said, calling attention to the softness of her finely developed bosom. "Come with me to the mountains. When the heat of summer comes, I will take you to my hunting lodges on Amana, Shenir, and Mount Hermon, as well as to the mountain of the leopards. You have ravished my heart, my sister, my bride. You have ravished my heart with one glance.

"Your soft words are like milk and honey. Your lips are like a scarlet thread." He described the delicate contrast between her lips and the natural beauty of her face. He continued, overly profuse in the praise of her beauty. "Your mouth is altogether lovely. Your—" His words were interrupted as she moved away from him to the windows.

He marveled at the freshness and perfection of her beauty as the light outlined her form beneath the too thin, shimmering gown. "Alas, such beauty is given to a young woman for such a short time," he thought. "She is like a gazelle standing beside a stream, delicate and mincing, ready to flee the lion or the leopard."

Her next words jolted him like none before. "Excuse me, sire, I must get some fresh air," Ammi said, finding herself light-headed from the effect of the incense. She turned from him and went to the doorway leading into the garden. She ran down the stairs, through the garden to the staircase, and ascended the stairs to the outer wall. On the apex of the wall she paused, staring at the basalt pavement below.

"God save her," Solomon breathed. "She's going to jump." From his vantage point, he could look down into the terraced gardens.

Shouts of confusion from his guards and a cloud of dust from a chariot coming down the road claimed his attention. The man driving the chariot maneuvered around and over the obstacles that had been placed for the very purpose of upsetting any chariots that might charge up to the palace. Solomon found himself admiring the skill of the driver as the chariot careened around and over obstacles. Amazingly, the wheels remained intact.

Only one man could drive a chariot with such skill. Ashur, clad in the full battle armor of a captain of militia, drove Tirsah and his brother toward the palace. The sash of blue cloth denoting his rank whipped in the wind. The chariot crossed the forbidden area and charged up to the wall of the palace.

Solomon saw that the uniform of the driver confused the guards. A dozen archers with bows drawn looked to him for a signal before releasing certain death on Ashur. Men rushed from all directions to position themselves between Solomon and the intruder.

One such soldier was Pithon. When he recognized Ashur through a peephole in the gate, he was beside himself, trying to clamber up the stairs to the top of the wall where he himself would shout to the archers to fire. Driven by his jealousy and hatred of Ashur, he cursed as he struggled to gain the wall above him. Pithon reached the next-to-last step, and then, in his haste, he stumbled and fell. His knee crashed into the unforgiving stone, leaving him writhing in pain.

"Come back, come back!" the daughters of Jerusalem shouted as they ran after Ammi. Without hesitation, Ammi leaped off the wall and into Ashur's waiting arms. Before she knew it, she was beside her prince in the chariot. Ashur turned Tirsah around, and they were away again, before Solomon's raised arm could descend.

Armed men in chariots came up at the shouting of the captain of the guard. They reined in their horses there below Solomon when they saw the archers standing at ease. "Shall we pursue them, sire?" they shouted.

"Will you kill him as your father killed your mother's husband?" The voice came from behind him and belonged to Queen Osoris. "You often confided in me that you would never make the same mistake that King David, your father, made. You also have told me that you have suffered greatly from having put your brother Adonijah to death."

"What you say is true. You have saved me from doing a terrible thing, Osoris."

Much of the anger drained out of King Solomon. He marveled at the courage of Ashur. Surely a warrior of such valor must be spared. Ammi had maintained all along that she was pledged to another, and there was the mystery of the ring. Her escape from him had been miraculous. He marveled that she trusted Ashur enough to leap from the wall as she had. If he had not caught her, she surely would have broken her neck.

"What does the maiden of Solem have that I do not?" asked Queen Osoris. "I know that we have different spirits and that I am unable to satisfy you, but I do love you as much as I am able."

"She is as magnificent as a company of two armies arrayed for battle," Solomon said in answer to the queen's question. He thought of that moment years earlier when he had looked down upon Pharaoh Siamun's chariots at Gezer. The last image he had imprinted in his mind was of Ammi's long black hair streaming out behind her as the chariot faded from sight.

The jealous Queen Osoris led the king away from the window and began to dance before him, letting her garments fall away. Her control while she seduced him had always been a tremendous attraction to him. She was able to maintain her perfect poise while disrobing, without smiles or undue self-consciousness. For pure sexual delight, she satisfied his lusts. She came closer to him, caressing his face with her hands. The rich fullness of her body pulled him toward her. Here, certainly, was one woman who wanted him.

* * *

Ashur drove the chariot recklessly back through the maze and was well down the road before he allowed himself a backward glance. Ammi clung to him, and the look they exchanged brought joy and happiness surging through him. He reined in Tirsah and looked back toward the palace. No one was following them. Tenderly he brushed the soft wisps of hair from her face, and then he embraced Ammi hard, their lips crushed together. The sweetness of the kiss was made infinitely deeper by the trials they had shared.

"I love you with all my heart. You are everything to me. They will have to kill me to take you away from me again," Ashur swore.

"Your love will be a banner of protection over me even till death, when we enter a new life beyond. We will begin it together," Ammi said.

That one embrace was all Ashur had hoped for in his wild charge to the death. Ashur realized with sinking heart there was nowhere they could go beyond the reach of Solomon.

Tirsah was limping slightly. Both of the horses labored to catch their breath. He dismounted from the chariot and bent down to run his hand over Tirsah's foreleg. Ashur looked back toward the city, but no one was pursuing them. The superbly conditioned horses quickly regained their breath. Ashur again put his horses to the gallop, but not at such a hard pace. He saw no sense in waiting around for pursuers to overtake them. Pithon, the king's avenger, would come after them. He would not come alone. The offense was too great, Ashur thought. Every moment together was precious.

He stopped at the Kidron River to allow the horses to water and to take a short rest. Ammi stepped down from the chariot to attempt mending her torn gown. When she looked up, Ashur was staring at her. She first thought he was staring at her flimsy attire. She was still wearing the dress of a harem girl. Instead, his eyes were fixed on her face. There was no condemnation in his gaze. Praise and love filled his eyes. He said nothing. No words were necessary. Ammi dropped her eyes, abashed that he was watching her, and then she met his in a moment of mutual admiration.

***

Later Solomon lay awake beside the sleeping Osoris. He thought again of the beautiful Ammi, but he knew that it was too late for him. "This is my portion in life. This is all there is for me," he thought despondently.

The king went into another room, alone, and sat amid his beloved musical instruments. He picked up one of the lyres. He lay back against the pillows, playing meaningless chords to himself. With great power had come a feeling of needing to account to no one, of needing no one. With great power had come loneliness. He had experienced the best that life could give. However, he had missed out on—how had Ammi expressed it?

"The all-consuming love of one woman for one man." As he lay staring into the darkness, he confessed to himself his great loneliness. "I began my life a wise and happy man," he thought. "What has happened to me?"

Now he was left with only a haunting regret. The women he had taken indifferently—and there were so many—now exacted their measure of revenge. His thoughts went to one and then to another: Abishag, whose high-strung temperament had attracted him and later caused her downfall; Sheva, whose breathless body he had found to be her only attraction. Would he always compare the last with the first?

Here again the prophets were correct in assuming that one woman for one man was the best course. If a man were successful in obtaining that one woman who fulfilled all his desires, he would have no comparison and no regrets. He would not be left with this aching void of wanting to retrieve moments from the past, of wanting to combine a body with a face, a passionate embrace, a seductive look, nebulous dreams.

The thoughts were ridiculous.
They left him with emptiness. He had
enjoyed a selection privilege that
most men would die for. All this had
dissolved into a wistful melancholy.
He was envied by all men but haunted
by bits and pieces of the past.

He thought of the signet ring. He
wondered why Ashur had been found
wearing the signet ring with the same
symbol he had adopted. The men he had
sent to Rabbah to find Jetur, who was
thought to have made his father's
ring, had come back empty-handed.
Jetur was dead. He had left no wife,
no sons, and no daughters. No one
remained of whom to inquire as to
the origin of the symbol of the ring.
The meaning of the symbol had apparently perished with Jetur and his
own father. Solomon had searched the
code at length until he found a
scripture referring to a star, the
symbol on the ring: "There will come
a star out of Jacob and a scepter
will rise out of Israel." Who was
this star that would rule Israel?

"I have searched all things under
the sun for happiness," he thought.
"I have gathered to me great riches

such as the world has never seen, golden shields coveted by all of the kings of the earth. I have built great palaces, hunting lodges in the mountains, gardens and pools of unsurpassed beauty. I have great power; all of the people of my kingdom, both great and small, bow down before me. I have studied until my wisdom surpasses all men who have gone before me, but now it is wearisome to me.

"I have given myself over to every pleasure: to wine, to my lust for women, and to the enjoyment of the offspring of these women, my sons and daughters. Again and again, I have looked on a beautiful woman and said to myself, 'If I have that woman, I will be satisfied,' but then I saw another and then another. I have indulged in every conceivable pleasure.

"But now, the limitations of the human mind and the eventual failing of the most perfect of bodies are painfully evident. The throbbing of the ever-present tooth worm has returned to remind me so. Now it has all come down to this, an emptiness of spirit."

There remained a great yearning—a yearning for what, he did not know. A search for completeness, he could not find—a search for the other half of one's self.

Was it possible that this mystery of love, of life, was a shadowy picture of the relationship Elohim expected to have with his people? Here, too, Solomon thought, the most important things in life were those of the spirit, as they were with the woman. The prophets called Elohim a jealous God, a God who demanded absolute fidelity. So might it be—a jealousy without imperfection.

Was the marriage and love of one man for one woman and the love she returned to him a picture of this greater love? Or was love only the search for love, an end in itself? Could a man even find happiness on earth with this one woman, apart from Elohim? Would this then be their only portion in life? Would they have no part in eternity?

When Ammi had spoken to him of her love for Ashur, she had spoken of her "loves." The word she used in his tongue was plural. Her words troubled him. This woman spoke of a love of body and of soul.

He felt a feeling of panic. He had satisfied his sexual drives with many women, but now he found that he had other needs. The women of the harem fulfilled his body, but not his heart or soul. Ammi had discerned that he wanted her for his own gratification. Was this love of which she spoke an emotion apart from the intellect? Must there be a tenderness of spirit, a wanting to give, to sacrifice, to die for? Could there be a difference?

Ammi apparently owned the capacity to love both with her physical being and with her soul. If two were to love each other in this way, then there would be coalescence of souls, a union of two spirits. This greater love would be free from any selfish motives, a selfless love. Love was the strongest emotion of the human heart and the purest. Was this the love that this young man and woman shared for each other? Did they know what they had? It was something for which he would give half his kingdom. He groaned inwardly. Was this why he had found no fulfillment? He felt a deep sense of despair. Of all the women he had taken, only Osoris had he attempted to love in this way, although Osoris herself had said that she was of a different spirit.

Solomon walked across the room and opened a scroll, words written by his father and left for him. The words leaped out at him with new meaning: "The sacrifices of Elohim are a broken spirit; a broken and contrite heart, O Elohim, thou wilt not despise."

He thought of his father and the words of Queen Osoris. She had surely saved him from doing a terrible thing. He felt no vindictiveness in his heart now. He smiled to himself in the darkness, thinking of the courage and devotion of the young lovers. Love indeed was stronger than death.

He rose and went into the hallway to locate one of the oil lamps. When he had pen and parchment in hand, he began to write. He went on to record these thoughts: "Let your fountain be blessed; and rejoice with the wife of your youth. Let her be as the loving hind and pleasant roe;

let her breasts satisfy you at all times; and be ravished always with her love."

Then, another and different thought led him to take another parchment upon which he began writing. When he finished recording the words, he took the signet ring and affixed his seal, making it an official decree. He summoned an officer of the royal guard and sent him out with the edict.

CHAPTER 15

The Chariot Battle . . . to the Death

*A*shur again stopped Tirsah and his brother, near Solem where a small stream crossed the road. He knew the place well. Clear waters meandered along the edge of a field and cascaded over a cliff. He had admired the little waterfall from below, on the Megiddon plain. The horses stood ankle deep in the shallows, drinking from the cool water. He watched them carefully to be sure they did not drink too much.

Tirsah snorted and lifted his head to look back toward Jerusalem.

Sounds of an approaching chariot caused Ashur's heart to sink. He did not have to see the man's face. He knew who he would be. The distinctive strip of black bear's hide Pithon wore confirmed his fears. Ashur was surprised to see that his old enemy was alone. He guessed the king's avenger must have outdistanced the other warriors.

Ashur guided Tirsah off the rutted road. He gazed around the field. A rock formation stood on one edge. A dense thicket of buck brush bordered the other side. A couple of trees grew in the field beside the thicket. The setting sun lay beyond the cliff's edge. He drove to the rocks, lifted Ammi from the chariot, and deposited her on the flat stones. "Stay here," he said, cupping her face lovingly with his hand.

"Ashur, I am afraid," she said, clinging to him. He had to remove her hands from his neck.

"I know," he said gently. "We knew it would come to this."

He turned the horses to face his adversary. Tirsah and his brother gathered themselves as though they

sensed the gravity of the situation. The few minutes of rest and
the short drink from the stream had
revived them.

Pithon's horses looked no fresher
than his own, and as usual, he drove
them without mercy. They attempted
to drink from the stream, but Pithon
lashed out with his whip, urged them
into the field, and roughly reined to
a halt. He paused a moment to put
away the whip and to take a javelin
from the carriage. Then he set his
matched team toward Ashur.

Ashur pulled gently on the leather
reins. The gallant steeds responded,
cantering toward the approaching
horses. "Attack, Tirsah," he commanded. The stallion went to a
full gallop. His brother followed
his lead.

Pithon threw his javelin first.
Confirming the errant flight, Ashur
flung his own javelin. Both missiles
sailed harmlessly over their tar-
gets and sliced into the ground.
The two chariots passed very close.
However, neither man had sufficient
time to take up another weapon.
For an instant, Ashur saw Pithon's

face. His features contorted with the unnatural hate Ashur could not understand. They retreated to opposite sides of the field to rearm.

Pithon immediately wheeled his chariot about and whipped the horses with his reins. They leaped forward as one, pounding hooves throwing up bits of earth. Pithon hurled another javelin. This time Tirsah was the target. The spear sailed over the horse's back, missing by the width of a hand. Ashur's second throw was almost simultaneous with that of his enemy. The spear pierced deep into the side panel of the chariot. Pithon broke off the point and tossed the shaft aside. Again they withdrew to rearm. The two well-trained teams turned, cantered, then charged again.

Ashur knew Pithon preferred the battle-axe. Sure enough, he saw Pithon take the axe from its place on the side of the chariot. His sword was useless to parry the huge weapon. Ashur tied the reins around his waist and took his shield from the side of the chariot. As they passed, Pithon wielded the battle-axe high overhead. Then he slashed low, intending upon landing a fatal blow to Ashur's midsection. Ashur was well aware of his exposed belly and confident of his ability to move quickly out of harm's way. At the exact moment, he knotted his stomach muscles and drew back. Superb reflexes prevented the axe from splitting him in two.

Lunging out, he struck with his sword and landed a sharp slash across Pithon's arm. The handle of the axe prevented a critical blow. At the sight of his own blood, Pithon's curses gave way to a bellow of rage. The combatants maneuvered around the field in a tight curve, withdrawing to ready their weapons for another pass.

Pithon immediately turned and whipped his horses into another attack. Taking a gamble on a practiced skill, he threw the heavy axe. This Ashur did not expect. The projectile glanced off the rim of the carriage and struck Ashur in his chest armor. Simultaneously the chariot bounced over a low place, and he lost his balance. His head and shoulder crashed into the side of the chariot. Ashur struggled to keep his footing on the rawhide floor. His father's innovative shock absorber, the rawhide, helped him maintain control. By grabbing the rim of the quarter round, he avoided falling from the chariot.

Tirsah and his brother were tiring and were slow in executing a withdrawal. The miles traveled through the day had taken a toll. Pithon, seeing this, began a chasing maneuver. He ripped another axe from its binding and sought to overtake them from the rear.

Ashur frantically urged the exhausted horses forward and guided them toward the two isolated trees near the cliff's edge. Horses and chariot successfully passed through the trees, and he turned them sharply away from the drop-off. Wheels grated on the rocky ground.

Behind him, the sound of thundering hoofs told Ashur that Pithon's chariot had also passed through the trees. As Pithon made his turn, the sun emerged from behind clouds and temporarily blinded him. He jerked the reins sharply. This caused one of his horses to stumble, throwing his weight against the side of his partner. The wheels skidded sideward on the rocky soil. The chariot slid until the right wheel went out into space. The horses, chariot, and Pithon teetered on the brink.

Pithon cursed loudly. Weight and momentum pulled all over the edge. Pithon leaped from the bed of the chariot as it went over the side. He fell heavily on the edge of the precipice, clawing for a handhold. Before Ashur could consider saving him, he fell away. The screaming stopped abruptly when he hit the rocks below.

Ashur dismounted and walked to the edge of the precipice to view the crumpled bodies. There was no movement, not even a twitch from the horses. The sudden ending to his conflict with Pithon stunned him. He had fully expected either to kill the man or be killed but could not have foreseen this ending.

Ashur turned to look back again in the direction of Jerusalem, then returned to Ammi. She wiped a trickle of blood from his chest with a piece of her torn gown. This made him aware of the pain in his ribs caused by the collision with the frame of the chariot.

"Pithon was an evil man, full of hate," she consoled. "I am glad, though, that you did not kill him. He killed himself."

***

The final rays of evening were casting shadows across the hills when Ashur and Ammi arrived on the outskirts of Solem. Tirsah was going lame, adding to Ashur's distress. There would be no fleeing now. Ashur stepped down from the chariot to examine Tirsah's leg. He ran his hand over the swollen limb. Ammi's emotions were moved with compassion, seeing the concern in his eyes. He had risked all for her.

"I wish you were as a brother to me so that every time I saw you, I could kiss you openly," Ammi said. "I could have loved you all this time without anyone disapproving. Come with me into my mother's house. We will be husband and wife. We will drink pomegranate wine together, and you will teach me of love. Your left hand will be behind my head, and your right hand will caress me. I said to the daughters of Jerusalem not to awaken my love until love pleases, and now she pleases."

"Come, my beloved, let us go forth into the fields together, or we will lodge in the village forever," Ashur proposed, giving her the chance to express a preference for where they would live. He tried to put aside the fact that they were fugitives from the king's wrath. "We will get up early in the morning to work in the vineyards together, and we will watch the etrog trees bloom. There will I give you my loves," he said, using the plural that Ammi used to express love to him.

"Set me as a seal on your heart, and as the signet on my hand," Ashur said to Ammi, referring to the signet ring he now wore on his finger. "For love is as strong as death. Jealousy is as cruel as the grave. The flames of love are as the *salhebhethyah*, the flame of God."

"Many waters cannot quench our love," Ammi responded. "Neither can the floods drown it. If a man offered all his wealth for love, he would be utterly despised."

* * *

Ammi's mother and brothers were retiring to the roof, as was their custom in the evening. Ammi's mother caught sight of them first.

"Look, it is Ammi in a chariot with Ashur!" she exclaimed excitedly. They ran down the stairs and outside. She embraced her daughter warmly. When they were all inside the house, Ammi related the story of her escape from the palace. She omitted telling them of the death of Pithon, the king's avenger.

"King Solomon let you ride away with Ashur?" her mother asked in an incredulous voice. "He must have allowed you to leave, yet I do not see how he could forgive so great an offense," she said fearfully, wringing her hands.

"I belong to Ashur, not the king. I will give my loves to him," Ammi said, maintaining her unshakable vow.

At this, one of her brothers spoke, adopting the recently learned metaphor-like speech of the court. "We have a little sister, and she has no breasts," said her elder brother.

"What shall we do for our sister in the day when she shall be spoken for?" asked the younger brother.

"If she be a wall, we will give her a rich dowry, but if she be a door, we will enclose her with boards of cedar, as a casket."

"Why do you not say what you mean?" Ammi asked angrily. "I am a virgin, and my breasts are like towers to my love. His desire is unto me. You did not think me too young to marry the king," she reminded them. "King Solomon saw me at Baal-Hamon and took me into the palace, where I became one of the daughters, but my virtue is still mine." Ammi continued, explaining how she had fallen into the king's hands but was successful in resisting his efforts to seduce her.

"I made a terrible mistake allowing you to be sent away as I did," Ammi's mother acknowledged. "Can you ever forgive me? I was so saddened by the death of your father that I failed to see how much you loved this young man and how much he loved you. He was willing to lay down his life for you. And you two—" She turned to face her sons. "You two had better make friends with your brother-to-be, or I will disown both of you! With your father gone, the decision is mine. You can also ask your sister for her forgiveness for the wrong that you have done her. You might have gotten both of them killed."

That thought sobered the two young men because they did love their younger sister. Both of them went to her and hugged and kissed her. "Please forgive us, sister. We thought you were too young for marriage, and then we were intimidated by the king," the elder brother said.

Ammi turned to Ashur, sensing that the time was right for him to make his marriage declaration. "I will marry your daughter," Ashur said to Ammi's mother. "If the king lets me live I will—"

Ashur was interrupted by an authoritative knock at the door. When Ammi's brother opened the door, outside stood a uniformed and stern-faced officer of the king. The family's frightened servant stood behind him. Ashur put his arm around Ammi protectively; she held him tightly, fearing the worst.

"Is this the house of the king's Royal K'nani, the sons of Dedan?" the officer demanded.

"You have the right place," Ammi's elder brother replied in a subdued voice.

"I have this message from the king," he said, handing a roll of parchment to the eldest brother. "A like message is being delivered to the house of Machir," he added, with an admiring grin directed toward Ashur, whom he recognized standing in the background. The officer turned and abruptly left.

Ammi's elder brother anxiously unrolled the parchment, which read:

DECREE AND PARDON

From the hand of the king of peace and ruler of all the lands of Hamath in the north to the great rivers in the south are written these words:

"I give this decree and pardon to Ashur, son of Machir, my brave warrior and captain of the militia, and unto Ammi, daughter of Dedan, my little sister. Let no man harm these, my children, expecting a reward from King Solomon, for that man shall meet with certain death. I order a hedge of protection about them wherever they may travel in this land. These words are written as a grace offering in memory of King David, my beloved father. Let these words be posted and obeyed throughout the land."

On the decree, King Solomon had affixed his official seal. The symbol that matched Ashur's signet ring was the Magen David, the six-cornered star, the Star of David.

CHAPTER 16

Ammi's Song

*T*he sound of trumpets signaled the beginning of festivities to a huge crowd gathered outside of Solem. Ashur's friend Sadoc had volunteered to be responsible for security. He moved through the fringe of the crowd until he came alongside the man he had been watching.

"Aren't you a stranger here in Solem?" Sadoc's face framed a disarming smile.

"Yes," the stranger replied. "I'm just passing through on my way to Jerusalem."

"Where are you from?"

"My home is in Hitti. I stopped here to inquire about some horses, but the man I wanted to see is involved in the festivities. They tell me his son is getting married today."

"You must be referring to Machir. His son is marrying one of the maidens of Solem."

"She is very beautiful," the stranger remarked as the wedding procession approached. "I have never seen so many people at a wedding ceremony before. He must be an important officer in your army. He is so young, though."

"Yes. They have King Solomon's blessing. The king sent his own sedan chair and a contingent of his royal guard. The daughters of Jerusalem brought her wedding dress from the palace."

"This place is very beautiful," the stranger remarked. "I have never seen a terebinth tree so large and a pool so clear."

"Our people call this place *Hephzibah*, which means 'God delights in you.'"

They watched as the crowd along the street threw hundreds of white rockroses ahead of the procession. Scarlet martagons, Ammi's favorite flower for its brilliant crimson petals and sepals, covered the palanquin.

During the ceremony, Ammi and Ashur stood under a canopy draped with more beautiful flowers—blue and violet pishtah and blue ketzah—and drank pomegranate wine.

***

They settled into a home within the protective walls of Machir's estate, as Nelmaah had always hoped. A year later, the celebration of their love was fulfilled with the birth of a child.

Years of unprecedented peace passed under King Solomon, king of Israel. And the legend of the wisdom of Solomon spread throughout the nations.

***

Three years after Ashur and Ammi's marriage, another stranger from Hitti appeared in Solem. The villagers were protective of their hero and reluctant to reveal where Ashur lived until a messenger was sent to warn him.

Ashur paused from his work to watch his young son follow Machir about, dogging every step the older man made. As Ashur watched in amusement, a sound came from the direction of the road leading to their home.

The stranger came into view, driving a dilapidated wagon pulled by a gaunt old horse. Ashur was not surprised by the man's arrival. He knew the man had asked his whereabouts within the village.

As the wagon approached, he stood to greet the stranger. His visitor was approximately Machir's age. He had a scar across his cheek and another on his arm. Ashur was somewhat alarmed to see the man reach into the wagon and bring a sword into view. However, the sword was in its sheath, and the man's eyes and actions did not appear threatening.

"You are Ashur, known as the son of Machir?" His words were posed as half question, half statement. The man spoke in a confident voice and chose his words carefully. This shed doubts on Ashur's first impression that the man was of low station.

"Yes," Ashur replied.

"I see the resemblance now," the older man said, peering closer and smiling.

"Resemblance?" Ashur questioned.

"Yes, you bear resemblance to your father, to your father by blood," the visitor said.

Ashur was stunned. After all the years, the words seemed anticlimactic. "You knew my father?"

"I was with your father when he died," the man said. "Your father asked me to come to you. This occurred many years ago. I could not come until now. May we sit? I tire more easily these days. The journey was long."

"Yes, please sit here." Ashur took the man by the arm. "Would you like for me to get you something to drink?"

The benches under the shade of the trees were rough-hewn, but comfortable. The man ignored his question. He shifted his body forward until his face drew near to Ashur. He began relating his tale.

"Your father's last thoughts on this earth were of you. He was a great man. I know that the most difficult and courageous thing he ever did was to give up his son.

"Let me go back to the beginning so you will fully understand. When our people were driven out of Egypt, we found protection in serving the kings of the sea peoples. We were there at Ashdod when Machir and the warriors of Israel destroyed the cities of Philistia. During the final conflict on the Sharon plain, the battle went against us. Your father shouted for us to flee, every man for himself. We were to gather at a prearranged place in the north. Your father and a handful of warriors were covering our retreat. Men fell all around me. I saw your father take an arrow in his chest and go down. I could not reach him."

The man became so impassioned with the story that Ashur felt compelled to grip his shoulder to steady him.

"When we reached the camp where the women and children waited, I was dismayed to see that so few of us remained. Only a handful of men straggled in. We prepared to go on to the north. Then your father entered the camp. He was wounded, but there was great rejoicing when we learned that the arrow had only pierced his shoulder. Your mother was overjoyed at his return. She tended his wound. We placed him in a wagon and fled into the wilderness. In a few days, your father, strong man that he was, fully recovered to lead us again.

"They hunted us now. Everywhere we went, the armies of Israel sought to kill us."

The older man shifted his tired body again and leaned closer. "What I am about to relate to you is what your father, my king, told me of his deliverance. When the arrow felled him from his chariot, he struck his head on a stone or some such object that knocked him unconscious. The enemy passed over him as we retreated. Your father was judged to be dead.

"When he regained his senses, he crawled into the shelter of a tree. The tree had apparently been blown down by a windstorm. The roots had been ripped from the earth, preventing the trunk from lying flat to the ground. However, the arrow protruding from his shoulder hindered him from hiding under the tree. Your father pushed the arrow on through his shoulder, broke off the head, and pulled the shaft away.

"There your father lay, under the deadfall, wounded and dying of thirst. After an hour or more of drifting in and out of consciousness, he heard the sounds of horses and chariots returning. The place where your father lay hidden was somewhat removed from the battlefield where most of the men had fallen. He heard the sounds of bodies being dragged away. The warriors of Israel set up camp. Your father said he almost despaired.

"After what seemed like hours, the clouds thickened and a light rain fell on the battlefield. Slowly your father's strength revived, and he began to hope to escape. Then he heard agonized screams as the warriors hamstrung the captured chariot horses so they could not be used for war.

"Again he heard the sound of footsteps approaching. They came so close that he was certain that he had been discovered. The man kicked at the tree trunk and ripped a branch from the tree. He heard this enemy warrior cry out to Elohim, the one God, as he kneeled down beside the tree to pray.

"Your father recognized Machir in the moonlight then. Only hours previously, he had tried desperately to reach him in the battle so he could kill the enemy leader. Our king said he could see Machir's face so clearly that he could see the tears form and overflow. Machir cried as he lamented aloud his king's order to hamstring the innocent chariot horses. He could not bear to see the poor dumb beasts tortured. Apparently, he left the camp so that his men would not witness his distress.

"Your father lay there listening to his sworn enemy pray for an end to the maiming and killing of man and beast. He heard him pray for his wife and the people of Solem and for the son that she had always wanted to give him. Apparently, this was a prayer Machir had prayed often.

"Your father felt his anger and hatred drain away. Only moments before, he had wondered if he had enough strength to take Machir's sword away and kill him. Although he had great respect for Machir, he had not expected to find that he was a man to be admired.

"Your father had counseled against war with the people of Israel and had rejected the gods of Egypt and Philistia. Now I know that he was right and the other kings were wrong. Our people are no more. All are gone.

"When night fell, your father crawled from beneath the fallen tree and circled the camp. In the moon-light, he found one of our chariot horses tangled in a thicket. That is how he escaped to rejoin us.

"We wandered for months. You were born in the wilderness area north of the Megiddon plain. Your mother, bless her heart, never regained her strength. She was born in Jerusalem and could have returned to her people, but she would not leave her husband. She became ill and died in a few days. You were suckled and cared for by one of the women of the camp who had lost her child.

"The seed for your father's thought and plan was planted that day on the field of battle. He knew that it was only a matter of time before we were hunted down. He was determined that you would have a life of your own. Your father and I, the woman that nursed you, and two other warriors left the wilderness camp and went to Solem.

"One of the warriors went into the village to inquire about the location of Machir's lands. He assumed the identity of a horse trader and apparently was not suspected. Your father was searching for a vantage point in the hills when he found the cave. We had to watch the house only for a few days before learning that Machir passed the cave when he was hunting.

"I killed an ibex on the hillside while the others watched for Machir. We took the skin and head to the cave and waited until Machir hunted again. Your father used the head of the ibex to attract his attention.

He left you in the cave in a basket with his signet ring. Then he fled out the other entrance. We hid in the hills to watch and to make certain that Machir found the basket—and you. Then we retreated to the north.

"Your father's prediction proved to be correct. They hunted us like animals. Even in the wilderness, our people were not safe. Enemy warriors attacked our camp and fatally wounded your father. His last thoughts were of you. He made me swear that one day I would bring his sword to you and tell you about him and about your mother. He loved you a great deal. He gave you up to save you. At that time, I did not believe any of us would escape. I fled to Hitti, where I worked for a man as his servant."

He paused and handed the sword to Ashur, laying it in his hands gently, almost reverently. Ashur traced the outline of the six-cornered star etched into the handle.

After a moment of deep silence, the man grasped the side of the bench and pulled himself to his feet. "I will return now to my home. My master is kind to me, and I have married a woman of the Hitti. I am an old man. No one seeks to kill me now. I came to Solem to try to find you and fulfill my vow. If it is all right, I will return to my wife and my children." The man was almost asking his permission.

Ashur finally regained his voice. "Of course. Thank you for coming so far to bring me this story. Surely you will stay with us and rest."

"No. Thank you," the man said. "I still do not feel safe in Israel. I will use the remaining daylight to head toward home."

Ashur watched the wagon and man's figure fade into the distance. He felt a kinship with the old warrior. He had learned that he was a king without a kingdom. King Solomon had adopted the coat of arms of an enemy of Israel. Machir had raised the son of his sworn enemy as his own. How ironic was the hand of God on the works of men.

His son returned to Ashur when Machir entered the house. "Who was that man, Father?" the boy asked.

"An old warrior who has found peace," Ashur replied, wrapping his arms around his son.

POSTSCRIPT

Flame of God is a work of fiction, but it is based on exhaustive research. I examined approximately one hundred commentaries/works at random that were available to me. Twenty-eight embraced a three-character Song of Solomon: Solomon, the shepherd, and the maiden. Twenty-three appeared to favor a two-character version: Solomon and the maiden. Others varied from a collection of songs, a collection of love poems, a wedding with Pharaoh's daughter, an allegory of Christ and the church, and as an allegory of God and Israel. Some were neutral.

I am indebted to a number of historians from whom I gleaned bits and pieces of interest. These sparked my imagination, made the book authentic, and are woven into the tapestry of my book. Many skilled people helped me with the novel. I agonized over whether to mention them here. I value those friendships too much to suggest that any one of them endorses the position I have stated here.

Scripture and common sense tell me that Solomon is not an example of pure marital love. He had sixty queens and eighty concubines in Song of Solomon 6:8. He had a thousand women in 8:12. Solomon violated God's instruction of 1 Kings 11:2. He married many foreign wives. His first wife was apparently Naamah, an Ammonite (1 Kings 14:21, 31).

Solomon was never a shepherd. He was raised in King David's palace. That he appeared disguised as a shepherd seems far-fetched.

Song of Solomon 8:6–7 is a problem for a two-character version. The Hebrew *salhebhethyah* is variously translated as "the flame of God," "a vehement flame," and as "unquenchable fire." Jealousy as cruel as the grave (8:6) appears to demand a third character.

Refusing the king entrance to her chambers (5:3) would have been unthinkable. King Ahasuerus removed Vashti for refusing to come when he summoned her. This led to Esther becoming queen in the book of Esther.

He (Solomon) grew mad in his love of women and laid no restraint on himself in his lusts, Josephus, *Antiquities of the Jews*, Kregel Publications, (182).

Solomon apparently never found his soul mate. (Ecclesiastes 7:28).

The Amplified Bible, Zondervan Publishing, Grand Rapids, Michigan, 1965, contains a scholarly rendition of the Song of Solomon.

The Five Megilloth (edited by the Rev. Dr. A. Cohen, MA, PHD, DHL, London: The Soncino Press, 1961) is an excellent three-character treatment of Song of Solomon.

Song of Solomon, Liberty Bible Commentary, Old-Time Gospel Hour Edition, Lynchburg, Virginia, 1983, is another excellent three-character interpretation.

All I have said here does not mean that I take a dogmatic stance, but certainly the three-character rendition should be in the forefront of the debate. Perhaps it is an asset that I do not have an allegiance to a seminary or any other group or denomination.

No other book in the Bible has so confounded the genius of man. What a fantastic book is the Bible. There is no other like it. The nation of Israel and the Jewish people are its proof.

Historical Development

This writer claims no originality in the development of the interpretation of the Song. The following statements are excerpts from commentators, which demonstrate the struggle to develop the interpretation.

"Ibn Ezra (1093—1168) distinctly states—that the lovers are a shepherd and a shepherdess, and that the king is a separate and distinct person from the beloved shepherd."— Christian D. Ginsburg, The Song of Songs, (46), KTAV Publishing House, Inc, New York.

"This is why this poem is called the Song of Songs, since it deals with matters of the loftiest and greatest kind, namely, with the divinely ordained governments, or with the people of God— in which God untiringly performs a host of staggering miracles and displays His power by preserving and defending it against all of the assaults of the devil and his world."—Dr. Martin Luther (1538), Luther's Works, Volume 15, Lectures on the Song of Solomon, (192), Concordia Publishing, Saint Louis.

"Of all the literary monuments of the Jewish people, it is the one whose plan, nature and general meaning are the most obscure."—Ernest Renan (1860), The Song of Songs, A Study, (1) London: Wm. M. Thomson.

"If the Canticle is an allegory, we must suppose that the author, having first conceived a clear spiritual theme, voluntarily made it obscure."—William Pouget (1847–1933), the Canticle of Canticles, (121),The Declan X. McMullen Company, Inc, 1948.

"According to the other view propounded first in modern times by J. S.

Jacobi (1771), developed in a masterly manner by Ewald (1826), and accepted by the majority of modern critics and commentators, there are three principal characters, viz. Solomon, the Shulamite maiden and her shepherd lover."—S.A. Driver D.D. (1910), Literature of the Old Testament, (37), New York, Charles Scribner's Sons, 1914.

"Well, if I had been born only to see through the mystery of the Song of Songs, it would have been enough."—Max Brod (c. 1918) Paganism-Christianity-Judaism, (160), The University of Alabama Press.

The following is an excerpt from Marvin Pope's commentary on the Song of Songs, (585), The Anchor Bible, Garden City, Doubleday & Sons, 1977. To demonstrate the difficulty of translation, Pope gives a sample of the English renderings of one of the pivotal verses: 6:12.

KJ Or ever I was aware, my soul made me like the chariots of Amminadib.

AT Before I knew it, my fancy set me in a chariot beside my prince.

JB Before I knew . . . my desire hurled me on the chariots of my people, as their prince.

(A note explains, "This difficult verse seems to mean that by a spontaneous impulse Yahweh places himself at the head of his people.")

JPSV Before I knew it, My desire set me Mid the chariots of Ammi-nadib.

NEB I did not know myself; she made me feel more than a prince reigning over the myriads of his people.

NAB Before I knew it, my heart had made me the blessed one of my kinswomen.

Living Bible Paraphrase Before I realized it, I was stricken with a terrible homesickness and wanted to be back among my own people.

(A footnote suggests another possible reading: "terrible desire to sit beside my beloved in his chariot.")

Young's Analytical Concordance to the Bible, Wm. B. Eerdmans Publishing Company, Grand Rapids, Michigan, 1972 defines *Ammi* (AM-MI) as meaning "my people," a symbolic name that the ransomed people were directed by the Lord to use (Hosea 2:1).